ARTIST AMONG THE MISSING

Books by
OLIVIA MANNING

The Wind Changes
The Remarkable Expedition
Growing Up (short stories)
Artist Among the Missing
School for Love
A Different Face
The Doves of Venus
My Husband Cartwright (short stories)

THE BALKAN TRILOGY:
The Great Fortune
The Spoilt City
Friends and Heroes

A Romantic Hero (short stories)
The Play Room
The Rain Forest

Olivia Manning

ARTIST AMONG THE MISSING

Heinemann : London

William Heinemann Ltd
15 Queen Street, Mayfair, London W1X 8BE

LONDON MELBOURNE TORONTO
JOHANNESBURG AUCKLAND

First published 1949
Re-issued 1975

SBN 434 44910 5

Printed in Great Britain by
REDWOOD BURN LIMITED
Trowbridge & Esher

Artist among the Missing

★

Part One

GEOFFREY LYND was jerked awake when the train stopped at Kantara. He was in the empty dining-car. He felt stupefied and the thought in his brain was 'Death'. It was always like that when he slept in the afternoon in Egypt. Only a cup of tea could pull him together.

He got to his feet. If this were the canal there would be no time for tea. The blinds were drawn. He felt his way through the stifling car to the door. Outside there was a blaze of daylight—no station to be seen, no shade. The black huts of the frontier officials were planted in sand.

People were descending in a listless, surly way. They were all being deprived of a siesta. Blinded by the scintillations of sun on sand, they trudged off unsteadily between the rails.

Opposite the train was a string of cattle trucks filled with Australians. Thin, lanky, their loins in khaki shorts, bare from the waist up and burnt a dark pink, the Australians lay on the floors of the trucks and stared with disgust at the new arrivals. Geoffrey knew who they were. Most of them had fought their way twice up to Benghazi, some had been in Tobruk; they had been sent for a rest to skirmish in Syria and now they were being rushed back to the desert. In their lolling indifference to him there was contempt—there he goes, on his way out of danger! The Pommy bastards, they can't do a darned thing without us!

He hurried up an incline to the front of the straggling

passengers. At the top a group of English privates stood back to let him pass. Their dispirited acceptance of return touched him more painfully than the Australian disgust. Because they troubled to straighten themselves and salute, he could scarcely meet their eyes. Well, he was in no position to explain or apologise. He went on, followed by his group of "politically compromised" army civilian employees. In the distance, between white banks of sand, he saw the startling turquoise of the canal. It looked too narrow. Standing up from it, like a toy ship moving on a rail, was a troop-carrier from India, red with rust, lined with the red faces of the watching men.

An Egyptian police officer stood by the main hut, his pressed tarboosh, his narrow waist, the curve of his breeches and the slender line of his boots excelling even the natural Egyptian elegance in dress. Geoffrey tried to shake off his shirt where it stuck to his ribs and shoulder blades. The Egyptian saluted and announced in English: "Every civilian must show in his passport, exit permit and frontier permit. Passports must be stamped further down the line."

Geoffrey had military passes for his own group. The others, who had chosen in the panic to evacuate themselves, crowded round an empty hut marked 'Passports'. The air-raid warning sounded. The refugees reacted instantaneously. Some fellah boys ran among them pointing out the shelters and snatching at baggage.

The Egyptian officer tilted up his face, its even brown skin and neat features held rigid by the fanatical vanity of his kind, and said: "We have a raid every afternoon at this time. It is arranged to meet the train. The 'planes will not be overhead for ten minutes."

Geoffrey made a note of his own calm. He watched a fellah boy run out from behind one of the huts. The boy's galabiah was blown by the hot wind so his body stood out as though naked. He tripped on a rail, paused to lift his bare, injured foot, and, seeing blood trickle out through the dirt, he broke into loud lamentations. Another boy ran to him at once and, tenderly sliding an arm round his shoulders, led him to safety.

"I had to leave my wife behind in Cairo," said Geoffrey.

"Ah! Then you are still confident."

Geoffrey, who had been unaware he spoke aloud, looked at the Egyptian in surprise. He hurried to say: "Of course. This is only a strategic withdrawal."

The Egyptian nodded agreement with no apparent irony.

"We are getting these Europeans out merely as a precaution." Geoffrey glanced round for them—they were all underground. The soldiers, also, had taken cover somewhere; there was an odd stillness about the place. Only the ship remained with her exposed look, her decks bare. A suggestion of sound grew into the purr of a 'plane.

"Not many," said Geoffrey.

"The others, no doubt, are busy elsewhere."

The raid began from the ground as a distant battery opened fire.

"Now," said the Egyptian. "It would be wise to take cover."

Geoffrey followed him down a slope leading from the hut to a private shelter. The growing uproar of guns indicated the approach of the 'plane. A thunderous series of thumps reverberated through the ground. Between outbursts of gun-fire came the pipping of a machine-gun and the whining lunge of the 'plane, then the noises grew distant again. Geoffrey and the Egyptian came up to the surface. The ship was sliding along as before. There was nothing remarkable to be seen but splashes of water already drying on the sand. The gun-fire passed from battery to battery until there was silence. The silence was held like a breath, then, suddenly, the 'All Clear' sounded. Passengers from the train began to re-appear—a muddle of women, most of them fat, in clothes that looked too thick for the climate, peevish children and little, self-important men who pushed a way through the crowd to get first to the huts.

Geoffrey's party, conscious of privilege, remained apart. They were first over in the ferry and had it to themselves. Two pretty girls, an Austrian and a Greek, kept close to him, indicating by a flirtatious exchange across him that they took for granted his peculiar devotion to them. On the other side a British constable awaited them. He accorded Geoffrey a certain conspiratorial chumminess, but towards everyone else his manner was an attack of sharp, nasal snaps and shouts. An Arab policeman, in shapeless khaki uniform and cossack hat of astrakhan cloth, wandered about with the air of an obliging man who cannot get it clear what is expected of him. There was more shelter from the sun on this side but no sign of a train.

"She's held up at Gaza," explained the constable. "All these troop movements've disorganised things. Scheduled five hours late."

"Lord! " Looking round at the pink, damp faces of his ten refugees—the two girls, an Italian, a Pole, a Rumanian woman, two Yugo-Slavs, a Hungarian and two German Jews—Geoffrey could see that under the stress of the journey their collective attempt to imitate British stolidity was collapsing: "It's an anxious time for them," he said.

The constable smiled the smile of a man who is habitually one jump ahead of his fellows: "Naafi over there, Major," he said.

The canteen shed was dark but as hot as the outer air. Geoffrey's group joined up behind a queue of officers and got mugs of strong, sweet tea. Everyone settled down at a table covered with crumbs, jam and spilt tea, and started killing off flies with folded newspapers. On the floor below ants, working in columns, carried away the dead bodies as quickly as they fell. Geoffrey was relaxing, in a sleepy stupor, resigned to waiting, when an Egyptian soldier appeared and asked him to return to the other side. Unofficial refugees without permits or frontier permits were demanding British protection. Geoffrey stood up automatically but the girls on either side of him pulled him down again. The Pole protested jealously: "Naw, naw, who are these people to trouble you? They do nothing but save themselves." He gave the soldier a push and shouted at him: "Yallah, Yallah!"

The soldier stood his ground, not looking down at the Pole, but looking at Geoffrey as at someone who must understand his position. He explained with dignity that he came from his officer.

"All right," Geoffrey dismissed him, "I'll be with you." He swallowed down his tea and went out again into the sunlight. It was late afternoon when the heat was heaviest but as he turned a corner he was struck by a wind that chilled the sweat all over his body. The town was on this side of the canal. People who had wandered out to see what they could find were returning in a disgruntled mood. The train was now known to have been delayed by the military and the waiting passengers shouted indignant questions after Geoffrey as he passed them.

When he got back to the Egyptian shore, the refugees crowded round him in a compact, sweating mass. In their different languages they started to explain why they had not had time to get permits or visas, but he pushed a way through them. He walked up the line to the station, where there was a military telephone. An hour or so later he had put through all his calls and could ring the Egyptian officer and the British constable to tell them that hundreds more refugees were now scrambling out of Cairo: "Instructions are to let them all through. They'll be rounded up in

Jerusalem." After that there was nothing to do but wait for the Palestine train.

The short, delicious evening had arrived. Geoffrey wandered out of the back of the station into a village that had grown unconsidered behind it. His wet shirt was cold in the evening wind. He leant against the station entrance and looked down the village street. There was no noise. The buildings were on one side of the road only—a few of two storeys with the shell-thin, dilapidated look of Egyptian offices and police-stations; the rest shacks, some of mud, some of twigs woven and hung with rags to keep out the sun. Between them were the usual bare spaces, covered with rubble and giving off that extraordinary stench which Geoffrey, when newly arrived in Egypt, had been surprised to learn was only urine. At first when it had come upon him overpoweringly in the noonday heat, he had resented it like an affront; he had tried to describe it—a bile-coloured smell, a smell that had in it disease and evil; but when he learnt it was only an ordinary human smell grown grotesque in this corrupting heat, he scarcely even disliked it. Here, mixed with the dusty odours of spice and burning cow-cake, it was the familiar smell of a village.

On the other side of the road, below street level, was a stream running into the canal. The water was out of sight but there rose from it a few coarse, white lateen sails. The riverside path was an evening promenade. The fellah youths walked in couples, fingers entwined like lovers, their white robes flickering and melting into the coloured distance. A café had placed its chairs and tables by the water-side; beyond them the translucent green of papyrus feathered out into the pink sky. Over the scene was a haze of heat and the first silvering of night as the sun dropped behind the station.

Some of the Egyptians eating their saucers of beans out on the riverside path were wearing the uniform of the

Egyptian State Railways, but here they were all villagers. They might live off the station and the ferry, and do well out of the traffic of these European wars, but here behind the scene was their true life, lived as though everything else was ridiculous.

Geoffrey, conscious of the impertinence of his own existence, felt here an intruder upon reality. He turned quickly and hurried back to the station and along the line to the frontier huts where his existence had propriety and his rank justification.

By now all the refugees had crossed the canal. He was the only passenger on the ferry. The porters sat in a group and watched him. He offered them cigarettes and they accepted with courteous movements of hands and heads, grinning shyly when they met his eyes.

"Germans coming," said one.

"Do you mind?" Geoffrey asked.

"Very bad men."

"You'll all learn to speak German."

"Hah!" the porters gave shouts of laughter, delighted by Geoffrey's amiability.

"You run away?" asked one, becoming at once more daring.

"No. I come back to-morrow."

"Not afraid?"

"The Germans won't come."

"Germans inside Egypt."

"Finish now. You'll see."

"Germans come to the canal," insisted one. "Last time Germans come to the canal," and the others laughed, glancing at Geoffrey to see if he shared the joke. He smiled to please them.

Dawn was breaking when the train reached Lydda. The stocky palms planted in the station asphalt had a wintry look. The refugees, waiting for the connection to Jerusalem, huddled shivering in corners away from the wind. Bands of yellow, splitting the black rind of the sky, lighted the unfamiliar sight of distant hills. Children whimpered disconsolately. Now that they had crossed the frontier the refugees were worrying about the future.

"What will be done for us?" they kept asking Geoffrey.

He told them everything was being arranged in Jerusalem.

One middle-aged man trotted after Geoffrey wherever he went, saying: "I have a weak heart. It is not good that I should go to Jerusalem."

Geoffrey turned at last and shouted: "Oh, nonsense!" surprising everyone by this show of impatience. He had spent the night awake in a crowded carriage and his head ached. He was looking for a porter for his party.

The man said doggedly: "It is not good, Jerusalem. It is too high."

The Greek girl rushed in now to defend Geoffrey: "Leave the Major alone. He has not come to be worried by you. He is here to look after us."

One of the unofficial refugees, who on the journey had kept in the background, now elbowed his way to the front of the platform. When the train came in, he seized hold of Geoffrey's porter and gabbled instructions.

"Excuse me," Geoffrey protested mildly, "this is my porter. He can't do two jobs at once."

"Shut your mouth," shouted the refugee, "do you think you boss me, too?"

Geoffrey, startled, let the porter be taken from him, but his charges, watching from the carriage into which they had all climbed, cried aloud their annoyance: "No, no," shouted the Italian, "you must fight, Major. These people have the manners of pigs." He came from the train and, flicking Geoffrey a patronising pat on the shoulder, bolted down the platform. After an uproar that silenced everyone else into attention, he returned with the porter, the refugee shouting hysterically at his heels: "It is not fair. It is persecution."

The Italian smiled up at the girls as he said: "Ah, Major, you English do not understand how to deal with them. You are too kind."

"They're all in a panic just now," said Geoffrey, excusing himself as well as the other.

"Nevaar mind, nevaar mind," the Pole shouted angrily from the window, "it is a folly to let them bully you."

Geoffrey said nothing more. When the luggage was in he climbed aboard. As he made his way down the corridor he heard from somewhere ahead the Viennese girl's penetrating whisper: "Major Lynd is nice, but he is not competent."

"If he were," said the Italian, not whispering, "would he be sent with us?"

Geoffrey stopped and stood in the corridor. While the train crawled upwards, he remained out of sight of the refugees. The only hope for him, he thought, was to get back to Egypt. He must return to his job at once. He must keep at the centre of the whirl of the emergency—anyway, within the radius of danger—and so avoid these intervals for reflection. During the last twenty-four hours he had been tranquil and good-humoured because a man of action. He had done well enough, but now he was being overtaken by his old inability to cope with human beings. He longed to return to his wife.

They were travelling at a snail's pace from the smooth foothills into dry and broken mountains that shot up out of sight above the train. After the sand-filtered light of Egypt, the morning here seemed to lie on the earth like a lustre. At every incurve of the hills there was an Arab village with the concave slopes above it terraced like an amphitheatre. The terraces were planted with olives, grey-green cloud-shapes against the pink earth.

"Hello, hello!" The Viennese girl had put her head round the door and seen Geoffrey. She came out to him, short and plump, swaying her hips along the corridor. He knew she knew he had overheard their remarks and he put on a reassuring smile.

"Ah, Major," she said very brightly, "we feared to have lost you. You are thinking no doubt this would be good to paint?"

"No."

"You see, I know about you. My friend knew about you in Athens, but she has heard that now you do not paint. Is that true?"

"Yes."

"What a great waste! No?"

He could scarcely speak from irritation. He said at last: "I have no time."

"But in Palestine you can paint, perhaps? My friend says here it is like Greece."

He wanted to tell her to mind her own business. Instead he looked from the window as though considering for the first time this resemblance to Greece. It had been lost for him as soon as he saw the Arab villages—stone cubes of houses growing from the rock with instinctive rightness like leaves on a branch; the Arabs in biblical dress leading camels that placed their spongy feet slowly and deliberately down the hill tracks. . . . He realised that was something he could tell her.

"This biblical quality repels me," he said.

"But in Greece," she persisted, "what was there?"

"Marble. A pagan country . . ."

She interrupted, laughing: "But now the Greeks are not pagans."

"Of course not." Did she suppose he was speaking of

the present? His unwillingness to talk was obvious and she countered it by putting her head out of the window and shouting: "Ah, the air it is so cool. Feel. It is like glass."

He put his head out and in spite of himself was exhilarated. When he drew his head in, his cheeks flushed, he said: "I wish Viola were here."

"Who?"

"My wife. She is still in Cairo."

"You have a wife in Cairo?" The girl adjusted her manner so subtly, a more masculine man would have noticed no change: "Really! How happy for you. I thought the English ladies had been sent to South Africa."

"Only those who weren't working. My wife has an important job."

"You are without children?"

"Yes."

"What a pity!"

He smiled: "Not at all. It is my wife's choice. She's still young."

"So!"

They stood some moments in silence, then the girl went back to her seat. He was unaware that she turned at the door of her compartment to give him a last glance. Had he seen it he would have remained unimpressed. He knew exactly the limitations of his power to attract women. At first they liked something romantic in his appearance; in his heavy mouth, light-coloured eyes and his black hair that grew quickly and curled before he could get it cut again. His nose was a little too long, his chin too short. A thin man, not over-tall, with the ability to fall into easy attitudes that gives a look of breeding. Beyond all this, women came up against—not so much a lack of response as an emptiness. Whatever it was they expected to find in him was not there. Perhaps it had once been there. Like a man no longer wealthy, he retained certain deceptive tricks of past affluence; but he had no wish to deceive. He would have spoken aloud to anyone what he was thinking then: "I am nothing now."

The train was levelling up on a mountain top. Trees, gardens and the first houses of Jerusalem were appearing; then the platform with miltary police at the gates. Everyone crowded out of the train. A sergeant came up to Geoffrey with a list of hotels in which odd rooms had been booked.

"No easy job, sir," he said, "finding accom. for your little lot. There's the Syrian do on, you see. Been crowding down here from all over."

"What about the others?" Geoffrey glanced round at the anxious, staring faces of the unofficial refugees.

"We've got a camp ready for them; we're trying to requisition a convent. They'll have to be locked up until we can screen them. You never know. Some queer types getting in this way."

The Greek girl was at Geoffrey's elbow. "Where will you stay, Major?"

"I hope I'll go straight back to Cairo."

"No, no, no. It is not possible," the protests mixed a coy flattery with self-interest. "It is necessary you remain to look after us."

"Don't worry. You'll be looked after."

While the refugees were demanding attention on one side of him he found that on the other a young officer in an oatmeal-coloured kilt was saying: "I see you don't remember me. My name is Joe Phillips. Viola introduced us years ago at your private view—you and she'd just got married."

For a moment Geoffrey's consciousness moved from the station to the white painted gallery with its grey carpet; Bond Street outside and the cool of an English summer day; the elegance, simplicity and leisure of peace. . . . Then the refugees closed in jealously. In a bewildered way Geoffrey indicated to the young man that he would soon be free.

The Rumanian woman was asking: "But what becomes when the Germans are here?"

"Everything's arranged." Geoffrey led them out to an army wagon awaiting them. They got into the seats but still leant forward, frowning and chattering at him. The Rumanian woman kept repeating her question.

He said: "You'll be evacuated through Transjordan to Basra. Then you'll be taken by sea to England." Before they could comment on the hazards of such a journey, he slammed the wagon door and signalled the driver to start. The refugees turned angrily in their seats; the Pole shouted: "Hey, hey, hey!" but they were carried off.

Geoffrey found Phillips at his elbow.

"I say," said Phillips, "what a bit of luck meeting you! I was just leaving my baggage here. I'm off to Cairo on the afternoon train."

"I'll probably be going on it, too."

"*What* a bit of luck!"

As they walked together from the station, Geoffrey could see the disappearing wagon with the faces of the refugees staring back at him. When it passed out of sight, he sighed as though he had thrown off a burden.

"Do you know Jerusalem?" asked Phillips.

"No." Geoffrey, obsessed by the need to arrange his return to Cairo, felt as though he were in blinkers. He tried to give his attention to his companion.

"Pity you won't have time to look around," said Phillips.

What did it matter? Geoffrey looked now and saw the main road running uphill between groves of stunted and beaten olive trees. At the top was a severe building in pinkish stone over which flew the Union Jack.

"Is that H.Q.?" he asked.

"Yes. The King David Hotel."

Geoffrey felt himself drawn to it as by a physical force. Before he could do anything else, he must get his return settled. If he missed the train, there might be a car starting out to cross Sinai by moonlight . . .

"Or what chance of a 'plane?" he wondered aloud.

Phillips laughed: "You're pretty keen to get back."

"Viola's in Cairo."

"Is she? *Is* she, by Jove! You don't say. I often wondered what became of you both. I was thinking about Vi on the boat coming out. I'd heard you were in Greece."

Geoffrey broke in indifferently: "I didn't know your regiment was here."

"It isn't. I've been on sick leave. The others're somewhere up in the blue. I've got to go and look for them. Is it true the Jerries have reached Sollum?"

"Reached it two days ago."

"And where are they now?"

"God knows. I've been told we'll try and hold that ridge between the Quattara Depression and the sea. We're putting everything we've got there—you included, I expect."

Phillips gave a sudden shout of laughter: "Wonderful. Thermopylæ. This is something like war. In England all we did was sit around with the women and wait to be invaded. But what happens if they get through?"

"We flood the moat round Alex and hang on there."

"What about Cairo?"

"Supposed to be an open city. Anyway, it won't be defended. That's why I've got to get back. I'm worried about Viola."

"Bad show, that. They should've got the women out straight away."

"Viola's doing an important job."

"*Is* she! Good for her. We used to be great friends. We were kids together, you know. I'd love to see her again."

"Of course you'll see her. We can put you up if you like."

"I say, really!" Phillips was panting a little, always half a step behind Geoffrey.

Geoffrey was unaware how quickly he was walking uphill. He kept his gaze on the hotel and talked from some part of his mind that had learnt to keep up, automatically, conversations of this kind. At last they passed through the revolving doors and were inside. Geoffrey, scarcely waiting to hear Phillips's offer to wait for him in the lounge, went straight up to Headquarters. For two flights the stairs were carpeted and the marble washed, then came the barrier and the squalor of military occupation. The Orderly Office door stood open. A crowd of officers whose leave had been cancelled were waiting round a desk at which an A.T.S. sergeant sat, refusing to be hurried. She glanced at Geoffrey: "Major . . . Major?" she queried remotely in a voice of extreme refinement.

"Lynd," said Geoffrey eagerly.

"Ah, yes, Major Lynd. 'Fraid you can't see Major Chapman before one o'clock, but I believe a signal came through saying you're to await further orders."

"But I must get back to Cairo."

She looked past Geoffrey and with her eyebrows interrogated someone behind him. Her disapproval silenced him. He went downstairs again, on edge with anxiety, yet empty because he could do nothing. Forgetting Phillips, he wandered through the lounge, which was spacious, new and light-coloured, with every door and window open to the morning air. It enhanced for him his own vacancy, a vacancy everywhere reflected on the faces of the Levantine visitors who had brought their idleness here for the summer. He went out to the terrace.

The terrace was already too hot for people used to Jerusalem; to Geoffrey, depleted by the Cairo heat, the air felt tender as silk. But his pleasure in it was scarcely tolerable. Nothing must deflect him from his determination to go.

He stared over the rich, down-sloping gardens of the hotel to the Old City that lay like a medieval fortress in a sort of crater. On three sides the hills rose around it; on the fourth they were riven by a valley that dropped to the Dead Sea. The scene, flat and colourless in this early light, seemed to him cardboard. He had taken one of the basket chairs that stood about the terrace, but he would have risen again and wandered off if Phillips had not come out. Phillips grinned and did not mention that Geoffrey had passed him as though he were a stranger. He asked: " How are things? "

" I don't know," Geoffrey looked down as though painfully ashamed that he had nothing more definite to say, " I haven't seen Chapman, but the girl up there—she seems to think I'll have to stay."

" Bad luck!" Phillips's face went blank in commiseration; he paused a moment, then asked happily: " Have you had breakfast? "

" No." Geoffrey had forgotten about that.

" I've ordered some. They'll bring it out here. I thought it might come in handy."

After breakfast, Geoffrey found the view taking on depth and significance. Here, he admitted, was not merely another Middle Eastern city. Among these white roofs with their little domes were the symbols not of Islam but of Christianity, and the innumerable, dark exclamation marks of the cypresses. The new stone city that was spreading over the hills seemed at this distance as severe, clean and permanent as a Cotswold village. Whether he liked it or not, he would probably have to get to know it.

He sighed and looked round at Phillips, who had been watching him. Phillips, too, began to materialise and

Geoffrey realised that, under the mask of sunburn that made all these young men look alike, he was probably no fool. He was certainly exceptionally good-looking.

"I suppose," said Geoffrey, "this place has its advantages. I might get Viola to come up on leave."

"If you have to stay, you could have my room at the club. It's not bad. I share a table with a couple of chaps, both majors—Clark and Lister—you'd probably like them. Brainy types. They've been quite decent to me, considering. I'm not up their street, really."

In all Phillips said there was respect for a senior officer but, at the same time, a certain ease. This was not an ordinary war-time acquaintanceship; because they had met once in the enviable days before the war, it had the solid basis of civilian friendship. Phillips asked: "You're Intelligence, aren't you?"

"I'm part of the notorious muddle inside the Cairo perimeter."

Phillips gave Geoffrey a glance of surprising penetration, then laughed as though to cover a lapse. Staring down between his bare knees at his feet, he said in a half-mumble: "At least in Intelligence you can keep your individuality."

"Perhaps. At a price." Geoffrey reflected that his individuality (whatever that meant) was not a thing over which he worried much. If he had been asked to dissect his own character he would have begun to wonder if he had any character at all. His moods, his ideas, his likes and dislikes, even his primary qualities, wavered and changed with circumstances. Until the war started he had been concerned only with the question of how well he was painting.

He said: "I felt I ought to fight. That's why I left Greece. I used to feel if I weren't a painter, then I'd be a successful man of action. But they wouldn't have me. I got stuck in an office."

"Pretty boring!" murmured Phillips.

"Worse than that. You just eat yourself up like a fox in a trap."

"Wouldn't suit me," Phillips's voice was worried with sympathy. He kept his head down but when Geoffrey spoke he would look up at him through long, sandy lashes. He said: "But you like Egypt?"

"Like it?" Geoffrey looked at his watch. He was keeping his attention with difficulty on Phillips's remarks: "It grows on one. I don't let it worry me; and I've got my job."

Phillips let his blue eyes open, then, dropping his lashes again, smiling nervously; he asked: "Isn't it rather beautiful?"

"I suppose it is; in a macabre fashion. If we ever get away, we'll remember it as beautiful, but here you're usually too irritated and frustrated to notice. After a couple of summers you feel only half alive."

"The heat does for you?"

"Yes, and your inside gets upset—it's inevitable; the food's filthy from flies and parasites—then you drink arrack or brandy to 'cure' yourself. You can't keep dieting, and that's only a temporary help anyway. Soon you've got a sort of chronic dysentery, and you get thinner and more irritable and more depressed and everything seems a burden. In Egypt you scarcely ever walk half a mile. It's too hot, but, anyway, you can't really be bothered."

"What about Vi? How does she stand up to it?"

"She looks wonderful, but . . ." his voice rose with a sudden explosive irritation, "she will ride on tram-cars. She even goes second-class with the fellah jammed all round her. She's crazy. She might catch anything."

Phillips smiled gently: "You worry about her?"

Geoffrey could remember moods when he was almost insane with fear for Viola's safety. He said: "I try not to. She does what she likes. I can't stop her. Anyway, we're trapped here. We've got to accept the place as it is. We don't stand a chance of getting away before the war ends."

Phillips shifted his feet in their large brown brogues and, still looking down at them, said: "It's rather a thing for me, you know, being able to talk to someone. When you've been on active service for two years, you forget what ordinary conversation's like. You learn a sort of formula language. I sometimes wonder if I'll ever be able to stop talking like a machine."

Geoffrey had no comment to make, so Phillips said quickly, stamping on the silence as one stamps on fire: "You didn't recognise me, did you? I was a different person when you met me in London. If I wasn't much else, I was a reasonably intelligent human being. You'd never guess what I used to do for a living?" Geoffrey shook his head. "I used to buy and sell antiques."

"In the country?"

"Yes. In Hertfordshire; where Vi and I grew up. Our parents were neighbours. You know, I wanted to marry her . . ."

Geoffrey did not know. He said nothing. Phillips rushed again into the silence: "There was quite a craze for your Greek paintings in London before I left."

For the first time Geoffrey's attention entered completely into the conversation. His expression was painful but Phillips, who was not looking at him, said: "I'd like to see your new stuff."

"I haven't any. I'm at the office from eight in the morning until one or two; then from five until eight at night. In the afternoons I'm too washed up to do anything. But it's not that. I don't want to paint here."

"But does everyone work those hours at G.H.Q.?"

"Yes. Seven days a week. God knows what we achieve by it; but we keep going as an excuse for being safe in an office instead of out in the desert."

Phillips laughed loudly at that: "I know where I'd rather be," he said.

"Well," Geoffrey said coldly, "you'll soon be there. And no doubt to a chap like you—off to join an almost defeated army—the war's more important than the individual."

Phillips remained good-humoured: "Like hell it is!"

Geoffrey laughed and Phillips, raising his head, laughed, too, as though some contact had been made at last. He said eagerly: "I say, I can see Vi in Cairo, can't I?"

Geoffrey got to his feet and said: "Must go up to H.Q. again."

"Couldn't we luncheon together?" asked Phillips.

"Yes. Why not? I'll see you down here, then."

Although it was not quite five minutes to one, the Orderly Office was empty. Only the typist's forage cap still hung on a peg. Geoffrey waited. When the girl came back she started at once putting a cover on the typewriter. Geoffrey stood patiently. She seemed not to see him and he had to break through her preoccupation to ask if there was a message for him.

With a hint of exasperation in her tone she repeated what she had said before. He was to stay in Jerusalem until further orders.

"When will Major Chapman be back?" he asked.

"Some time after five." She took down her cap and twirled it in her hand but still Geoffrey could not go. He asked: "If I came in this evening, could I put a call through to Cairo to my wife?"

She made a movement with her lips that was almost an audible click of disapproval: "Sorry, sir. We've had strict orders: 'No personal calls to Egypt until further notice.' Must keep the line clear for important signals."

"Yes, of course. And there's no civilian line?"

"No, sir."

He went, defeated, as he had expected to be. Any other

fellow, he told himself, would have had the girl on his side in no time; the call would have been fixed up somehow. Not he, of course.

When he turned the last flight of stairs he looked down on Phillips's face smiling up at him. His jealousy struck him like a sickness. He had to pause and pretend to go through some papers in his wallet. As he did so, he stared with disgust in at the muddle of his own nature. He hated his humility in this world which had no use for him; he was resentful, yet hated his resentment. In spite of that, when he met, not contempt, but Phillips's forbearing friendliness, he could not respond. He was filled with distrust and bitterness. . . . When he looked down again, he saw that Phillips was no longer smiling; his eyes, fixed on Geoffrey, were troubled. Geoffrey, seeing Phillips vulnerable, was at once remorseful. He ran down the remaining stairs and caught the young man by the arm. As they walked to the restaurant he said: "Yes, do go and see Viola. I'll give you our address and telephone number. Tell her they're keeping me here indefinitely—and for God's sake, tell her not to be a fool. She must leave if things get any worse."

"Trust me," said Phillips.

Two hours later, when his enthusiasm had long failed, Geoffrey, seeing the young man off on the Cairo train, reflected that Phillips could not be in Cairo longer than twenty-four hours. And had he even a thirty per cent chance of surviving the next battle?

Phillips, leaning out of the carriage window, said: "What a bit of luck, meeting you! I'll give Vi all your messages. Trust me."

The train drew out and Geoffrey turned on his heel so that he need not see again Phillips's warm, embracing smile.

The refugees settled down happily enough in Jerusalem. Throughout the modern city there were Jewish cafés, run in the European manner, where they could spend the morning drinking coffee, playing chess and gossiping. Because they had nothing better to do, they were always early enough to get the coveted window table and they would pack their chairs together round it and watch the passers-by. It seemed to Geoffrey that wherever he walked someone would tap a window at him. Turning his head unwisely, he would find one of them rushing out to seize him by the arm and pull him into their circle.

"Hel-l*o*, hel-l*o*," the younger German-Jew shouted one morning from the steps of the Viennese café, "Hel-l*o*, Major Lynd, we are so much wishing your company."

"Not now," Geoffrey tried to move away, "I must go to the King David."

"Oh, no, Major," the two girls cried from within. "Is your work so important you cannot take a little cup? Come in, come in!"

"Come. Come into the café and join us."

Geoffrey was drawn into the hot, damp atmosphere of the café and a seat squeezed for him into the circle.

"Now, Major, tell us please what is being arranged for us?"

"I've told you. If the Germans get through, you'll be taken to Basra."

"And if we get to Basra? What then?"

"Boats to England."

"So!" Would it be safe, such a journey? Would they be safe in England, did he think? What if the Germans invaded England?

Then the piping rise and fall of the Austrian girl's voice: "We have been here since two weeks and still we nothing know. In the cafés they say that here is a cul-de-sac. The Jews tell us when the Germans come the Arabs will rob and kill us. To go to Basra in cars is very dangerous, they say. The Arabs will await in the desert to overpower us."

"Nonsense!" said Geoffrey. "Anyway, you will have military protection."

"But the Arabs have it arranged, and they are strong."

Geoffrey said weakly: "The Germans won't come, anyway. We will hold them in the Western Desert."

"Ha!" said the Pole, his voice filling the café so that people turned to look, "can we be sure of that? They have come a long way."

"How is it," asked the Rumanian woman, making a boxing movement in the air, "how is it you English cannot fight more good?"

Geoffrey shrugged his shoulders, feeling helpless before this friendly aggression.

"I would ask you," said the Greek girl, "about my room. For a little while, all right! But to stay like this, week after week! It is too small, and now so hot. One can smell the cooking."

"That is nothing," burst in the Pole, "all rooms are little here. It is the Ghetto. The Jews like to crowd in such small spaces. But me, I suffer with a hotelier who charge extra for everything. He say the army pay only for room and food, all else is extra. A towel is extra, a clean sheet, extra," he whacked the table with his large hand. "To kill the bugs, extra!"

"The bugs," shouted the Viennese girl. "Now let me tell you, Major; here is a matter for you! I have been eaten from head to foot."

"Move to an Arab hotel," said the Pole.

"What!" the Viennese girl's voice soared to a pinnacle of scorn, "are there no bugs in Arab hotels? I ask you, Major—are there no bugs in . . ."

"Naw, naw," roared the Pole, "you do not understand. I am not making propaganda. Here the Arab hotelier is the old hand; he knows a clean hotel, good business. Here

Jews are amateurs; everyone, amateurs. They tell us, in Europe, they were bankers, lawyers, such and so on. Perhaps. Anyway, here they are hoteliers, shopkeepers, laundry keepers—and what do they want? Money, money, quick, and get out of this vulgar job. Look at these laundries—where are such prices?"

Everyone shouted about the laundry prices, then the Greek girl carried on: "But everything here costs so much. This place is too dear for us. What can we do here, Major, with everything so dear? And not good, either. No quality. In Egypt we had such nice little sweet cakes, such nice chocolate, fruits and the food so good! Here, nothing; nothing but paying money for nothing. Something should be done for us, Major."

"You brought us here," accused the Italian, joking and yet not joking.

Geoffrey tried to move back from the table: "I must be off."

"Naw, naw," the Pole caught his arm and it seemed to him that in the crowd about him there was something like menace. He struggled up from among them, then finding himself free, unharmed, caught his breath and tried to laugh. He said: "I want to get back to Egypt as much as you do. I'm doing my best for you."

"We know, we know," they reassured him quickly. They smiled back at him and he saw them become in a moment harmless, well-intentioned and reasonable.

Out in the street he hurried from a sense of freedom, but as he approached the hotel his pace slackened. He went up the stairs slowly.

"Nothing for you, Major Lynd," said the typist before he had time to speak.

"I suppose my wife hasn't rung through?"

"'Fraid not."

After that nowhere to go but the King David bar until

he could return to the Officers' Club for luncheon. The uncertainty of his position kept him restless and yet idle. He thought if he were told he must stay another fortnight, say, or another month, then he could plan his time; he would set out to visit the sights of the place; he would go to Bethlehem, to Jaffa, Hebron, Nazareth . . . but his nebulous future gave him too much time. He could do nothing but waste it.

The club was in a requisitioned Arab house a few hundred yards from the hotel across the olive groves. At meal times Lister was usually silent behind a newspaper. Nicholas Clark, in a hurry, would stare critically at Geoffrey and sometimes ask in an offhand way:

"Any news to-day, Lynd?"

"No, nothing. I'll probably have to stay here until something happens in the desert."

"Nice holiday for you, anyway. Wish I could fit in a spot of leave before the autumn."

Clark always kept his arm on the table so that he could glance every few minutes at his wrist-watch. His arm was broad from wrist to elbow and covered with a golden fur of hair. His wrist-watch, as big as a pocket watch, was set in a two-inch leather strap. Although his face with its strong, regular features, was handsome, Geoffrey's instinct was against it. He could not like Clark; he felt in his presence apologetic and ill-at-ease. Clark's endless activity seemed to him a comment on his own inactivity.

Clark always left the table first. When he went, Lister, a fat man yet a remote man, would put down his newspaper and uncover a large face decorated with a large, fluffy moustache. If he caught Geoffrey's eyes he would at once shift his gaze and stare sternly at the traffic of the dining-room. Two or three days passed before he spoke; then he asked:

"Still no news?"

"No, but they can't keep me here long."

"Lucky for you. This place is worse than the worst small provincial town in England."

Now that Lister had spoken to him, Geoffrey found he had no difficulty in speaking to Lister. He said: "I wouldn't mind where I was if I had my wife with me. But she's still in Cairo."

"You're worried?"

"Well . . ."

"Don't worry," Lister gave Geoffrey a sweet, sombre smile: "She'll get out all right. We're becoming quite expert at evacuating our nationals. Before I reached Middle East I was evacuated from Yugo-Slavia, from Greece and from Crete. I was in Italy when the war broke out. Always got out just in time. We're beginning to understand the arts of defeat."

"You think she'll be all right?"

"Women always get looked after—and if they don't, it's remarkable how well they can look after themselves."

"You think so?" Geoffrey as he spoke recognised the absurdity of his question. He expected Lister to say: "My dear fellow, you ought to know. She's your wife," but, instead, Lister grunted reassurance: "'Course she will," he said as he got unsteadily to his feet. He rocked a little, balancing on a walking-stick. In brown corduroy trousers and a short-sleeved shirt that had faded from khaki to lemon-yellow, he might have been anything; then he put on his cap, the peak sloping over one eye, gave it a tap at the top, and became a British officer.

"Be seeing you," he said, and limped off.

"God," said Clark one night at dinner, winding his watch, frowning for a safragi, "I don't know where we're going to put all these fellows coming up from Egypt. They're clearing them out down there in preparation for the next round. All very well, but we're overcrowded and short-handed. Half the time I'm nothing but a stretcher-bearer myself."

Lister was not at the table. Clark talked into the air, his eyes cold as pebbles, but Geoffrey knew he was the person being accused. He said desperately: "I suppose I couldn't be of any help?"

After a long pause Clark grunted: "Anyone could help who didn't mind giving a hand with the stretchers."

"Of course I don't mind."

Clark grunted again, saying nothing more, but when he rose from his meal it was evident he expected Geoffrey to go with him. They left the club together. Inside the house the air had been sticky with heat but beyond the black-out curtain that kept out the air was the cool night lit by enormous stars. Geoffrey and Clark took the short cut to the station across the olive groves. The path, where the dusty earth had been trodden from the rock, glimmered under the trees. Geoffrey, who did not know the road, stumbled after Clark, who walked sure-footed at an athlete's pace and with nothing to say.

Ambulances stood in the square outside the station. On the half-lit platform English women, wives of government officials, were waiting with a tea-wagon. Civilian volunteers and stretcher-bearers from the military hospitals were drinking cups of tea. No one was talking. There was silence, almost apprehensive, as the train slid in. When it came to a standstill it stood like an empty train, dark, without sign of life.

The man standing beside Geoffrey muttered: "What's happened to the poor bastards? All died on the way?"

The windows were open. From somewhere inside the train came the voice of a stretcher-bearer: "We're all in. If any of you fellows can walk, for Christ's sake do it."

Clark opened the carriage door and shouted: "We've brought help."

The stretcher-bearer leant out, his face ashy-yellow in the yellow glimmer, and jerked his head to the right: "The worst cases are in the rear."

Clark's party moved down to the end of the train. Geoffrey and a corporal entered the last carriage. A heavy stench of drugs hung in the hot air. The men lay like corpses beneath the little blue buttons of light. Geoffrey leant over the first stretcher to warn the occupant that they were about to move him, and met only the gaze of empty eye-sockets. A fragile beak of bone stood up, the only feature on a skinless face.

For an appalling moment the elaborate structure of Geoffrey's self-control disintegrated and he nearly broke into tears. He regained himself instantly and looked at his companion. The corporal swallowed in his throat and whispered: "Tanks."

Geoffrey helped him manoeuvre the stretchers out one by one. Competently, he thought, competently. Now he was as hard and cold as ice, as competent as a professional. . . . The women trundled up the tea-urn. The first of them gave a look at the men lying on the platform. Her face went blank. After a pause she called on rather too high a note: "Anything we can do here, Major?"

"Better leave them alone," said Geoffrey.

The tea-urn went back to the other end of the platform. The air was full of the shocked excitement of feminine voices, refined English voices jollying the exhausted men, putting up between themselves and the reality before them the transformation screen of good fellowship.

Girl ambulance drivers occasionally appeared on the platform to give a hand with the stretchers. They came and went with the nonchalance of old soldiers. In an hour or so all the wounded had been taken away and there was tea for the helpers who remained. Some of the ambulance girls returned and, finding the job finished, joined the tea party. Geoffrey noticed one of them talking to Clark. She was a tall girl in khaki trousers and battledress tunic; her short hair caught the light and shone like a sovereign. He had seen her before somewhere. Yes, of course, she was often in the louge at the Continental.

He had to give his attention to the corporal, who was earnestly and slowly describing his home and family in Liverpool; when he could, Geoffrey looked back to make sure the girl was still there. He must talk to her about Cairo; she might know something about Viola. He began to be on edge with fear that she would go before he could intercept her. The corporal's story seemed interminable. Not really listening, Geoffrey kept his expression interested but took a moment off now and again to keep an eye on the girl. She and Clark seemed to be exciting one another; Geoffrey could hear their voices and Clark's surprising laughter.

The girl was standing like a man, one hand in her pocket, a cigarette hanging from the corner of her mouth, talking loudly with an unselfconsciousness that made the government wives seem genteel. The wooden masculinity of Clark's face had come to life and his eyes shone. Geoffrey knew quite well that this was a developing relationship he should not interrupt, yet when he could he had to cross over to where Clark and the girl stood. At first neither appeared to notice him.

The girl was talking rapidly: "Hell, of course—but someone's got to do it. It's the kids I feel sorry for; they've seen nothing like it before. The worst job's bringing in the dead. You get that as a punishment for being drunk or late on parade. Some of the kids were so scared they were drunk all the time. You'd pack in the bodies—pretty far gone, they were, in that heat—and by the time you'd got them to base, they'd be running all over the floor. Then you'd have to scrub out the ambulance.

One of the orderlies said to me: 'If you've got a cut and any of that stuff gets into your hand, you're a goner.' So I—I'm a sergeant, y'know—asked for an issue of rubber gloves. Our C.O.—a silly bitch who'd been a head prefect—lectured me for cosseting the girls while the brave boys were dying all around us. I said: 'We're not taking risks for the fun of it. We may be unpaid—but we're not bloody amateurs. We're doing a job of work.' Then one of the kids went off her rocker a bit and tried to shoot herself, and we got the gloves. My God, those female C.O.s give me a belly ache! There's no fool like a middle-class female fool and the army's full of them." She paused, lit another cigarette and stubbed out the old one. She slid her large, yellow eyes round to give Geoffrey a curious glance, then added rather breathlessly: "Always talking about 'the officer class', and 'playing the game', and . . ." Her voice trailed off; she was conscious of Geoffrey at her elbow and Clark swung round on him with a look that said: What the hell do you want?

Geoffrey blundered in with his question: "Have you come from Cairo?"

"Why, yes," she and Clark stared in surprise at Geoffrey's irrelevance. He swallowed in his throat. The excitement between them had been evident enough, surely they must know he would not interrupt without good reason.

"How are things there?"

"Oh, settling down," the girl was not unfriendly, but not encouraging: "Even the Egyptians doubt if the Germans'll get through now."

"I suppose you don't know Viola Lynd?"

"Why, yes," now she showed some interest, "we bump into one another at parties. Friend of yours?"

"She's my wife."

"Oh, I see."

"I was wondering—have you seen her lately? She hasn't

written to me and I thought . . . You might know if she's all right. Hope she's not lonely? "

The girl laughed in a riotous reassurance: "Is any woman lonely in Cairo these days? Anyway, not Viola. She's fine."

"Oh! That's all right, then." Now he should move away, but it was difficult to move away just like that. He stood wretchedly.

The girl watched him with her large, full mouth twisted down a little: "What are you doing here?" she asked.

"Nothing much." Then he added untruthfully and knowing that Clark would know it was an untruth: "Job at H.Q."

"You're one of the lucky ones." She spoke without malice but Geoffrey reacted as though she had spat at him.

"Do you think so?"

Clark and the girl exchanged glances. Clark's annoyance was obvious, yet the girl spoke to Geoffrey, detaining him because she wanted him to go; and somehow excusing him by what she said: "You're a painter aren't you? Someone told me Viola's husband had been a painter."

"Didn't know that." Clark stared as though Geoffrey had changed before his eyes; his tone became more patronising than usual: "Ever want to become a war artist?"

"No."

"What about camouflage? Useful job!"

"The only thing I wanted to do was fight."

The girl sighed slightly. She was doing her best to keep the conversation normal but her voice grew lame as she spoke: "I expect Viola would rather have you with her."

"I'm not so sure of that," said Geoffrey.

"Well, well, well!" Clark lifted his head and said briskly to the girl, "How about a drink?"

"Fine idea!"

"A drink will do you good." Clark stepped past Geoffrey and caught the girl's elbow; he was careful to exclude Geoffrey as he said: "The King David all right?"

"I suppose I must be going, too," said Geoffrey. Neither answered him. He looked at their backs as they moved away and said: "Good night," but they did not reply.

"Darling, thanks for all your letters. I've been expecting each day to hear you were on your way back. I hope if they intend keeping you there indefinitely, they'll give you something useful to do. I know how chaps can be kept hanging around between two worlds, one dead, the other powerless to be born, etc. It happens under my eyes every day.

"Here life is almost normal. A few days of panic, double whiskies and philosophy, then by some miracle the Germans held and the air clears at once. I believe quite firmly they won't get through this way. More likely to come down through the Caucasus. The English are hopeless in everything but an emergency. This is a 100 per cent emergency. All the men and armaments we've been crying out for for months are being sent in shiploads, almost too late. The troops have disappeared off the streets. Enough rifles to go round now. I expect you've seen Demetrios who's in Jerusalem with the Greek refugees. Must rush to dress for a party. All love, Viola."

That was the first letter he had received from her since he left Cairo six weeks before. Geoffrey lay on his bed and read it through four times. He put it down beside him and lay with his hand upon it, his eyes shut. He was exhilarated with relief at hearing from her, yet more disturbed than before. His letters to her had become a repetition of the question why she did not write to him. What was she doing? Was she safe? Was she well? Was she happy? Every few days he had asked if he might telephone her and been told it was impossible. He had felt as though his letters were being thrown into the sea. Now that she had written at last it was like someone waving a casual hand out of the midst of happiness.

He suddenly turned on his bed in agony and buried his face in the pillow. For a moment his sense of persecution touched an unbearable point, but he saw it as persecution by his own inadequacy. He loved Viola, yet at the thought of her freedom or her happiness he felt only jealousy.

The vague, intolerable pressure of self-accusation devolved slowly into a sort of pebble weighing down the substance of his mind. He fixed his attention upon it and named it: he had upset the refugees. He relaxed slowly as he concentrated upon the incident and relived it . . .

The rapping of the café window, the net curtains pulled aside, the familiar voices: "Oh-ho, Major Lynd, come please into the café and join us . . ." The faces peering between the café curtains, all now seeming set in a caricature of peevish self-interest, and then the Italian running out with the playfulness of a bear. . . .

For the first time he had rebelled and refused to be dragged inside, so the Italian stayed out on the pavement and held on to his arm and proclaimed a solution of their grievances. They had reached it all together. They were suffering too much. The army was responsible, therefore the army should requisition a house for them that would be properly run with good food and service and laundry, and no expense and a nice sitting-room, "private for them."

The Italian circled one of his hands round and round from the wrist as he enumerated the items. Geoffrey, watching the movement of the plump, yellow hand, felt all his frustration detonate into rage. He answered: "For Heaven's sake leave me alone. Do you think of nothing but yourselves? I'm sick of the lot of you."

The Italian, startled and surprised, let go of Geoffrey's arm. Geoffrey, surprised at himself, strode on. His anger disappeared almost at once, but he knew it would not be forgiven him. It might be forgiven someone else but it would not be forgiven him. All his long effort at patience with them was now wasted; for the rest of their stay he would have to face their bitterness and embarrassment.

Now, as he remembered the hurt surprise on the Italian's face, he sat upright and said: "Damn the whole lot of them. If it weren't for them, I could go back to Viola."

He started to scribble on his writing pad: "Darling, why don't you write more often? Tell me everything you do. Who have you met at these parties? Have you seen anything of the young man Joe Phillips?" He paused and his anxiety stood out hideously from the paper. He crumpled it into a ball and made up his mind not to reply for two days.

Doors were opening and shutting throughout the club. It was four o'clock—time to take a cold shower, dress and go down to tea. Everyone went back to work at five o'clock. He could, if he liked, go and hang round other men's offices; or he could stay where he was. He went to the window and stared out at the mat of morning glories hanging on the opposite wall. He knew the behaviour of these flowers by heart. In the early morning they were blue —a very pure, deep blue; ultramarine rather than cobalt; by mid-day they were a red-purple, and in the evening heat, before they closed to die, they were a pinkish-mauve. Next morning the new buds were open, a new display of blue turning to purple, to pink . . . What, he wondered, happened to the blue? How was the red introduced? The red, of course, must have been there all the time, so the blue could not be so pure a colour as it seemed. Supposing one mixed a little rose madder with the ultramarine? Considering this, he turned and became aware of the room. He forgot the flowers in an anguished consciousness of his circumstances. He began to wonder how he could excuse himself from sharing a table with Clark and Lister. He did not suppose they would care if he simply went and sat elsewhere, but he could not do anything as simple as that.

The club house had been built by a wealthy Christian Arab family and might have been furnished in the Tottenham Court Road. His bedroom walls were covered with one of the little stencilled designs the Arabs used instead of wallpaper; the furniture was fumed oak; the curtains green casement cloth. In one corner was a wash-hand basin with running water. Instead of going out to stand in the queue for the showers, he splashed himself with cold water from the basin and looked in the glass at his own thin body. His lungs had once been tubercular; he had imagined himself cured until the M.O. rejected him. He had felt a new vitality when he arrived in Palestine from Egypt but that had soon passed and now, like everyone else, he felt continually tired and irritable.

By the time he got downstairs Lister and Clark had started tea. Clark had been down to Tel-Aviv the day before and he was describing some processions he had seen there. Lister put his paper aside to ask: "But what on earth are they in aid of?"

"It's this way," Clark leant forward and spoke earnestly. "The Jews here didn't believe a lot of the stories of persecution in Europe. They thought they were propaganda to get them to join the British Army. Now some letters have got through proving it all true—and they demand that we do something to save their relatives. Hence the processions."

"What do they want us to do?" asked Lister, weary and patient, "I mean, other than we are doing?"

Clark grunted impatiently: "We could exchange

German prisoners for Jews." Lister said nothing. After a pause Clark turned to Geoffrey and gave him the usual critical stare: "What do you think about all this?" he asked.

"I don't know."

"If you'd heard the stories I've heard . . ."

"I have heard them," Geoffrey broke in, but Clark went on:

"I have met men who've actually been in these horror camps and . . ."

Geoffrey made a sudden violent movement and said: "I've heard about them until I can't bear to hear any more. I can't pity anyone any more. It's too much for me."

Both Clark and Lister looked at him in surprise and he flushed slightly.

"God!" Clark threw down the knife he was holding and turned his face away.

Lister said: "Lynd is right. There is a point beyond which pity dies. Most of the people who go round saying how sorry they are for everyone really feel nothing."

Clark turned to Lister with a disgusted stare: "You're a damned anti-semite."

"I sometimes think," said Lister mildly, "I'm less anti-semitic than you are. I have no violent feelings about the Jews one way or the other. I'm suspicious of your sort of hysteria. Young men are dying in every country in Europe and you react by getting hysterical about the Jews. There are good Jews and bad Jews, honest Jews and dishonest Jews, clever Jews and stupid Jews—but suffering is not peculiar to their race. You make me wonder what's behind this hysteria."

"Behind it? I hate cruelty, that's all."

"Who doesn't? You're a doctor, so you're probably a repressed sadist. My guess is, you're attempting to work off a feeling of guilt."

Clark got to his feet. His expression was that of a man not to be provoked into a reply. He picked up a leather Sam Browne belt from beside his chair and buckled it on.

Lister said: " . . . and, by the way, you're probably the only officer left in Middle East who hasn't changed to a webbing belt."

Clark's nostrils dilated: " And what do you deduce from that? "

Lister shook his head; the whole of his large, soft body began shaking with laughter so that he could not speak. He wiped his eyes. Clark turned on his heel and went Geoffrey, looking after him as he strode through the restaurant, saw him a handsome man, a man who knew his own mind, a man right and justified in the face of the world.

Geoffrey said nervously: " I think I'd better find myself another table."

Lister was still laughing to himself: " Why? " he asked.

" I think Clark would rather I went. I get on his nerves."

" What the hell do you care? He often gets on mine."

" But I made a fool of myself one night at the station. I was worried about my wife."

" What's the matter with her? "

" Nothing."

" You're getting a *cafard*, aren't you? "

" I'm hanging around here with nothing to do. I belong nowhere. Chaps at H.Q. are sick of the sight of me."

" Humph." Lister handed his newspaper to Geoffrey and finished off the tea in his cup: " I wouldn't mind doing nothing for a bit. And I wouldn't have a scruple. Let the fools fight the war—they enjoy it—and they're the ones who come to the top in war-time. When the war's over, down they go again and then they moan that people don't appreciate the sacrifices they made. Hell, they love it.

Having the time of their lives; a lot of them'd keep the war going for ever if they could. Anyway, don't leave this table. If you go we'll only have to have someone else, and I don't mind you. That's all that matters."

Geoffrey smiled without much enthusiasm. There had been a time when he could have laughed at Clark for a fool. Then he required his world to meet his standards; now he was gone down before the standards of a world that was meaningless to him. He blundered about in it, never really understanding how he was required to behave. Forgetting Lister, he pressed his eyes with his hands, then looked up and saw Lister watching him as from a considerable distance.

"Haven't been sleeping lately," he said. "Must get to bed early to-night."

Lister said: "We all become bloody neurotics out here. But there are compensations, you know. Now I . . . I've been to Palmyra and Baalbec," he smiled so that his round face lit with innocent, almost infantile, pleasure, "and in the autumn we hope to get to Petra."

"Who? You and Clark?"

"Yes—and I suppose anyone else who might like to come."

Geoffrey saw this as a polite inclusion should he wish to invite himself along, but he made no comment. It was all too far distant to mean anything. He would not be here in the autumn. He might be in flight with the rest of the Middle East, but more likely he would be returned to Viola and the routine of life in Cairo. He scarcely knew where this place was of which Lister spoke.

"Is it in Sinai somewhere?" he asked.

"Petra?" Lister smiled at the name. "Southern end of Transjordan." He began scrambling up from his chair. He was going bald and there were blue smears under his small, pale eyes, yet he was only thirty-eight. Clark, probably older, looked ten years younger than Lister. Having got successfully to his feet, Lister started bending slowly to pick up his cap. Geoffrey handed it to him. He took it, laughing at himself, and waved it as he went. Clark left the room with his usual stride. Lister, putting his gouty foot tenderly to the ground, went with the aid of a stick.

Soon all the men at the other tables had gone off, too. Geoffrey had been to H.Q. that morning; he could not go again. To keep up appearances, he crossed the olive groves to the King David and hid himself in a corner of the terrace at the back. He had brought a volume of Gibbon's "Decline and Fall of the Roman Empire" but he could not concentrate upon it. At last he was driven by restlessness and boredom to wander out to the street. In the greenish twilight he went down St. Julian's Way towards the Mamilla Road and decided to eat alone in a restaurant.

A convoy of trucks, colourless with dust, stood nose to tail down the hill and up the Princess Mary Avenue beyond. One had its bonnet open and the men were bawling from truck to truck:

"Hey, Ernie, come and take a shufty."

"Looks as if you've had it, chum."

Further along, men, not concerned with the breakdown, had started singing. Geoffrey recognised the song from the tune of "The Lincolnshire Poacher" before he could catch the words:

"Oooh, Roosevelt's a non-smoooker,
And Churchill smokes cigars,
But, don't you see,
They both agree
On imperialistic wars!
But Uncle Joe's a worker
And a very decent chap,
Beeecause he smokes a pipe and wears a taxi-driver's cap."

As though he, a staff officer, must represent for them all the evils of British imperialism (often described to him by Viola), Geoffrey felt the men were shouting their song at him. It was scarcely modulated, never stopped, as he passed the trucks one by one. There might, he thought, be less bitterness in the desert now, but these men on their way there voiced the bitterness there had been and the near revolt. Rommel was still to them more of a hero than any English commander. Geoffrey, in spite of himself, glanced up at the trucks. One or two of the men saluted but most of them looked the other way. They had a similarity of appearance, like brothers—not tall, hair bleached fair by the sun, skin burnt to a dark pink by the wind and sun; red throats, red, thick arms and legs out of shirts and shorts washed till they looked like rags. Below the knees puttees and hoof-thick, metal-tipped boots. There was about them signs of a change from disgusted indifference to some active resentment. They knew they were the ones done down every time.

Well, he had nothing to complain about. He had been made a 2nd lieutenant, a 1st lieutenant, captain and major all within a couple of months because Bagshot's establishment provided for a major to do the job. Had Bagshot, an old regular who took a charitable view of everyone, been ambitious to build up his establishment, he might have dragged Geoffrey after him to the usual lieutenant-colonelcy. As it was, here for no reason at all, he walked a senior officer; someone apart from these men on the lorries—someone it would be dangerous to strike, dangerous even to avoid saluting, yet most of them avoided it. They had no illusions about him. He felt that his whole appearance was one of guilt, not only for his rank, but for his physical difference. He was too thin in face and body, too elegant in person; he felt his Celtic darkness to be a reproach.

"When Rommel roared on Alamein
And shook the British line,
The whole of Cairo beat it to
The land of Palestine . . ."

Oh Lord! Someone had added a new verse . . . He looked down the length of the convoy, that had probably come from Baghdad, and would have turned back and escaped into the hotel had the lorries not started up one after the other. The line began moving. The song drifted out of hearing and he forgot about it. At the bottom of the hill he saw on the other side of the Mamilla Road a figure as familiar and alien as one repeatedly encountered in a dream. His instinct was to hide but the convoy prevented his crossing to the left and the woman had already seen him. She waved and came hurrying towards him—a delicate, adolescent shape in trousers and jacket; cropped hair, face sallow and lined, with dark, monkey eyes.

"Why, Geoffrey! You are in this town? How strange to see you an officer."

He pretended surprise as though he had not recognised her at first: "Maria! What are you doing here? When did you leave Greece?"

"I am with Demetrios. We arrived two months ago in a caique. We are all in the Hotel Splendide. It is very dirty, there are bugs in the beds and no service—but the bills! They are splendid indeed! Two of us in one room with bad food, we each pay £P45 a month." She caught Geoffrey's arm and gave it a shake: "But this is wonderful! To find an old friend here. Come with me to the Splendide."

He hesitated, unable to think of any excuse not to go, and she looked at him closely in the late twilight: "What is the matter with you? Are you ill?"

He shook his head.

"But you are . . ." she snapped her fingers in the air, seeking a word: ". . . without sparkle, without—what? Vitalness."

"Well, I'm a sort of soldier. It's a dull profession."

She put her arm through his and pulled him on. He held back: "I don't want to go."

"What's the matter with you? You *are* ill."

"I'm not ill, but I'm dull; I'm dead. I'm just nothing any more. I've nothing to say to people."

She laughed, holding to him: "Do you think they will accuse you?"

That was exactly what he did think, but he did not answer.

"And how is Viola?" Maria asked.

"Oh, she's wonderful," in his enthusiasm he relaxed, letting her lead him on. "She looks wonderful. Egypt agrees with her, and she's got an important job."

"Indeed!" Maria's voice had a little edge on it, "that should suit her very well."

She started pulling him up some steps to a gateway in a wall. He stopped, unwilling to see anyone from the past in which he had been a personality.

"No, no," she gave him a tug, laughing, her grip so strong he could have escaped only by force. He had to go on. They went through a courtyard to the old stone house that had become the Hotel Splendide. Inside the porch there was complete darkness. They passed into a hall where there was a smell of cooking and Maria threw open the door of a lighted room. The Greeks were sitting in a semicircle inside. They all looked up, smiling politely when they saw the stranger but not recognising him.

"You have forgotten him?" shouted Maria.

Demetrios, sitting in the midst of the circle, said: "It is Geoffrey. But such a pleasure. Such a pleasure!" He raised his large body out of the tight-fitting basket chair and gave Geoffrey his hand.

There were some dark-eyed young men, restrained in manner; a heavy-featured girl, wife of one of them; two or three older men . . . Geoffrey shook hands with them all.

"You remember Spiro, of course," said Maria. "Agamemnon, Andreas and Tempe? You met them in Athens, surely? Nanos? But Mr. Marco you do not know; he is from Alexandria."

Demetrios, who was holding a book, made one of his slow movements: "They have all come to be with me," he said.

"Say rather, to sit at your feet," said Marco, a middle-aged man who spoke English languidly and with an English accent.

"Mr. Marco, the savant," said Demetrios, "a notable Alexandrine. Please, Geoffrey, sit down among us." He wedged himself back into the basket chair and the others sat round him. Now they looked at Geoffrey as though they were expecting something from him. It seemed in a moment clear to everyone that there was nothing to be got and at once, in order that he should not be embarrassed, they started talking quietly to one another. This, to him, was worse than their expectation.

He said to Demetrios: "What were you doing? Did I interrupt your reading?"

Marco with an elaborate flourish said: "We were reading poetry."

Demetrios wriggled in his chair. He was a young man growing fat; he had a stiff, elderly look but his hair was still black and his eyes moved blackly in the waxen pallor of his face. His voice was very gentle. He lifted the book he was holding and said: "Think of us! Exiles reading poetry to one another."

"Continue," said Maria, "continue."

Demetrios looked at Geoffrey. "Yes," said Geoffrey, "please go on."

Marco said: "Demetrios was about to read one of his own poems."

Demetrios looked down at his book and after a pause, in which the room sat in silence, he started to read quietly in Greek. Geoffrey, understanding only imperfectly, watched Demetrios, who, with his eyes hidden, seemed too sombre, too discouraged a man for a poet. Only when he lifted his sloe-black glance his spirit was visible. Geoffrey covered his own eyes with his hand as though absorbed by the poetry and there came into his mind a picture of a taverna on the lower slopes of Pendele where he had gone with Demetrios to a party in spring. He was conscious of the sun on his hands, the sound and clarity of running water, the taste of retsina and the smell of the pine-trees that grew distorted over a windy hillside. There were cyclamen flowers dotted over the ground and tortoises of all sizes moved across the paths in the pine woods. Far below, the salt-white city sparkled under a mist of heat . . . Suddenly he thrust the memory out and, shaken, resentful, glanced round as though for harbourage at the black-out curtains, the chipped, dirty paint of the 'cubist' furniture and the dust that lay like a bloom over the crinkled wallpaper. He breathed with a sort of bitter gratification the smell of stale cooking-fat and tobacco smoke.

"Do you understand this poetry?" one of the young men asked him.

Geoffrey, looking up startled, realised that Demetrios had finished reading: "Not all," he said, "tell me what it was about."

The young man replied willingly: "There is a man on a ship, you understand, and it is night. He can hear other passengers but he cannot see them. All are travellers, travelling blindly. He does not know where he is going but he knows that somewhere near there are some islands. These are the islands he has been seeking."

Geoffrey asked: "Does he still write poetry? Can he write here?"

"Ah, yes," replied the young man with enthusiasm, "Here, because he suffers, he writes magnificently."

Geoffrey felt his desolation must be visible to them all. He started to rise, saying: "I must go now." Maria gripped his shoulders and thrust him down again. He said urgently, angrily: "No, Maria, I must go. I have work to do."

She kept her hands on his shoulders, bending her face to him, and whispered: "You can't go. We celebrate Spiro's birthday in the Old City, if you please! He will be hurt if you go."

"But I want to go," he said like a child held against its will. He tried to shake off her hands but his tone made her laugh: "What is the matter with you? We would open our arms and take you among us."

"I no longer belong."

"You are an artist."

"I am nothing."

"What is the matter with you? You used to be such a man! I was in love with you myself. Come, now jump out of this mood."

Geoffrey turned his face from her wretchedly. She might as well try and goad the dead to walk.

She was determined he should stay and he had not the strength to resist. The others were talking among themselves. He leant back, glad to be unnoticed, wishing Maria would leave him alone. Feeling him relax, she took her hands off his shoulders, but she went on talking.

"Tell me, Geoffrey, did you like Demetrios' poem? Do you know those islands?"

He answered stupidly: "I once spent a holiday on some islands off the coast of Ireland. Just rocks out in the Atlantic."

"Were they like our islands?"

"Yes, very. I often think of them."

She was watching him closely. He thought she knew too much. He grew tongue-tied.

"Yes?" she encouraged him.

He did his best: "At times I remember places I've known—in England or Ireland, or sometimes in Greece—like complete pictures. It's not just like remembering a scene, it is like suddenly walking into one. Then it disappears and I find I'm here in the Middle East." He stopped abruptly when he noticed the others were listening.

"It happens to me, too," said Demetrios.

"At times," said one of the young men, "I wake up and find tears on my face."

Another said: "These are lost years for us all."

Maria laughed at them: "And why did we leave Greece?" she asked. "Because we wanted to get away—and not only from the Germans; but from the family ties, the conventions, the politics—the politics! I have always wanted to be free like an Englishwoman. I have chosen not to marry. But in Greece I was in prison; so were you all."

"I felt more free there," said Geoffrey, "than I have ever felt anywhere."

"Yes; but for us—a prison. These poets here, they must always be pricking their hearts to keep them tender. Look at our Demetrios! Look!" she tilted up Geoffrey's face, "look at this painter here! What do they say? 'Suffering is my stock-in-trade'."

"Only the raw material of a stock-in-trade," drawled Marco, "How they must labour to convert it."

Geoffrey was trying to move out of his chair. Feeling

were he on his feet he could escape more easily, he slipped his shoulder from under Maria's arm and managed to stand up. But as he stood, the others stood, too, and Demetrios said gently: "Come with us, Geoffrey, to celebrate Spiro's birthday."

Outside in the street, moonlight as brilliant as blue limelight cut the road into blue and black. At the end of the street, above the crenellations of the city wall, an enormous moon floated flatly in a silver sky. They walked on the dark pavement. Maria, keeping a hold on Geoffrey's arm, said: "You did not want to come?"

"You are quite wrong," he assured her, then added: "What a pity Viola is not here!"

"Why? To protect you?"

"She's so alive."

"Come! You're not yet dead. Do not deplore yourself. We are delighted to have you with us."

They passed through the Jaffa Gate, then from the moonlit square before the Citadel into the dark, deserted alleys that led to the Christian quarter. Glimmers of light came from the Greek cafés on the Via Dolorosa. When the party burst into their chosen café, two men in shirt sleeves and a Greek priest sitting at a table turned like disturbed conspirators and murmured a restrained, almost reluctant, welcome. Spiro, the host, went and shook hands with the three and whispered impressively to the proprietor. A table covered with pink paper was already prepared for the meal. There were saucers of hors d'œuvre and salad, and bottles of arrack and mavrodaphne.

"Come now, Geoffrey," said Spiro, placing him opposite Demetrios.

Geoffrey felt their friendliness, their willingness to count him as one of themselves, but he could make no response. His every movement was stiff with effort so painful that he wanted to cry: "Let me go." When anyone spoke to him, he turned apologetically and smiled like a man in a state of acute suspense.

For a little while he talked across the table to Demetrios about some Greek painters still in Athens, but the party was gay and getting steadily drunk, and Demetrios, his sloe-black eyes brilliant in the sallow expanse of his face, was soon drawn into the gaiety. As Geoffrey was forgotten the others began to talk Greek, shouting across to one another, making jokes that were meaningless to him even when he could understand what was said.

The little café with its blue-washed walls oppressed him and he longed desperately for Viola. He longed for her to protect him, just as Maria had said, and he felt her now the only link between himself and reality.

The climax of the party came with the appearance of a parcel for Spiro and a bunch of rose-buds drooping at the necks like dead pigeons. Spiro had to make a speech. He stood on his chair and said his sentences in bursts like public speakers he had heard, sometimes throwing out an arm with a dramatic gesture that was a signal for applause, sometimes throwing up his eyes and wiping sweat from his brow, a signal for laughter. Then he became very serious and spoke of Greece. The tears streamed down his young, plump face and Maria, too, began to sob; then he joked again, toasts were drunk in the syrupy mavrodaphne and it was over. At last they were all out again in the cool night air.

When Geoffrey parted with the Greeks at their hotel he promised to visit them soon. When he was safely alone he said fiercely to himself: "Never again, never again." He was filled with bitterness and anger, telling himself it was all right for Demetrios who had nothing to do but write the poetry of exile, he—but he had nothing to do, either. He had nothing to do, and did nothing. There was no justification for his existence.

He saw his own emptiness with such clarity he suddenly cried aloud: "Viola". He hurried under the tranquil moonlight, through the empty streets, until he got to the club and could shut himself in his room. There, with no hope of sleeping, he threw himself on his bed and longed for the comfort of Viola's body as a child longs for its mother.

A few days later Geoffrey was called to the office of an elderly colonel who spoke almost as though requesting him to do him a favour: "Major Lister has suggested you might be willing to give him a hand. Believe you're used to dealing with aliens—quite good types some of them, quite good! You know what his job is? P.R. mostly, but he's started one or two of these Arabic propaganda vehicles. He says you can read a bit of Arabic—not really necessary, anyway. We're expecting a chap out in the autumn to take all that over but if you'd like to give a hand meanwhile . . . If you'd *like* to . . ."

"I'd be glad to."

"Well, then, why not start straight away, eh? Why not straight away?"

"Thank you," said Geoffrey.

Lister's office, which seemed always growing and changing in character, had spread into a half a dozen rooms throughout the upper floors of the King David. His private office, one of the large, balconied rooms at the back of the hotel, was papered with enormous photographs of old Arabs, old Jews, Arabs on horseback, healthy Jewish girls holding bunches of Jaffa oranges, Palestine scenery and camels. When Geoffrey entered, a young Arab in a smart European suit was sitting on the corner of a trestle-table, talking into a telephone receiver. He slammed down the receiver quickly and stood up.

"The Major?" he looked at his watch with an exasperated swiftness of movement. "The bar is open."

As Geoffrey went he heard the receiver lift again. He found Lister in the bar talking to one of the officers who were always appearing there for a day or two on some mission from Cairo. Lister raised his eyebrows at Geoffrey: "All right?"

"Yes," said Geoffrey gratefully. "Thank you very much."

"Fine. Have a drink."

The officer from Egypt was describing the restlessness of the Germans held on the west of the Quattara Depression while the English accumulated materials for the attack: "They're bringing up engineer-types every day. We watch them through field-glasses while they poke about the Depression trying to find some means of getting their stuff across."

"What does it look like, the Depression?" asked Lister.

"Nothing much. Just a—what would you call it? A depression," he gave a yelp of laughter.

"I'd give anything to see it."

"You'd be bloody disappointed when you did." The officer looked at Geoffrey: "Haven't I seen you in Cairo?"

"Yes, I belong there."

"What are you doing up here?"

Lister answered: "Temporary job; very important, very hush-hush."

Geoffrey stared into his glass. For a moment he was irritated by this defence, then he flushed; he felt flood over him a love of Lister. He saw Lister a personality like Viola to which he could flee from his own failure. He stood back in shadow, saying nothing, letting him talk. Lister drained his glass and sighed: "Suppose we'd better be getting back to work?" He took Geoffrey's arm.

Geoffrey was given a desk in Lister's office. His job was

to plan and design a new magazine for troops, and collect material for the first number.

"If you want anything," said Lister, "Jamal here will get it for you. Scissors, paste, paper, coloured paper, pencils, paint-box? Just tell Jamal."

Jamal, who was Lister's civilian secretary, worked in busy silence while Lister was in the room. As soon as Lister went, he sprang up and crossed to Geoffrey: "Anything I can do, Major? Anything you want? Just make mention of it. I do everything around here, you know."

"Oh!" Geoffrey smiled, "doesn't Major Lister do anything at all?"

"Major Lister! He is a very busy man; a very important man. Naturally he has not time to do anything; he must depend on me. I do all for him. I love him." Jamal pressed the region of his heart with a long, soft, olive hand, "I love him like a brother."

"I can understand that."

The telephone rang. Jamal answered sharply: "Major Lister's office. . . . Speak up please. . . . No, Major Lister is not here. . . . You say the telephone is always engaged. Naturally—we are a very busy office. Who is that speaking? Ah, Mr. Abdulhadi. How are you this day? . . . Yes, thank you, well as can be expected. . . . No, I fear not. . . . No, quite impossible. . . . Is that so? Well, I will consult with the Major personally and see what can be arranged." Jamal put down the receiver and ran his fingers through his short, black curls: "He says we requisitioned his house because he is a Moslem. He says why do we not requisition the house of the next-door Arab who is a Christian?" He shrugged his shoulders, "What is to be done?"

"What will you do?" asked Geoffrey.

"Nothing. I am a Moslem, yet I shall do nothing. The Major would not wish to be worried by such things.

Besides, Mr. Abdulhadi is not a friend of my family." Jamal settled himself to an occupation that seemed to consist of shuffling papers together, putting them down, then picking them up and reshuffling them.

Now he had a job, Geoffrey felt a sense of release. At last he was free to explore the town. At sunset on his first free evening he followed the long medieval wall of the Old City that ran downhill, blank as a prison wall, to the Damascus Gate. Here the Arab buses paused in a reek of petrol before starting out for Jericho and the Dead Sea. Oranges, bilious in colour, were stacked beside the Gate that rose beautifully, fortress-square, its great door open, up from the filthy roadway and everlasting piss-smell of the Arab world, into the tender blue. The gate was a single magnificence. Beyond it everything dwindled into Moslem indifference. Among the slip-shod shops and houses, lights were coming on; the cafés were putting chairs out on to the pavement. From all the wireless sets came the nasal monotony of some Arabic epic.

Geoffrey turned off from the cobbled lane to rough ground that brought him to the wall steps. As he ascended he could feel the evening wind blowing in from the hills. At the top was a pathway formed by a wall's width; on one side the road to Jericho, on the other the little yards of the stone box houses built at all levels. At times the hillocks inside the city rose in a muddle of rocks, gardens and houses to overhang the wall, then dropped again to a pigeon-holing of yards as dark as wells. Donkeys were being tied up for the night and hens shut in. On one of the roofs, on a level with the wall, was a gazelle, tiny, delicate, wild, moving its small feet nervously as Geoffrey approached. When he paused to admire it, an Arab in the yard below called up, offering it for sale. Geoffrey asked where did it come from. The Arab said he had brought it that day from the wilderness.

"What will you do with it?" asked Geoffrey.

"Eat it," said the Arab, then, seeing Geoffrey's expression, he gave a laugh that was half an apology.

Dark-skinned Arab women wrapped in black moved bare-footed into their dark doorways with petrol-cans full of water on their heads. In the open spaces Bedu had camped and were settling down for the night. Some were already lying on their backs under striped rugs, staring up at the sweep of the brilliant sky. Their eyes turned to watch the movement of the stranger on the wall. When Geoffrey waved down to them they responded instantly with an identical gesture.

Beyond Herod's Gate he came to a stop at a corner of the city that overlooked the Mount of Olives. A violet shadow lay over the hill's pink dust and touched the shoulders of rock so that they were as white as bones. Here and there were groups of small, starved olives. A little patch, carefully doctored, was Gethsemane; behind it rose the onion domes of the Russian church.

Almost every afternoon Geoffrey had looked towards this hillside from the hotel and had seen it dry and shabby in the heat. Now in the twilight it had taken on a new quality like a stage-set lit by limes. As he watched, the colour deepened rapidly yet the sky remained brilliant as a crystal. When he looked the other way the olives planted within the city walls seemed no more than a thickening of the twilight. Below them cabbages, planted in rows like steel-blue ribs, were bloomed as by phosphorescence.

Forgetting everything else, he considered the quality of the light here that for this moment between daylight and dark made the stones of the city seem translucent. It absorbed him, a problem in painting; then, remembering, he turned from it with resentment. He started back along the wall, his thought fleeing to Viola as from accusation.

In the houses the windows, small as postage stamps, were black or showed a flicker of light reflected up from the floor. There were slight movements in the darkness of the alleyways. The tethered gazelle was still standing, pulling at its cord, too nervous to sleep. Geoffrey swung his head from it and stared deliberately down at the traffic passing over the glossy Jericho road. It seemed to him that by refusing to feel for the gazelle he was defeating something, but he did not know what. He was filled with chaotic bitterness that gradually took the shape of an intuitive suspicion that Viola had been relieved by his leaving Cairo. He touched the walls on either side as though uncertain of his balance and could scarcely see where he walked. She had not written again or telephoned. He was suddenly convinced she did not care whether he came back or not. Probably she hoped he would not come back—yet, until now, he would have said they were happily married.

He had reached the top of the steps that led down to the sûk. He stood still, trying to pull himself together, trying to see the situation dispassionately and to consider if it could be mended. When they married, she had seemed to him a mere adolescent. It had not been unreasonable to put the claims of his art before her sociability. But when the situation had changed—when he had ceased to paint and she had become a woman in a responsible job—he had remained unsociable and complaining about every new invitation they received. He must have hung on her like a weight. Yet he had never really realised how his personality had fallen until he was ordered off with a troop of refugees while she remained behind indispensible. It seemed to him now that when he said to the Viennese girl on the train (and admitted the fact for the first time): "My wife has an important job", he had admitted to the world his own failure.

But she must have realised it long ago. When he went

she had felt, what? Relief, release? And now, perhaps, dread of his return? What could he do? Turn again into the man he had been? Even if that were possible Viola would remain unchanged. Then, what? Submit to his own failure, cease to be himself even in his faults? At the thought he felt a passionate revolt. In that moment he could have murdered Viola. The impetus of his emotion drove him pell-mell down the steps and he ran until he was brought up by the crowd in the road below. Bland faces stared at him curiously and his spirit fell. "As though it were her fault," he thought, "as though I could blame anyone but myself!" In a desolation of guilt and self-disgust, he wandered back to the club.

Geoffrey worked in Lister's office but Lister himself was seldom to be seen there. He worked, when he worked at all, secretly, out of reach of visitors and telephones. He told Geoffrey that he could do a great deal in a very short time and that served as excuse for and explanation of his absence. Jamal's chief duty was to protect Lister from callers. Unless instructed otherwise, he never knew where the Major was and he had a natural talent for avoiding giving information to anyone.

Lister had said once that Jamal's only occupation was telephoning his friends, but now that Geoffrey was in the room he did no more than shuffle papers and occasionally sigh deeply. Geoffrey knew he was oppressing Jamal by his presence and he was discomforted until one day Jamal lifted the receiver and, with an air of caution, rang up someone to whom he spoke rapidly in Arabic. All the time he kept his glance on Geoffrey, but Geoffrey appeared to hear nothing.

Next day Jamal telephoned three friends and soon enough he was spending his days tilted back on his chair, his broad face bisected by a smile, and saying into the receiver:

"Yes . . . No . . . Ah, you cannot surprise me! Is it so? Dear me!"

When Lister entered, these conversations would end abruptly, but Lister did not speak or look at Jamal. Usually he went straight to his desk, took out a whisky bottle and two glasses, and poured out a drink for himself and Geoffrey while Jamal moved about restlessly waiting for an opportunity to speak to him. Lister would sit on Geoffrey's desk, gazing sombrely at Geoffrey's work, and Jamal would fidget at his elbow: "Major Lister, please, sir, there is a matter here. Most important," and clicking his tongue when Lister did not look at him. Sometimes Lister would finish his drink and go from the room again without having paid any attention to Jamal. When he did look at him he would speak with impatience, even annoyance: "Well, what the hell is it now? . . . No, tell the bastard he can't have it. I'm busy. I don't want to hear any more about it," yet Jamal seemed satisfied, seemed indeed to glow with something more than satisfaction. When Lister was gone, Jamal would settle down to shuffle papers uninterruptedly for as long as half an hour.

Geoffrey was content merely to be occupied. He could work for hours with his mind blank and his hands active, like a craftsman. Lister, sitting on his desk, would watch him as though his application were both a mystery and a joke.

"That's the stuff to give the troops. Nice girl on the front cover. Going to look all right, eh? What about coming down to the bar when it opens?"

When his work became tedious, Geoffrey would join Lister in the bar. The fact that Viola had not written again ceased now to be so urgent an anxiety. He could remind himself that she never wrote to anyone. Her parents were always sending cables to enquire if she were alive or dead. Still, she could send a telegram. (The telegram was her usual method of communication.) Or she could ring him from her office. She did nothing.

Knowing his own temperament, how for short times in his life he had been possessed by some woman's beauty so that he was scarcely sane, he imagined the same thing could happen to her. Imagining that not only her body but her every waking thought might belong to some other man, his content would collapse. His jealousy would come down on him like a blow. There was no escape from it except into the understanding that might exist between himself and Lister. That might exist. . . . He did not know for sure.

Usually when he got down to the bar, he found Lister, who kept bottles in every room in which he worked, already rather drunk. Like Viola, Lister always found someone to talk to in bars or public places. If he were alone he was usually depressed.

"God help us, another bloody week-end. What a country! Three Sundays in a row—Moslem, Jewish and Christian! How this place gets me down."

"It's the heat," said Geoffrey.

"No, it's not the heat. I'm used to that. I've lived round and about the Mediterranean since I left Oxford. I'm always depressed if I have to stay any length of time in one place. I've been here over a year," Lister was sitting at the bar on a stool which his backside overhung on three sides, "The only thing that makes life tolerable is travelling and seeing new places. I'm determined to get to Petra next month."

"Is there anything to stop you?"

"Transport. They're pretty sticky at the moment. Then there's Clark. He doesn't do anything to help. I don't think he really cares whether we go or not." Lister moved his bleary stare from the window to Geoffrey; he said diffidently: "Perhaps you'd like to come?"

"Yes, if I'm still here. The situation's easier. I suppose they'd let me leave Jerusalem for a few days?"

"Four days, five days, no more. I expect you'll still be here."

"At this rate, I'll be here for ever. Will you go to Aquaba?"

"Shouldn't think so. We'll be lucky if we get transport to Ma'an."

"I remember," said Geoffrey, "I used to have one of those engravings of pictures of the Levant by Roberts. An island in the Gulf of Aquaba." He described the picture as he saw it in his mind: the island small and jagged like an iceberg, was crowned with a medieval castle and set in a sea as flat and colourless as glass. In the foreground was the mainland sand that might have been snow. It was like an arctic place, frozen into silence—and yet across the sand went Arab drivers and a string of camels with all their trappings.

Lister leant towards Geoffrey, looking slightly to one side of him, and listened with a smile. His eyes, usually flattened by sadness, seemed to deepen. He whispered: "I wonder if we could get there," and stared beyond the walls of the bar to some other sight distant in time and place. Geoffrey smiled, feeling in his relationship with Lister an excitement that had almost a quality of romance.

After that Lister took to inviting Geoffrey to go with him when he wandered round the Old City: "I haven't exhausted it yet," he said, "this is the first year it's been in bounds. When it's no longer new to me I'll just go quietly crazy."

"Perhaps you'll get posted."

"That's what I pray for. I keep asking for Cairo. I could spend months on those Qait Bey mosques."

They were walking in the evening sunlight down the

Jaffa road towards the main gate of the city. The crowd moved round them in the narrow cobbled street, wafting about in the air a smell of sweat, paraffin, oranges, latrines and spice. Among the dark and light faces, the peoples of all countries of the Levant and the priests of half a dozen denominations, went the British troops swaggering in their nervousness of alien surroundings and in the long-ingrained consciousness of British superiority.

"There," said Lister, giving Geoffrey a nudge, "did you hear what those chaps were singing: 'Don't you see they both agree on imperialistic wars'? What sort of war do they think the next one will be?"

"You think there will be another?"

"Don't be a fool! Another? Why, this war will never really come to an end. We'll never know peace—not in our lifetime."

Geoffrey caught his breath. He felt himself beset on all sides. He felt hopelessly outnumbered by life. As he paused, trying to recover himself, he instinctively lifted his hand to strike the silly face of an Arab who had blundered against him . . . Lister, limping ahead, was warding off with his stick anyone who came near his gouty foot. He glanced back—the profile of a fretful baby hidden beneath a fierce moustache—and shouted: "What's up?" Geoffrey dropped his hand and the Arab, unaware, slid past.

Inside the city there was still a languid activity. The shops crowded their wares out into the narrow alley of David Street. At the top of the highest buildings there were bands of sunlight but everything else was in shadow. Here Lister, moving with new energy, forgot to limp. His feet, long and flat in delicate hand-made shoes, turned out jauntily on either side as he made his way down the steep slope of the sûk. Geoffrey, looking at Lister's large, curved back with love, began to smile. Here, he thought, were the two of them tramping the streets like beggars, drawn together by discontent and seeking compensation for their losses.

Lister waved his stick in the air to point out a classical archway or the broken lion head of an ancient fountain: "Look there! Among the muddle and dark ignorance of Islam! Look, the incongruity is delightful, isn't it? Have you been inside the big mosque yet? It's full of pieces pilfered from classical ruins, but the Arabs think they made it all. They're so gloriously unaware of anything outside their own world. You find them living like rabbits in the ruins of Athlit. In the Cairo mosques there are classical pillars, even lotus pillars. Ask the caretaker where they came from and he'll tell you his great ancestors made everything. They're so naïve. I can forgive them anything."

They passed from the raffish Moslem quarter into the Christian quarter that had a severe air of life lived circumspectly behind walls. In the Via Dolorosa there was a smell of scented tapers and shops filled with decorated candles, crucifixes, boxes and camels carved from olive wood, blae glass bottles of Jordan water and hampers full of the dry, curled up, little plant called Rose of Jericho. At the door of one shop stood massive coffin lids. Here, behind the closely packed stone houses, was the Church of the Holy Sepulchre, its façade almost hidden behind the scaffolding that held it upright. They entered into chilly gloom.

"Black as hell in here," said Lister as they felt thei way to the rotunda that had been built by the Crusader over the marble sepulchre. Scaffolding here shored u the blue-painted walls and rose into the distant dome.

"Whole place is smoked black by religion," said Liste "They say there's no smoke without fire—but that's wha religion is nowadays. Smoke without fire."

Lister's voice, thin and penetrating, echoed round th circular walls. Some privates, led by a padre, turned t stare and listen. The padre gathered them in and raised his voice: "Here you will find eighteen large pillars. Count them, lads, if you wish. Supposing we do it all together—one, two, three . . ."

Geoffrey, pink about the ears, turned his back on the faltering chant of the soldiers, but Lister, unaware of it, talked on loudly: "In my youth, you know, I was something of a connoisseur of all this Byzantine stuff—but now I've had it. Can't take it at all. Look at that ikon. See what I mean? That black-faced bastard in the gold armour?" Lister's laughter, at once whole-hearted and melancholy, followed the soldiers who were being led into the darkness of the outlying passages and chapels. Faces glanced back. Lister followed them:

"Up these steps," he said, "is the site of Calvary."

The soldiers were ascending, their boots striking like flints on the stone steps. At the top was a landing heavily draped and decorated with twisted pillars, chandeliers and witch-balls. The main altar, site of the cross, was aglitter with spangles and candles.

"Calvary up here," said Lister, "the tomb just over there—and downstairs you can see the cave where Queen What's-her-name discovered the cross. All under one roof. You couldn't ask for more than that, could you? Now look at this wax doll with all this jewellery—gifts of the faithful. Incredible, isn't it? Genuine stuff, mind you, valuable—but the most execrable taste."

The padre in opposition was doing his best: "Now, lads, let your hearts dwell on the sacredness of this spot of spots . . ."

"Have you had enough?" asked Lister.

"I think so."

"Oppresses you?—this Byzantine gloom and tawdriness?"

"No, I don't really mind it."

"I agree, it's all part of the show. But a little at a time," Lister made the descent of the steps, putting his good foot down first and bringing the other after it. They left the church: "You'll like what I'll show you now," he said. He led Geoffrey through the courtyards and in by the gateway of a Greek monastery.

The white buildings with their blue woodwork, glimmering through the delicately coloured evening light, reminded Geoffrey of Greece. A young monk, pale, black-bearded, with innocent eyes, came to them smiling. Lister explained in classical Greek that they wished to climb to the basilica roof. The monk, getting the gist of it, smiled more broadly and replied in Arabic. Lifting his black skirts in his hand he led them with agility up the narrow iron stairways and across the bridges between the buildings to the highest roofs and the foot of the last flight that led to the roof of the church. He ran up, unlocked the gate at the top, and left them alone. When he was out of ear-shot, Lister whispered loudly: "The Abyssinians live in holes up here. They're not rich enough to own a space inside—not that there's any for sale. Our idea of a world war's nothing compared with what's been going on here for centuries. Last Christmas the Church of the Nativity was almost wrecked in a brawl caused by a Greek Orthodox priest putting a toe over the border of an R.C. preserve."

They stood by the glass dome of the rotunda and peered down through the church at the sepulchre glimmering in the twilit well below. The padre and his group of privates had returned to view the sepulchre in peace. Lister spoke down into the echoing darkness: "Look at those poor devils trailing round down there." The padre's face was turned up, a white oval in the gloom, and Lister moved away unconcerned. He said: "The religious muddle is old. It's unimportant now. It belongs to the past. It's indistinct with antiquity, like those black ikons, and who cares? It's just a muddle for which we've found a formula. The last of its real power went with the break-up of Imperial Russia—by the way, I'd like to tell you some delicious stories about the goings-on of the Russian priests here. Rasputin was only one of them. But what are all these churches now? Just pools left by the receded tide. Stagnant pools. The medieval world suffered from religion just as we do from politics. Now politics . . . I hope you're not politically conscious?"

"Well, I try to be to please my wife, but my mind just slides away from it."

"Your wife is, though?"

"She's quite intelligent," Geoffrey said with pride and yet with apology. "When I met her she was a student of languages at London. She could speak German, French, Spanish and Italian almost perfectly—yet she'd never left England until we went to Greece. Out here she learnt Greek, Turkish and Arabic. Extraordinary, really! You know, some people who aren't remarkable in any other way have a gift for absorbing languages. I never appreciated it until . . ." Geoffrey paused and did not go on. There was a long silence, then Lister said slowly, soberly and in a tone of great reasonableness:

"I see it this way. Most human beings—ninety-five per cent at least—are incapable of development beyond the age of fourteen. The world depends for its advance on the other five per cent. It's not that the others don't get a chance—you get them in all classes; they just happen to be like that. Members of the five per cent come from all classes, but they de-class themselves. If one comes from the working class or the middle class or, even, the aristocracy—though an aristocrat might have hung on to his privileges in the days when there were privileges—he de-classes himself and joins a sort of isolated class of intellectuals. He just can't help it. He just can't take the other ninety-five per cent for any length of time. That's a fact, isn't it?"

"I suppose it is," said Geoffrey, bewildered by these revelations.

"Centuries ago, when people were rigidly class-bound, it was a different matter. Then a genius of the people stayed with the people and you got a folk culture—ballads, legends, what have you. Nothing like that to-day; far from it. Now this 'government by the people, of the people, for the people' poppycock—there couldn't be such a thing. Ninety-five per cent of the people are incapable of thinking for themselves, much less governing themselves. You'll always get some of the five per cent on top. I see no point in overturning the social system for a set of morons."

"It's a question of justice . . ." began Geoffrey.

"Oh, justice! You're as likely to get justice from the wicked capitalist who can be denounced and thrown into prison as from some sea-green incorruptible of a dictator whom no one dares cock a snook at. Give me a good old fallible government that can be thrown out at the next election, and an opposition to keep it in order, and a . . . What was I talking about?"

"Political philosophy."

"Philosophy, yes. Take Kant, Hegel and all the rest of them. Before you start on them you imagine you're going to find some vast intellectual grasp of life and the universe resolving in conclusions of a profundity you've never met before. And what do you get? Just the same sort of superficial meanderings that pass through your own mind when you're lying in a warm bath looking at your toes. Don't you agree?"

"I don't know. I've never tried to read any of them. I thought they'd be above my head."

"Exactly. That's what their reputations are based on—people thinking just that."

"Ninety-five per cent of people thinking it," murmured Geoffrey.

Lister laughed. He went on talking but Geoffrey, ceasing to listen, wandered over to the edge of the roof and watched the pink and blue light deepen over the roofs and minarets and the black peaks of the cypresses. The hills beyond the city were flushed with violet. Looking at them Geoffrey said suddenly: "That probably did not exist."

"What?" asked Lister.

"The perfection of reason. I was thinking of classical Greece."

"A civilisation built on slavery." Lister descended the steps slowly and cautiously, "and in all these years we've found no substitute for slavery for a few—except slavery for all."

They could see beside the monastery a small garden, formally laid out in squares with round clipped orange trees and young cypresses like a garden in a Persian painting. The greens were growing dark and shadowy. Some monks were moving slowly about among the bushes. When the two officers came down, the young monk opened the monastery gate. He was holding a dahlia, velvet black in the twilight, and as they left he handed it to Lister. Lister stuck it in his cap.

The shops in the open lanes were being boarded up but in the old roofed sûks acetylene flares hissed, dazzlingly white, before the cafés and confectioners.

"Let's go in here," said Lister. They went into a small café where there were half a dozen bare tables and chairs. The radio was snapped off as they entered.

"What were they telling you?" Lister asked the Arab who, with crimped, hennaed hair, flannel trousers and khaki shirt, came to their table. The man looked blank. Lister jerked his thumb towards the radio: "That the English have lost the war? That the Germans will be here to-morrow? That Hitler is a Moslem? That you should kill us all off here and now?"

The Arab, still blank, shrugged his shoulders and asked: "Café Turc?" He went behind a counter and poured coffee from a brass pot into little cups shaped like egg-cups.

Lister swallowed his in one mouthful then sat back and stared at the passers-by: "The remarkable thing is," he said after a long pause, "that in spite of this chaos, we know what reason means. We're not just lost in our jungle. We know north, south, east and west. In theory we can conceive of perfect order brought out of chaos; or we can imagine a vast area of perfect reason just beyond chaos. Remarkable thing, really! As you say, it has probably never existed, yet the idea of reason is born in every one of us."

"And what good does it do us?" asked Geoffrey. "It makes us wretched. The animal in the jungle is content with the jungle; he doesn't want to get out. But we want to get out. We're lost because we can't find the way out. We can conceive north and south and eternity beyond, but we can't get out."

"Eternity beyond? You believe that?"

"No, but I want to. We've given up believing that beyond chaos there is eternal order; for us there is nothing, only death; yet we can't reconcile ourselves to chaos—and there's only a handful of idealists who honestly believe we can bring order out of it. We're discontented, and hopeless—that's what's wrong with us."

"Meaning we're incurable neurotics?"

"But I'm not a neurotic," said Geoffrey, "I go quietly on and somehow remain normal." When Lister made no comment, Geoffrey added: "Of course, I've got my wife."

"You're lucky in that," said Lister.

"You've never been married?"

"Yes. She left me. She wanted a settled life and I dragged

her around the Mediterranean until she was sick of it." Lister leant forward suddenly, distracting Geoffrey from this subject: "There!" he said, "Look!"

Geoffrey looked out into the sûk. A small boy was sidling past, spider-thin, in black stockings with black alpaca tunic and black hat. An auburn curl hung on either side of a face as green as a water-lily.

"A Pharisee in the making," said Lister, "asking to be persecuted. God, a couple more."

Behind the child came two young Orthodox Jews pulling at their long side curls, sliding their eyes towards the two officers, their adolescent faces pallid and spotted, a vestige of virgin hair on their chins, a certain swagger of sex and foppishness mixed with their air of self-congratulating sanctity.

"Never do a stroke of work," said Lister. "Too damned holy. They pray all day and get paid for it by the superstitious. You should see the old bastards in their fur hats going round the Jewish shops on the Sabbath to see no one tries to open on the sly. The European Jews hate them and yet they're afraid of them . . . Again, you see, these stagnant pools of religion!"

"Is Clark right when he calls you an anti-semite?"

Lister laughed: "I'm not anti-anything."

"You like the Arabs?"

"They're ruffians, but they're consistent ruffians. Once you've got their behaviour pattern, you know where you are with them. That's why the English officials like them. But don't listen to anything I say to Clark—it's all just to keep him going."

"You like him, don't you?"

"Can I afford not to? In this bloody little town I'm lucky to find anyone who can talk sense. You know, he's not so bad. He's harmless."

"Is he?" Geoffrey was beginning to feel Clark a shadow

on his life as he had once felt the school bully. "I suppose he's definitely going to Petra?"

"We've both asked for leave in the autumn. We'll have a few days for Petra, then later we're thinking of going to Cairo. I expect Clark'll come, but don't let that stop you. If he bores you, shut him up. He's a lonely creature, really. Like all the rest of us, he wants to be reassured—he wants to think the world loves him."

Geoffrey smiled. He was filled with pity and tenderness. not for Clark but for Lister and Lister's charity.

Clark only once came into the bar when Lister and Geoffrey were drinking together.

There was an epidemic of bubonic plague in Haifa among the dockside Jews and Arabs and one or two British police became infected. As the heat increased in the late summer it was feared the plague might reach Jerusalem. Clark was excited: "My first opportunity to see a case," he said as soon as he saw Lister. His whole personality seemed warmed as though by happiness.

"I thought everyone was injected against it," Lister said.

"Yes, but that doesn't mean everyone's immune. Oh dear, no. I want to try this new M and B treatment. I believe it'll cure anything if it doesn't kill you doing it."

"Is there any danger of the plague reaching Egypt?" asked Geoffrey.

Clark had his back to Geoffrey; now he looked over his shoulder: "They've always got it at Port Said and Suez, but it's kept dark. If anyone could see statistics of disease in Egypt, the English would bolt in a body."

"I can't get my wife to take any precautions."

Clark turned round: "People survive," he said, "the English constitution can stand most things. The majority of English out here die of drink. What's she like?"

"Quite healthy, strong . . ."

"She's probably as strong as a horse." Clark dismissed the matter and went on talking to Lister. For a moment Geoffrey saw Viola dispassionately, a gentle woman, soft-bodied yet strong, and as safe as any other man's wife. He had never known her ill—but that very fact thrust him back into anxiety. Ailing women lived for ever. The strong and the beautiful could fall like elms.

That afternoon when he went back to the office he found Jamal's telephone gossip intolerable. Who else in the world would put up with it? He had stood it now for nearly a month. Although during the month he had ceased to hear a word of it, he now began to suffer like toothache every nuance of Jamal's voice that ranged from wriggling and giggling to self-important indignation.

He had often wondered, listening to the chatter of the fellah women who squatted on the floors of the Cairo tram-cars, or of the servants under his window, or of the Jewish girls speaking Hebrew or German in the Jerusalem cafés, what it was they all found to talk about. Now he realised it was not that they had so much to say as that they could, without self-consciousness, go over and over and round and round a subject a dozen times, and interest and wonder would remain.

It was a Saturday afternoon. Jamal was telephoning his friends to describe an outing he had made on his free Friday. Geoffrey was convinced that it was this very afternoon Viola would choose to ring him. Supposing she wanted him urgently, or he was wanted urgently on her behalf. Supposing she had got Bagshot to order him back to Cairo; or supposing she were seized with one of those rapid, fatal diseases of the East? A man he saw dining one night at the Turf Club had been stricken with infantile paralysis and by the next night was dead and buried. Geoffrey might return to nothing but one of those dry, naked graves in the English quarter of the cemetery . . .

" For God's sake," he shouted, " stop this idiotic nattering, Jamal. You may be holding up an important long-distance call."

Jamal put down the receiver at once. His face turned red. He picked up some letters and, breathing heavily, sat staring at them.

Geoffrey's anxiety collapsed at once and left him exhausted. He felt Jamal's anger like electricity in the air. Nothing Lister did or said made Jamal angry, but for that one protest Jamal could have murdered Geoffrey.

After a long silence Jamal found breath to mutter: " If a long-distance call came through, the operator would interrupt."

That was true, of course. Geoffrey had known it all the time. All his anxiety had been about nothing. Now it was diverted to his own stupidity and he saw Jamal's anger as a terrifying force that could turn Lister, too, into an enemy. At last he had to go and find Lister. He found him in a converted bathroom at the end of a passage where he shut himself up to work.

Geoffrey said breathlessly: " I'm afraid I've annoyed Jamal."

" Annoyed him! " Lister looked up vaguely from his work. " He's there to do what he's told."

" I spoke to him about this endless telephoning."

" Quite right," said Lister, not interested, " kick his backside if you like." He returned to his papers and Geoffrey went.

Outside in the passage Geoffrey leant against the wall. He felt like a man who had passed through a storm. For the first time in his life he wondered if he were completely sane.

The first rain came early in September. The clouds piling up blackly behind the Jerusalem hills met and broke over the city. After the torrent, the sun returned. The pavements steamed in the heat and the air was full of the smell of the drenched rosemary bushes in the Y.M.C.A. garden. It was no more than a short interruption of the summer, but a few days later a fur of green came up and fitted itself round the washed, white stones that littered the Palestine soil. The Mountains of Moab, hidden by haze all summer, appeared suddenly at sunset, their gilded surface carved like a peach-stone. This was the autumn.

The battle of El Alamein had been fought in the desert. The Afrika Corps was in retreat, tension had relaxed and everyone knew that this was a turning point in the war. Lister and Clark had been offered a lift in a staff car from Amman to Ma'an. Geoffrey, who daily expected a signal recalling him to Cairo, was to go with them if he could.

The Arab employees in Lister's office gave him a victory party to which Geoffrey was invited. It took place the night before they set out on the Petra trip.

Geoffrey sat in the lounge of the hotel waiting for Lister. For want of something better to do he listened to four officers on leave from Cairo who were talking loudly behind him:

"Yes, climate's oke, but give me Cairo. I like a bit of life."

"Well, I wouldn't say 'No' to six months of the Holy City"—a familiar voice that one.

"Wouldn't you, now? And what about that smashing blonde I saw you with at Mena."

"Not my property, old chap. The husband's away."

Geoffrey twisted in his chair to see the man who spoke—the man caught his eye and gave him a comic salute. They'd met somewhere in Cairo. Geoffrey, very red, collapsed back into his chair. He tried to hear more about the blonde but the conversation had suddenly been reduced to whispers. He stared into a memory of the Mena House garden as he had last seen it in the crystalline brilliance of moonlight, the paths feathered over with the shadows of the palms. Viola in her white evening dress, her skin golden so that in that light her face, shoulders and arms seemed darker than her hair, walked with a young officer from light to shadow, from shadow to light, through a perfume of orange flowers . . .

Lister came down the stairs and said at once: "Your signal has come. You're to return to Cairo."

"You mean I'm to go at once?" Geoffrey asked.

"No. Any time within the next ten days. Jamal can warn your party and make arrangements. You're free to come to Petra if you like."

After a pause Geoffrey said: "I'd like to come."

Lister lowered himself down into a chair. A little, fair waiter, whose coat-tails touched his heels, came to their table and stood aloof, fingering his white tie. Lister ordered drinks and, when they arrived, said "Well, here's to the fleshpots! Steaks, cream-cakes, belly-dancers, tarts!" He sighed and drank, "I'm sorry you're leaving us."

Geoffrey could think of nothing to say. He felt empty. That afternoon he had for the first time been allowed to telephone Cairo. He had got through to the flat and Viola's voice, remote, small and broken by atmospherics, was the voice of a stranger. He had asked was she looking forward to seeing him soon, and she answered without enthusiasm: "Of course."

He roused himself to say to Lister: "Do you really want those things— belly-dancers, food . . . ?"

"I don't know," Lister laughed, "they compensate if you've nothing else. You've got your wife. You don't know the god-awful emptiness of these places if you're alone. What has one got here? Damn all. The British officials are too dim to be true—they try and build Balham on Israel's dry, unpleasant land; the Jews propagand and accuse you; both the Jews and the Arabs bore you to tears.

There are no women on the loose except a few feather-brained typists. There's no night life because it's a holy city. In Cairo at least you can have a good time."

Geoffrey said: "I don't know that I'd recognise a good time if I were having one."

"I thought you'd be delighted at getting back."

"I am . . ."

Lister waited.

Geoffrey said : "I used to be a painter; now I'm nothing. When you're nothing, you can't enjoy yourself. You hang on to someone else and make a nuisance of yourself. You spoil things for them and they want to get rid of you. It's understandable. If they've any sense they do get rid of you." He spoke with a nervous decision of manner that kept Lister from interrupting him: "I want to go back," he said, "but why the hell should my wife want me back?"

Lister frowned and moved uneasily in his seat: "Where's that fellow, Jamal?" he looked towards the door, "he could have fetched a dozen cars in this time."

At that moment Jamal entered wearing a navy-blue pin-striped suit with built-up shoulders; a brilliant tie hung to his waist. He glanced round with self-conscious hauteur, then, seeing Lister, crossed the floor importantly: "I have been seeking petrol," he said.

"Sit down, Jamal," Lister looked stern. "Tell me what you will have to drink."

Jamal glanced towards the Moslem Soudanese sufragi, then bowed to Lister, touching his brow and his heart: "Thank you. Nothing."

"Then we may as well go."

A large Ford stood outside. Lister asked Jamal: "Do you drive well?"

"Not so well as my brother. He drives very fast. How will you have yourselves?"

Lister sat in front. Geoffrey had the back seat to himself. Jamal, a tense expression on his face, thrust his foot down on the accelerator and the car bounded off. A brittle wind blew through the car windows. It seemed as though summer had gone in a day. The atmosphere was on edge with storm; dust curled up under the olive trees. Black, grey and silver clouds, darkened by twilight, were in continuous movement over the hills.

"You'd miss this in Cairo," Geoffrey said to Lister, "we get no weather there."

"It's a thing I can do without."

Geoffrey leant towards the luminous and windy air. The olive groves were deepened by this light as by an added dimension. A tribe of Bedu, men and women in black trimmed with sombre reds and browns, slashed at the trees with sticks.

"Getting in the olive crop," said Jamal. "A picturesque scene, you think?"

"These filthy Bedu disgust me," said Lister, "they do everything the easiest, most destructive way. They're like their own bloody destructive goats—and they have just as much sense of the beauty of nature. It's sheer animal incomprehension. The only thing they can appreciate is a horse, and that's because it's valuable."

Jamal shrugged his shoulders. Lister turned and spoke to Geoffrey: "There's a little mulberry tree near the club. One morning when the fruit was ripe I found the tree torn to pieces, literally torn to pieces. It will take a year to recover, if it ever recovers. Those apes of Arabs were standing round chewing and grinning, their faces plastered with mulberries. A waste of time talking to them. They'd as much sense of what they'd done as a dog would have. Less. A dog doesn't believe he's always in the right—they do. They're lords of creation."

Jamal fidgeted unhappily: "They could be taught better," he said.

"They have been taught," said Lister. "One day I caught up with a girl who was whacking a donkey along. She'd just picked up a sharp flint to use as a goad but when she saw me, she hid it in her dress. She knew all right."

"Perhaps we do not feel for beasts and trees," said Jamal, "but we feel for one another."

"Do you? The Egyptians do, perhaps, but you Arabs, especially you Moslem Arabs, you're a sour lot, full of pride. Would you feel much sympathy for your unmarried sister if she followed her instincts as you no doubt do yours?"

Jamal gave Lister a bewildered glance, then, comprehending, his ears turned red: "Really, Major!" Some moments passed before he recovered sufficiently to speak, then he said in shocked tones: "Such a thing is different. It is a question of honour. I would not wish to kill her, but the other fellows would jeer at me so I would have no choice."

"Hah! you don't like criticism," Lister turned again to Geoffrey and said in confidential tones but without lowering his voice: "The English here have a policy of treating Moslem customs and prejudices with respect—but, you know, the average Englishman has a sneaking envy of the Moslem attitude towards women. It makes him feel inferior because his own women have the upper hand. Homos always go into ecstasies about this part of the world," Lister laughed, "and it's all so romantic. There's nothing more romantic than an Arabic love song. Jamal," he commanded, "sing us one."

Jamal was driving like a maniac; he made no response. They were out on the open Bethlehem road. On one side the country, divided by dry-stone walls into fields and orchards, fell down to the wilderness of the Dead Sea. The last steel-silver light touched distant bowl-shaped valleys and extinct volcanoes, then it was suddenly dark. They skirted Bethlehem and came, out of complete darkness, upon the dazzle of a lighted café.

"How odd! Out here," said Geoffrey.

Jamal jumped down to open the car door: "Lighted in your honour," he said. "We had hoped to have our party in the garden, but, alas! the weather has let us down."

The garden was an open, gravelled courtyard planted with a few young pepper trees. One end, roofed with dried grass and paved, had become a three-sided room. There the party awaited the Englishmen. Jamal rushed ahead, shouting importantly, still angry. Everyone turned—a dozen or so men, three Christian Arab girls and a Jewish girl with red hair. They gazed towards Lister. Geoffrey, walking in his shadow, felt that to all of them Lister was no ordinary Englishman. Their attitude was not merely the friendly respect for authority usual among Arab employees, there was a glow of affection about it, a pleasure in him. They moved forward to surround him and one of them produced, like the result of a conjuring trick, a large cigar.

"Thank you, thank you," Lister took and sniffed it. The young men started clicking their petrol lighters but Lister waved them away: "Later," he said, "later," and stared round sternly.

"A drink, Major?" asked Jamal, and Lister smiled as he stood head and shoulders above the Arab youths.

From somewhere at the back of the café came Halil Bey senior Arab liaison officer, short, plump, perfumed, elegantly dressed, his feet in pointed shoes. As the oldest most distinguished Arab present, he acted as host. He had been educated in Europe and had a humorous, easy-going manner unusual in Palestinian Moslems. He led the two officers over to the bar. The party would have been described by the Arabs as being in the English style. Ladies were present and there were tables and chairs. Bottles of arrack, cognac and wine were crowded together on a buffet, and a bottle of whisky stood apart for Lister.

Lister drank his first whisky in a gulp, then, sipping gently at a second, he gazed round with an expression of warm benignity. The young men, who had been waiting for this, carried him over to the couch of honour prepared for him.

Geoffrey, left alone with Halil, felt denuded. Halil stood smiling, a gold and amber cigarette holder between his teeth. When he realised Geoffrey had nothing to say, he excused himself and went to see what the ladies would drink. Geoffrey, who had taken a glass of neat arrack, wandered round the fringe of the café to a position where he might see and be unnoticed. He looked at Lister, who, sprawling on the sofa, shoulders propped against the wall, had half a dozen young men round him laughing, then went out into the dark area of the garden.

He had once seen with painful clarity the possessiveness that had probably destroyed his marriage—yet he must bring it even to his relationship with Lister. Why? Because there was no justification in himself. He had no contact with life in his own right. Now he knew that for certain. He stared into the darkness around him as into the inadequacy of his own nature, then, in despair, returned to the lighted café. He would not look at Lister again. He watched the girls, who stood together drinking glasses of lemonade.

Lister was the main point of interest but the girls were a close second. They inspired in the young men the best European manners. The Arab girls stood together, all pale-skinned with round, black eyes and dark, crisp hair, their European dresses hanging badly on their plump figures. They had little to say yet seemed self-possessed rather than shy; when they smiled it was in confidant awareness of their desirable femininity. The slim Jewish girl, with her delicate, freckled features and smart silk dress, sailed out to meet admirers, laughing and talking rapidly, taking the lead and queening it among the diffident, lascivious young men who had been brought up to expect little from women but compliance. They were captivated.

Geoffrey wandered off to the end of the terrace where there was an open fire and an old Arab cooking kebab. The cook greeted him in Arabic; he gave the conventional reply, then they both watched in silence the skewered pieces of lamb and kidney lying above the coals. After some moments the cook said in English: "I see you like arrack! Some think it sanitary for the stomach."

"It does no harm," said Geoffrey.

"One or two a day, perhaps not."

"But three or four?"

"Not so good."

"And more than that?"

The man threw up his eyes: "More means death."

Geoffrey laughed and the silence came down again. He watched the pink and blue flames, sheened with silver, that wavered over the orange glow of the burning charcoal. A scent so rich it verged on taste came from the roasting meat, whetting his hunger that was already edged by the sharp taste of the arrack. He could feel on one side of him the heat of the fire and on the other the outdoor wind that had a frosty chill as though it came off snow. He had felt nothing so cold since he reached the Middle East and, freed from the weight of heat that deadened the mind, he was transported suddenly by a creative excitement. For some reason it brought back to him his only memory of his mother—a winter's night with snow on the window-ledge and she no more than a shadow in the dark nursery, bending to kiss him so that he smelt the perfume of the Parma violets in her muff. The memory had returned to him repeatedly through his childhood. It came most acutely when he was ill. Once his aunt, who had brought him up, put some violets beside his bed. Half in delirium, he had imagined himself the son of a king, sleeping in a tower that stood alone in a snowbound landscape. The indoor warmth, the frozen outer world, the perfume of violets, had filled him with a sense of luxury he had never forgotten.

Now, with the wind glancing against his side, he was nostalgic for a region beyond reality. He saw, as though in childhood delirium, the picture he had described to Lister—the robed Arabs, the camels with their trappings passing through a world so glass-still with frost that their tread might splinter it.

Something moved near him and he was startled by the impact of reality. He gulped down his arrack to hide the fact that he had spoken aloud. The cook had shouted, scattering some small boys who had been watching Geoffrey with wide, delighted eyes. They ran to the shadows of the garden and there fell together giggling.

Geoffrey made himself smile: "Your grandsons?" he asked.

"Yes." The old man made a gesture of exasperation and pride.

Halil came to ask if the meat were ready yet.

"Aye, aye, aye," grunted the cook.

Halil took Geoffrey's arm and led him back to the tables where there were saucers of *taheena*—ground sesame mixed with oil, lemon and garlic; bowls of salad, olives and fruits; and the flat rounds of Arab bread that served as plates. All the first restraint of the party was broken down by now. Jamal was drinking cognac from a tumbler. Lister, sprawling on his divan, called to Geoffrey to join him. Then kebab was brought round on bread. Lister forked down two helpings and refused a third. He dipped his bread into the *taheena* and ate noisily.

"Good?" asked Geoffrey, still on his first pieces of kebab.

"Never tasted better," said Lister with his mouth full.

A group of professional singers had arrived while Geoffrey was at the fire. They were gathered on two divans near Lister. The chief singer—introduced as George, a Christian Arab from the Lebanon—opened his mouth very wide and with every muscle in his face strained into an expression of suffering gave out a cry that seemed to the two Englishmen unbearably sharp. The note lasted so long that connoisseurs in the audience wriggled in their seats and murmured ecstatically. The cry broke off abruptly, the chief singer lay back breathless against the wall, and the others took up the song. When George had recovered he opened his mouth again and everyone leant forward in expectation. Among the performers was a very pale girl in shabby European dress who gazed fixedly but expressionlessly at the chief singer. Lister whispered to Jamal, who sat intently on the edge of a chair: "Who is that girl?"

"Ah," said Jamal with enthusiasm, "she is the wife of the great singer. With him she ran from her parents in the Lebanon. When they first came here they were yet unmarried but in love, and when they sang together you could feel how deeply it came from their hearts. Now she does not sing; she has been ill."

The girl, noting their interest, bowed acknowledgment with great dignity. She looked ill. Indeed, thought Geoffrey, she looked dying.

While George sang, Jamal murmured: "Wonderful, wonderful. When the song was over, he crossed the room to talk to some friends beside the buffet.

Another singer with a zither sang a modern love song, repeating over and over again: "Who is Romeo? Who is Julietta?" George relaxed while his wife whispered urgently at him and the others joined in the new song. Suddenly the party was startled by Jamal's pursuing with uproarious shouts of anger a quiet, middle-aged man who had been standing beside him. No one near Lister had noticed the cause of the trouble. Jamal was caught and held, and while he gazed round wildly, struggling vaguely and shouting, others patted his shoulders and smoothed his arms.

"What's all this?" asked Lister. Halil came and explained that the quiet man was the café proprietor. Jamal had asked for a hookah and been told there was only one and that was reserved against Halil Bey's requiring it. ("Not that I would wish it," explained Halil, "I am too glad that Jamal should have it.") Jamal had then expressed contempt for a café that possessed only one hookah and the proprietor had made a remark about Jamal's family that could be taken either as an insult or as a piece of good-humoured banter.

"To impress the visitors," another young man whispered to Lister, "to do something that would be noticed, you understand, he asked for a hookah."

Others around were saying that with English officers present, Jamal should have overlooked the remark. One said: "He made this scene to attract the attention of Major Lister."

Geoffrey said to the youth beside him: "They are fond of Major Lister."

"He is a man with a heart," the young man placed his hand tenderly over his own heart. "To us he is an Oriental. He feels with us." Then, bending forward and smiling, he waited for Geoffrey to carry on a conversation so successfully begun, but Geoffrey could think of nothing more to say. The young man, infected by Geoffrey's self-conscious silence, got out a silver tooth-pick and cleaned his teeth. In a moment he found an excuse to move away. Lister was talking to Halil on his other side. Geoffrey found himself isolated again.

He leant back against the wall and smiled round miserably. It was on such an occasion as this that Viola used to protect him; now she was no longer a refuge; she did not want him back. He realised he had loved her for her ease in the world—that was something he had never admitted before. Because his own means of communication had been difficult, he had despised anything so simple as Viola's. Now he knew it had the simplicity of an art that was completely beyond him.

All revolt had died in him. He could blame Viola for nothing. Suddenly his defeat in life so overwhelmed him that he began to feel an exhilaration of relief. There was nothing left to resist and he felt drunk. When Jamal came over sheepishly and sat at Lister's feet, Geoffrey spoke to him with such an easy friendliness that Jamal looked at him with suspicion.

"Do you like working for the English, Jamal?"

Jamal shrugged his shoulders: "Yes, thank you."

"You like the English?"

"Some, like Major Lister, I like very much; others . . ." Jamal shrugged his shoulders again. He sat sullenly for a few moments before he succumbed to his old desire to make an impression. He drew out a large handkerchief of red and yellow silk, blew his nose, then started speaking rapidly: "I understand the English. I went to Victoria College. I learnt Latin, Greek and cricket. When the war is over my father will send me to England to make my studies in commerce."

"But at the moment you are learning German?"

Jamal jerked up his head, and his nostrils and lips quivered with anger: "That's a lie," he said, "whoever told you . . ."

"No one told me. I saw you in the office writing in your exercise book."

Jamal opened his lips as though about to shout a denial

then he relaxed. He waved his handkerchief nervously as he spoke: "Well, what are we to do? The Germans may come here; we must look after ourselves." He began to talk excitedly: "Between the Arab and the English there is love. You promised us freedom in our own country; you betrayed us. We do not betray you—but we must look after ourselves."

"When you go to England, will you stay there?" Geoffrey asked.

"What?" Jamal was at once bewildered and angry that Geoffrey made no comment on his defence. He set his lips tightly and swallowed once or twice before he answered: "Stay there? No. This is my country. I have here my family, my friends and my fiancée. I could not live elsewhere."

"Have you any Jewish friends?"

"Naturally. I am a civilised man. I have one or two Jewish friends, also civilised men. We meet and talk in cafés."

"Do you ask them to your home?"

"That would be impossible. My father would not permit."

"But isn't the prejudice breaking down now? Surely the younger Arabs are not unwilling to accept the Jews?"

"That I cannot say," replied Jamal with caution. "I am a man of heart. I feel for these people who have been cruelly treated, but I do not see why they should all come here. This is my country. It is a small country. There would be more room for them elsewhere."

"But they don't want to go elsewhere. They, too, believe that this is their country."

Jamal bit his lip and did not reply. He sat frowning straight ahead of him.

There was a movement at the other side of the room. The girls, after standing apart all evening, consciously demanding and receiving respect, were now departing. Jamal made this fact an excuse to get away from Geoffrey. He leapt to his feet and Geoffrey watched him as he crossed the room and began bustling about among the girls, finding their coats, shaking their hands, making jokes.

The Arab girls seemed relieved to be getting away. The Jewish girl went with them, but none too willingly. She stayed to the last moment, giggling with the men, going and coming back to wave farewells until the taxi hooted impatiently and she had to run to it. All the younger men followed her to the gate and two went with the taxi as escorts and protectors.

Jamal remained on the other side of the room. Geoffrey knew that his attempt to talk with him had been a failure —and yet his failure left no sting. He did not care. He looked for a new distraction with the sublime amiability of indifference to hurt.

Now the girls had gone a change had come over the party. The woman singer retired through a door at the back of the café and her husband sat on his couch alone and gazed into space. When he at last opened his mouth to sing, the cry that came out was like the howl of a bereaved animal.

With no women to impose restraint, the men leant forward, eyes glazed, mouths open in abandonment to their sensuality. The atmosphere quivered with excitement; Geoffrey felt himself drawn into it as into a sort of opium state of exaltation and wisdom. He watched the hand of the boy in front of him tighten round the wrist of a friend. Deprived of women, they had learnt all the compensation of symbols. No reality could give them more satisfaction . . . There was, Geoffrey saw, a hint of escape in that, a thread of light at the end of a tunnel—then it passed and he could not remember what he had been thinking about.

Everything became clear and simple for him as though he were watching a children's play. The singer had thrown back his head and was giving his long, sharp note—he stopped abruptly; everyone gazed at him, expecting him to do it again, but he remained silent, looking at no one. Now the other singers took up the chorus and the audience began clapping to the rhythm of the music. One of the two young men in front of Geoffrey—a plump youth, pale-faced, with a plump, soft-looking body tightly fitted into his navy-blue office suit—started to click some tin castanets in his pocket. The other turned round; those furthest from him began calling to him, those nearest patting and coaxing him, but his face with its slight smile remained unchanged. He let himself be lifted from his seat and pushed out into the middle of the floor, but there he stood slackly without moving, looking softer than a woman and more persuadable. His eyes slid round to the two Englishmen and although he appeared to ask no question, Lister nodded to him and smiled encouragement from a mild, drunken agreement with everything.

The zither player changed to another tune. The audience formed a circle round the dancer, leaning towards him and clapping up to him. He lifted his hands above his head, crossed his wrists, then began to dance very slowly, moving his feet a little, clicking his castanets and giving a slight jerk of his soft waist. Fixing his glance on one of the young men, his smile deepening and becoming at once ironic and significant, he began shuffling round slowly, his body still, except for the movement of his feet and the rhythmic, lascivious thrust of his hips. When he had turned completely, he progressed a little to pause before another friend and the smile, the dance, was for him.

The circle clapped as though hypnotised, then someone standing outside shouted a joke; the others laughed, and at once the dancer began caricaturing himself. The spell was broken. The clapping died down and it was all buffoonery. Two or three others began imitating the dance, making the same movements but clumsily, with a masculine jerkiness. One man, rolling his eyes, wriggling his hips, made a play of courting his friends with indecent gestures. The others chaffed him. The joke was becoming an improper one.

Lister glanced at Geoffrey, aware, beneath his apparent inertness, that this was the time to leave. The two rose from the divan. Polite attempts were made to persuade them to stay, but not seriously. Everyone knew their departure was when it should be. Jamal, always a little separate from the others, bustled importantly to the car.

Lister, limping and swaying into the shadows, waved the red tip of his cigar in large gestures of thanks and farewell and, when he got into the car, called out in unintelligible Arabic. He leant from the window but Jamel, thumping down on the accelerator, cut off the farewells and applause of the others. The car rushed into complete darkness.

Lister lolled in the back seat with Geoffrey: "Nice boys," he said. "Nice boys." He sucked at the stub of his cigar and after a long interval spoke as though out of an excess of bliss: "To-morrow," he said, "we start for Petra."

While the three of them were walking down towards the Damascus Gate next morning, Clark said to Geoffrey: "What's the matter with you?"

"Nothing," said Geoffrey, smiling to himself. He was feeling almost light-hearted in the relief of his indifference to everyone and everything.

"I suppose you're patting yourself on the back because you're going back to Cairo?"

Geoffrey laughed. Clark, annoyed that he was coming with them, made a disparaging noise in his throat: "Filthy place—Cairo," he said, "full of disease." When Geoffrey laughed again Clark turned, as though provoked by Geoffrey's indifference, and looked at him with an expression at once ironical and threatening. Geoffrey thought: "He can't bear the sight of me. If he could, he would stamp me out like an insect," and yet he did not care.

At the garage they became involved in an argument about the fare to Amman, which had gone up during the last few days. Clark and Lister together gave way to one of those rages that attack the English in the Middle East. Geoffrey stood in the background as though it had nothing to do with him.

Clark's strong, athletic body seemed to vibrate with anger: "I won't pay more than thirty piastres. No one's ever paid more."

The proprietor, a fat, elderly Arab, struck the side of his right hand across the palm of his left and shook his head. "Half a pound," he said. "All this week, half a pound."

"Why? Why fifty piastres now?" shouted Lister, too angry to repeat the 'half a pound' phrase. "Last month thirty piastres. Many officers go last month—thirty piastres. Why?"

Four friends of the proprietor, sitting on the ground outside a hut made of flattened kerosene tins, exchanged delighted glances, then grinned up at the Englishmen.

"Tyres," explained the proprietor. "Very scarce. Very expensive."

"We'll go by bus," said Clark.

"Hah!" shouted the Arabs, "bus only goes to Jericho." They sat up to assure the officers with a sort of paternal patience rather than triumph: "Only taxi and Post Car."

"How much taxi?" asked Lister.

"Each person half a pound," yelled the Arabs.

"And how much for Arabs?" Clark yelled back.

"All the same," the proprietor said indignantly, "Arab, English, Jew—all the same. You'll see. You'll see Arab pay half a pound like you."

Lister started to laugh: "It's no good. The East always gets the better of the West."

They got out their fifty-piastre notes. The Arabs, sitting on their feet, their grimy robes carefully caught between their legs for decency's sake, smiled approval that the business was settled. Only Clark grumbled on remorselessly: "I hate to be done," he said, "I hate to be done."

"What does it matter?" asked Geoffrey from his ease and remoteness. "The difference is only four bob."

Clark swung on him: "It's a matter of principle."

Geoffrey shrugged his shoulders: "We lose money, they lose time. Which do you value most?" He sauntered off and Clark glared after him like a man who had been mortally insulted.

Lister looked at his watch, then glanced round: "Where's the Post Car? I bet it's been and gone."

"Not here yet," the proprietor soothed him. "An minute come."

Lister and Clark followed Geoffrey to the garage gat and stood and watched the traffic of the Jericho Road The weather was fine again, the sun hot. On the dust verge of the road two British N.C.Os. sat on their pack smoking, not in the leisured manner of the Arabs, bu with an air of deep-seated boredom, of spirits represse until they had almost died of inactivity. Althoug there was no cause for hurry, Clark muttered with im patience and began to wander in circles round the garag enclosure.

The proprietor brought out from the hut three dirt wooden chairs: "Sit down, sit down," he said in pityin tones. They sat on the chair edges, nervous of bugs, but in a moment were up again, made restless rather than enervated by the heat. At last the Post Car swung out of the road into the garage. It looked like any other big, black, glossy taxi with which an owner could now make a fortune in a few months, but it had 'POST CAR' painted in white letters around it. The Arab driver showed no consciousness of being half an hour late, but with the indifference of someone in an official position lit a cigarette and left the proprietor to deal with the passengers. The three officers sat in the back; the N.C.Os. took the two middle seats; the seat beside the driver remained empty.

"If he doesn't get another customer," said Clark, still feeding his impatience, "we'll be here all day."

About ten minutes later an Englishwoman arrived. Catching together her long, tussore-silk coat and holding down her waist-length strings of beads, she got in beside the driver. She put her parasol of green-lined tussore into a corner of the car and opened a beaded vanity bag. She spoke to the proprietor in Arabic. He replied. She immediately became indignant. Her large straw hat decorated with a fringed scarf, swung round and she stared at the five Englishmen through gold pince-nez: "How much did you pay?" she demanded.

"Fifty piastres," they replied in chorus.

"It's disgraceful—the profiteering going on in this country because of a war that's got nothing to do with them." Her delicate, pink face, her bun of grey-fair hair and her hat quivered as she spoke. She was holding a fifty-piastre note in her hand. All in a moment the proprietor had snatched the note, the driver started the car and, turning in one movement, carried them off. The woman looked out of the window as though nothing had happened but the hand she raised to her hat was trembling.

Lister mumbled: "What a life we live in this country! What a hell of a life! We're always in a rage about something. Geoffrey's right—what do twenty piastres mean to any of us, yet we were ready to do murder for them."

Nobody answered. As soon as they turned their backs on Jerusalem, the N.C.Os. opened picture magazines and became absorbed in them. The car passed through Bethany with its delicate pepper-trees and descended into the naked wilderness of Judea. Here nothing lived and there was no movement but the shimmer of heat over the distances. The sun poured down between the terra-cotta-coloured hills on to the road that dropped rapidly in unceasing curves to below sea-level. As the air condensed the passengers began to sweat. Their heads seemed to swell and a nauseating pain pressed on their brows and ears. The two corporals lost interest in their magazines. One pushed his copy of *Cavalcade* in front to the Englishwoman and said: "Like to have a look?"

She turned, smiled and gave a businesslike nod: "Thank you." She went through the magazine in a couple of minutes and returned it at once: "Is this your first visit to Transjordan?" she asked.

"Not exactly," the corporal gave a modest laugh, "we're stationed there; been there some time."

"You like it?"

"Well," the corporal laughed again, twisting about with shyness, "not much night life."

The other one also laughed: "Not even a cinema," he said.

"No, I suppose there isn't." The Englishwoman turned away again. The corporals began to nod and were soon slumped together asleep.

In the distance, between the golden foot-hills, appeared the dark flower-blue of the Dead Sea. It disappeared again behind rocks, then, suddenly, the road swung clear on to the wide, flat plain of the Jordan. The river was invisible somewhere among the dry mud flats that stretched to the Mountains of Moab. In the distance dust columns whirled into the sky, long, white and swaying as they raced into sight and out of sight again. The surrounding hills, softly eroded and coloured grey-blue, flamingo-pink and rose, floated round the plain as though upon mist.

"God!" said Lister, his face looking oiled, his shirt saturated, "I believe you could touch this heat." He put his hand out and drew it back quickly and gasped.

The driver, with a straight road before him, accelerated, glancing at the wavering speedometer needle and smirking with pride when it touched 150. Even at that speed the wind seemed to be holding them back. A dark patch in the distance began to grow until they saw it was the Jericho oasis. They passed in a moment from the arid plain into a jungle of green. Lister leant out, astonished at this vast fertility: "There ought to be tigers," he whispered.

The banana orchards grew a little below road level so that the pointed leaves were massed to the sight, a delicate silken green almost hiding the bunches of green bananas. Behind them rose tall date palms with clusters of magohany-red dates. The houses, hung with blood-purple bougainvillæa, could be glimpsed among the foliage of the orange groves. Beside the iron gateways were small, dark hibiscus trees dotted over with flowers of red or fuchsia-pink. The wind seemed to have dropped and there floated into the car a scent of flowers.

The Englishwoman looked round and spoke over the heads of the sleeping corporals: "Such a delicious fragrance, don't you think? The name Jericho means 'scented air'."

Lister said: "I've been told the Jericho women are the dirtiest and laziest in Palestine."

Everyone stared out to get a glimpse of them but the

street was deserted. Only in the market place a few Arab lay in the shadow of their fruit-stalls and as the ca passed in a cloud of dust they indolently covered thei faces.

"Tigers," said Lister urgently, "tigers, elephant monkeys, tarantulas, scorpions and giant spiders. Danger.

"None of those," said Clark, "is as dangerous as th common fly."

"I suppose you've got some bloody medical book in you rucksack?"

"I've got Manson," Clark said. "One must have som thing to read."

Beyond the village the driver made speed again. Geoffre watched the speedometer needle slide over the figure 16 touch 170, tremble there and move on. It meant nothing. few miles on was the Allenby Bridge. The car stoppe with a jolt and scream of brakes and the corporals wok up.

"We'll be half-an-hour," said the woman. "Put the ca into the shade."

The driver appeared not to hear her. He jumped out an speaking for the first time, said officiously: "Passport Give, please." Only the Englishwoman had a passpo and when he put out his hand to take it, she moved away: "I will take it myself," she said. He glared at he his round face twitching angrily, but she left the car ar walked calmly down the road to the huts. A milita policeman came to examine the army passes. The corpora got out to have a talk with a policeman they knew. List said: "Now let's have a look around."

Flies had settled on them as soon as the car stoppe "Bloody flies," said Lister. "In England they're qui happy playing round a chandelier, but here they've on one interest—the human body." Geoffrey watched one them moving through the sweat and hairs on his han

The fly was a greasy grey colour under its transparent wings and so large it was like a fly seen through a magnifying glass. Geoffrey looked up and, seeing Clark watching him with a cynical smile, he smiled back. An awareness had grown between them that was almost physical and eclipsed Geoffrey's attachment to Lister. He got out into air so hot and damp it had a tangible density. They walked together past the frontier post to the bridge.

The frontier huts, painted with some dark preservative, stood deep in dust beside the road. Their windows were unglazed and it was possible to look straight in at the bare card-tables, the soda-water bottles stacked on the floors and the camp-beds hung with mosquito netting. Police and officials could exist down here only for a few days at a time.

Lister, eager to find something to look at, limped on ahead. As he went he twitched his shoulders against the irritation of the sweat trickling down his back. His shirt was sodden.

The three of them leant in a row over the side of the bridge. The river, brown and heavy as melted chocolate, slid between flat banks where some feathery trees grew grey with dust.

"What is that perfume?" Geoffrey asked.

"It comes, believe it or not, from those tatty tamarisks," Lister peered towards them. "There used to be leopards here; not a sign of one now. They've all been exterminated. Humanity's closing in on everything. Soon there won't be a wild creature left."

"Good thing, too," said Clark. He threw his cigarette end down into the slow eddies of the water. Dragon-flies, monstrous, flashing their kingfisher-blue, whirred over towards it and dipped at it. Two butterflies the colour of sulphur appeared and dodged around one another into the darkness beneath the bridge. Lister watched them, his mouth slightly open, an infantile intentness in his stare.

"Let's go back," said Clark irritably as though to interrupt this intentness. He started walking back at once and Geoffrey was drawn to follow him.

A car from Amman was standing at the Palestine frontier. Police were taking out the leather seats.

"They won't find any hashish there," said Clark. "The Arabs aren't good for much but they do show some ingenuity in dealing with hashish." Clark talked directly at Geoffrey, a thing he seldom did: "They seal it up in a metal container, make the camel swallow the container then, at the end of the journey, kill the camel. Or—you know those fat-tailed sheep? Well, they cut all the fat out and fill the tail with hashish and drive the sheep with a herd over the frontier. Then they've another nice little trick! . . ."

Geoffrey managed to listen without flinching and at the end returned Clark's smile with an innocent disinterestness.

When they had crossed the bridge and passed through the Transjordan customs, they came into a region of new strangeness. Here the putty-white mud hills, smooth as flesh, were shaped like breasts and thighs. When the car rose out of this moon landscape and began to ascend the hills, the weight of the heat was slowly lifted. The ridges rose in jerks until they reached a height where even the interior of the car grew cool. The road followed the hill brow on one side of a valley; on the other the crags shot up out of sight of the occupants of the car.

"Like Tibet," said Lister, putting his head out to look at them.

"How do you know?" asked Clark.

"I just know. This might be Tibet—the Gobi or Shamu desert," he sank back into his seat and repeated tenderly to himself, "The Gobi or Shamu desert."

There had been no rain here. Everything—rocks, earth and the stalks of last spring's flowers—was the colour of a dead rose. Not a thread of green except in the valley a long way below where the margins of the little Shu'ieb were brilliant with grass and leaves and the pink of oleander flowers. The road dropped and met the valley where the widening river watered fields and pomegranate orchards. Among the black-green glossiness of the leaves, the pomegranates hung like globes of pink light. Children ran by the car holding up branches of fruit. Lister called to the driver to stop but he took no notice, and when the car sped past the children flung stones and shouted curses.

Houses began to appear, multiplying and pushing back the green until they formed a village street. The car stopped. The Englishwoman with her umbrella and parcels got out. A boy came towards her wheeling a lady's bicycle. She nodded at the soldiers but the driver started off before anyone could speak.

"What a place to leave an old lady." said one of the corporals, turning anxiously to look out of the back window.

Lister said discouragingly: "Old ladies are safe anywhere." The corporal slid back and was silent. Soon both he and his friend were asleep again.

The car climbed until it reached a plateau of cornland from which a valley fell on one side to rise beyond in ranges of rose-brown hills. The corn had been cut and the camels grazed over the fields in the evening light. They bent their necks slowly down to the thorn bushes, moving away from the car slowly, deliberately, but with a show of being unaware of it. Other camels, pressed into service, came in slow trains down the road, their bells clinking, their feet pressing the ground deliberately like blotting-pads, their knees bending with a slow-motion grace, each head swaying, the lifted face, superior as a dowager's, bristling with indifference to criticism and disdainfully critical.

The evening wind was pouring across the plateau and the corporals stirred and awakened. Everyone came to life. Some ox-carts, laden with girls from the fields, laboured towards the car and the girls bent to laugh in at the men. The men sat up in astonishment.

"Such girls!" cried Lister.

Round-faced, golden-skinned, rose-cheeked, large-eyed, black-haired—all laughing. Occasionally one Arab woman in a crowd would possess this beauty—but here were fifty of them all alike.

"Circassians, of course," said Lister, "planted here by the Turks."

"Not bad at all," Clark's large face was transfigured with smiles, "not bad at all!"

Geoffrey, for the first time since the war had absorbed him, felt a glow of beauty over the world. He sat up in the car, his eyes brilliant, and the corporals, looking back at the girls, caught his glance and laughed. He laughed back at them. Everyone began talking good-humouredly, so that even the driver relaxed sufficiently to grin over his shoulder and say "Amman" when Amman appeared.

At the Philadelphia Hotel, Clark became angry again because the prices were higher even than those at the King David.

"Look at it! Look at it!" He waved his arms at the dark hallway with its enlargements of photographs of Petra and Jerash and its dusty leopard skins. The manager, short and fat in a dark suit, his hair stiff with brilliantine, gazed round him, bewildered.

"Three of us in one small room with brass bedsteads and a cracked mirror . . ."

Lister interrupted quietly: "You're shocking him. To the Arabs here this is the height of sophisticated luxury. Don't spoil it. Don't hurt his feelings."

"Feelings be damned!" shouted Clark. "He knows how to profiteer."

"Please?" the manager turned to Lister. "The gentlemen are not satisfied?"

"Quite satisfied," said Lister. "Besides," he added quickly to Clark, "there's nowhere else to go."

Clark opened his mouth to speak and shut it again as a young Arab of unusual good looks, magnificent in his expensive robes, came up the steps to the door. As his eyes flickered self-consciously from side to side, the effect of the impact of this western-style hotel on a nomad country became clear to all of them.

"Let's go and look at things," said Lister.

"Not me," Clark was still angry, "I can't bear the smell of the Arab world. I'm going to have a drink on the terrace."

"I noticed a little Waaf out there," said Lister.

Clark strode away without speaking. Before the others followed, the manager touched Lister's arm and showed him a photograph of the Petra Treasury. "Please, Major," he said, "I wish to make an advertisement. Tell me—is it 'rose red' or 'red rose'?"

"'Rose red'," replied Lister at once.

"And, please, Major, what means this 'half as old as time'?"

"It's poetry," said Lister.

"Ah!" the manager nodded and went satisfied to his office.

When they left the hotel they noticed Clark had already got into conversation with the girl on the terrace.

"How does he manage it?" murmured Lister.

Geoffrey, who had felt oddly that day something of the

attraction of Clark's masculinity, said nothing. He was a little piqued that Clark had been so easily distracted from tormenting him.

The town was bare with wide roads and small, square houses; the wealthier houses were dotted over the hills among young trees that were limp from the long, thirsty summer. Down in the naked-looking sûks there was little to buy and the prices were high. Standing gazing about them on the pavements were groups of young nomad Arabs in from the country. They were still and quiet, yet seemed on the alert like wild animals; all small, elegantly made, like delicate girls in their white robes. They had slender hands, painted eyelids and long curls, but their eyes, black and brilliant as jet, staring with animal directness, were the eyes of men. With them stood soldiers of the Frontier Force in tight robes of pink-and-white check cotton, black curls on their shoulders, their small waists and narrow hips held in massive leather trappings from which stuck pearl-handled pistols, swords and every sort of ornamented knife.

"Now," said Lister, "these are the real thing. These give you hope for humanity. How different, eh?, from those puffy, squint-eyed, syphilitic bastards you get in towns in Palestine! "

He turned with admiration, gazing warmly at the young men, who looked back with the cold, watchful stare of the tiger.

"I love them," said Lister. "One might start a new world with them."

"What would Clark think of them? " said Geoffrey.

"Clark! " Lister echoed with disgust. "He'd hate them But he's not a romantic. He can't see that these people however destructive, have a beauty and dignity that gives them a right to existence. He's all for those gross Jews with their backsides bulging out of khaki shorts. The Jews drive tractors and make the desert blossom with Brussels sprouts. He'd give Transjordan over to the Zionists if he could. God, what a thought! "

The Arabs, disturbed by the admiration they were arousing, made slight, nervous movements, touching their dagger handles, shifting their feet and flickering their eyelids as though they felt that some response was required of them.

Geoffrey took Lister's arm and moved him on, but he kept staring back and asked excitedly: "Hell, who taught the Jews to drive tractors? The Arabs could learn."

Geoffrey laughed: "That's what Jamal said."

"Oh, Jamal! "

"You love their simplicity. They'd corrupt in knowledge."

Lister sighed and with one last yearning look at the Arab youths let himself be led away: "Yes, I love their simplicity. The Palestinian Arabs are already corrupted, but these are untouched. They are simple and pure. I believe in them because I must believe in something."

In the main square there were a few large shops. One with a red-and-white-striped blind attempted an air of the French Riviera and displayed perfumes, shirt silks and ivory-backed brushes at exorbitant prices. Lister and Geoffrey wandered round and round, looking and re-looking at the shops, unwilling to return to the hotel and not knowing what held them until Lister said: "No black-out."

"Of course."

They lifted their faces and gazed round at the lights and the colours of the twilight. They went upstairs to the flimsy wooden balcony of a café and sat watching the life of the square. A blaze of light came from an open-fronted barber's shop in which were painted chairs, paper roses, bottles of green and violet oils and pictures of the

Nubian hero Antar. Next door was a lemonade seller displaying glass barrels filled with sherbet. Up over the hills the lights were looped on wires from house to house.

Geoffrey and Lister remained until the hills had disappeared against a black sky and there were only the lights in mid-air.

When they went back to the hotel for supper, they found Clark had eaten his meal and was sitting in a corner of the bar with his Waaf. He did not appear to recognise them. When they went to their room he had disappeared and he did not come to bed until after they were asleep.

Next morning they were awakened at five o'clock. A staff car driven by a sergeant was waiting for them. They left the town in the early sunlight and met flocks being driven in to market. The Arab herdsmen leaned down from their horses to gaze curiously into the car.

Clark scowled up at them: "What do these savages want?" he asked. As the car was held up by the rough-coated, frightened sheep and goats, he leant out and shouted furiously at the horsemen. The Arab nearest the car replied at once, reaching in a moment a crescendo of rage, while those not involved sat impassively watching the row. In a few minutes it was all over. The flocks had passed, the Arabs galloped on and Clark lay back panting in his seat.

Geoffrey felt unendurably irritated by Clark's behaviour. The sublimity had passed from his mood and his despair was like something dead within him. He had begun to feel a foreboding about Petra. If he could, he would have turned and gone back to Jerusalem.

Clark had not yet recovered and kept saying angrily: "Bloody savages."

Lister drew out his hip-flask and handed it to Clark.

Clark took a long swig and passed it in front to Geoffrey, who drank and passed it to the driver. After that the car itself seemed to proceed more easily.

On either side of the road were the stubbled remains of cornfields. In the distance, corn-coloured and cream, a frieze against the grey-blue sky, were grazing camels followed by their stumbling, tender young. In this crystal-pale light everything was a monotonous sun-colour, the colour of the stubble, the parched earth and dead end of the year.

An hour passed before they got beyond the cornfields. The first police post stood on the desert earth, crenellated and bastioned like a child's drawing of a castle. The Arab policeman peered into the car and then waved them on: "Beyond," he said, "only desert."

Out on the desert road they were thrown about like dice rattled in a box. Lister asked the driver: "Does it get any better?"

"Get's worse, sir. Except for Palmyra, this is the worst road in M.E."

"That's something," said Lister, not ill-content.

"What happens if we break the back axle?" asked Clark.

The sergeant laughed good-humouredly: "Then we've had it, sir," he said.

The desert stretched out of sight into the heat haze of the horizon. It was flat like a mud bottom left by a receded sea, and littered with rocks and lava pebbles. Here and there grew greyish bushes and rosettes of dark, rubbery-looking leaves. Occasionally there were asphodels like the dry, grey husks of dead flowers, their long stalks pushed up leafless from the ground. The road ran straight ahead like a line drawn with a finger on felt. The car managed to rock and bump its way forward at a good speed.

"Must get to Ma'an before dark," said the driver. "Mustn't run off the road."

"What difference would it make?" asked Clark. "The road doesn't look much better than the desert."

"You'd be surprised, sir. If she went off the road she'd go arse over tip quick as look at you."

"Would she now," said Lister. His tone sounded heavily sarcastic but the sergeant merely smiled to himself as though he knew all about Lister.

Here and there beside the track were the bones of creatures abandoned by caravans. The bones lay white on the fawn-grey sand—curved vertabræ tipped by the small, delicate skull of the camel or the long, white frontal bone of the horse.

"Look, look, a lake!" said Lister.

"No, sir, a mirage."

"Really, a *mirage!*" Lister leant forward and gazed at it, lips parted.

The mirage grew as they watched it until it was like a sea, flat and silver, lapping in always a few yards ahead of the car. Out of the sea rose rocks, distorted and oddly magnified so that they seemed like distant piers and breakwaters. Geoffrey, gazing out of the windscreen mile after mile, fell into a dreamy drowsiness, so that he imagined the mirage to be the sea beside which he had grown up. He drifted about on memories that filled him at once with nostalgia and dread, and carried him at times towards some region of the forgotten past from which his instinct was to flee. It lay in darkness, just behind the radius of memory, and with an old cunning he deflected his consciousness from it always just in time. As a safeguard, he concentrated the weapon he had forged against it—his skill as an artist. Whatever was wrong with him, he could do something that astonished people. At school, even if he were physically weak, not good at games, possessed of no unusual intelligence or personality, he could do something that astonished people. That justified him to himself if not to others. They did not understand the importance of his ability. It was only when he went to an art school, where talent was everything, that he could feel at home in the world. There, somehow, miraculously, he had had added to him, intelligence, vitality, wit and importance; miraculously—but too late. He had always to apologise for himself and claim his right to existence through the fact that he could do one thing supremely well.

He remained lost in the mirage until it began to dwindle within itself. The sea lost substance, became like a glaze over the desert, like the quiverings of heat, then was gone. Geoffrey, awakened, gazed round him in a stupefied way, then said to excuse himself: "Do you think we could get to Aquaba?"

"Aquaba!" said Clark, frowning as though Geoffrey were a difficult child, "what's it like?"

"I don't know." Geoffrey, disconsolately lost in reality, put his head down into his hands.

"You feeling the heat?" asked Clark.

"Yes."

The sergeant broke in at the right moment: "I've been to Aquaba. Very colourful place. The sea's a smashing colour."

"Peacock-green," Geoffrey lifted his face.

"Exactly," the sergeant agreed admiringly.

"You can't get down there?" Lister asked.

"No sir. Not this trip. Got to be back at Amman by Sunday."

They passed another toy castle, like a cardboard stage castle, shut and deserted on the barren ground. Here the single track of the Hejaz railway came close to the road and went away again. At noon they reached a village—a few huts by the rail, no tree or hint of vegetation, only a handful of concrete huts, the naked line and the bare grey-yellow, broiling desert. The sky, white with hea could scarcely be glanced at. In the midst of the villag area lay the body of a donkey. It was swollen like a barre and when they passed it at a distance of a hundred fee the stench struck them like a blow.

They stopped at the main hut and an Arab police office appeared. They asked if they might eat inside and h smiled and said his home was theirs. They sank dow on to the forms by the wall, glad to be still, glad to b out of the sunlight, their bodies still trembling from th car's shaking. The policeman went into an adjoining she and put a kettle on a kerosene stove. When he returne he went behind a greasy wooden counter and touched som instruments, then smiled towards his visitors. Geoffrey watching sleepily, saw that the man wanted to draw thei attention to the fact that he was lord over the mysteriou means of communicating by telephone and of tran mitting telegrams. Geoffrey nodded his appreciation an the man's smile broadened over his handsome, simple face He stared about anxiously as though considering wha more he could do for his guests, but the room was bare He hurried to attend to the kettle.

Geoffrey noticed that the hut was dirty—not untidy, fo the man had been trained like a soldier; the other hut would be worse than dirty, they would be squalid an full of vermin; the sanitary arrangements would be casua the dead, swollen donkey, polluting the air, would lie ther until turned to bones; the children gaping in at the doo were filthy, their eyes clotted with flies; and yet this Ara moved among it all with a dignity that seemed in som way to place him beyond responsibility. That, of cours was the solution of everything—to escape responsibility, t live like a visionary in the regions beyond guilt.

The policeman brought them mugs of tea made stron

and sweet in the army manner. When they thanked him he offered in the fulness of his heart to kill and roast a sheep for them. They dissuaded him from this and he took his seat on a bench a little way from them and, smiling contentedly, watched all they did. As host he would not eat with them, but he tried to entertain them by questioning them about every yard of their journey.

When they returned to the car, that had had to stand in full sunlight, the seats were too hot to touch. They lay inside feeling the leather burn through their shirts, and were thrown endlessly back and forward and from side to side so that sleep was impossible. Lister and Clark argued vaguely for want of something better to do. Geoffrey heard Lister's voice as in a dream:

". . . and in England if you're poor, you may be clean. If you're rich you've got to be clean. But here rich and poor are as dirty as they like. Being clean is merely a foible the sophisticated few have picked up from the West . . ."

Suddenly Clark shouted, "Oh, shut up!" and the voices ceased.

Towards evening Lister pointed with excitement to a hill in the remote distance—a pink pyramid that slid for a little round the horizon then dropped out of sight. Later they passed another hill, long and low, its flanks ridged so that in the long fall of the evening light it stretched back from the road like a giant millipede. They turned to stare after it, commenting on its golden colour and the rich red-purple of its shadows, watching its shape change as they moved from it until the crick in their necks forced them to face again the flatness ahead.

At twilight they gazed down into the hollow in which Ma'an was built. There was a stream somewhere but no look of an oasis. The town might have been a collection of square pill-boxes left behind by an army. The car descended between limestone crags that were iridescent in the shadows, and came level with houses like sugar cubes tossed on to the sand. In the main street there were a few shuttered shops and the occasional flutter of a white galabiah as an Arab passed, almost invisible in the blue light.

Lister stared out eagerly from side to side: "Is there really an hotel here?"

"Yes, sir. Not bad neither. Beer, whisky, Guinness even. It's where the railway ends."

"How do we arrange about this taxi to Petra?"

"You speak to the hotel manager, sir; he'll lay it on."

They passed out of the town through another limestone region, then came on a group of larger buildings beside the railway terminus. One was the hotel. Before it was a cement space in which were two fountains, quite dry; the front door stood open between them.

The sergeant, who had come down on an errand from his commanding officer, the nature of which he kept to himself, put out the baggage and saluted: "Call for you Sunday, sir," he said to Lister, "six-o-o hours. O.K., sir?" and drove off into the darkness.

"At last," said Lister, entering the hall like an explorer. "At last."

In the narrow passageway a group of Arabs in shabby European clothes sat playing tric-trac.

"Hah!" said Clark irritably, "the local aristocracy." The Arabs, seeing Clark was speaking of them, smiled and saluted like soldiers. Clark said: "I wonder how much they're going to rush us here?"

"More than the Philadelphia," said Lister, "and don't waste your time grumbling, there's nowhere else to go."

"I bet it's filthy."

"No worse than most places. The manager's certain to be Lebanese or Armenian."

They were taken up to a room furnished with ten small

beds and a tin wash-hand basin. They washed and went down again and found the manager behind a counter in the hall. He stood there, fat and pale, his face shaped like a pear standing on its broad end, and around him were goods that had not been seen on the civilian markets in the Middle East for years.

"Chivers' marmalade," said Lister, "tinned sausages, Lux, Johnny Walker, Gibbs' S.R., tinned pineapple—all pinched from the Naafi, I don't mind betting. You see, I was right, he's Lebanese—Christian, Levantine, a different race. The Moslems are lean like the Bedu and usually handsome." He asked the price of the whisky.

"A bottle—six pounds fifty," the manager glanced away indifferently. He had a self-importance that set him apart from the smiling, eager Arabs whose tric-trac counters clicked monotonously out in the hall. "Want a bath?" the manager asked with his back half-turned to his guests.

"How much?" asked Lister.

"Twenty piastres each person."

"Good Lord! And supposing we all use the same water?"

"Sixty piastres the three."

"Then no bath."

"As you wish. Eat in there." He pointed casually at a room leading from the hall. It was a bare dining-room with one big table.

While they waited, Lister wandered round examining pictures of King Hussein and the Emir Abdullah. There were cheap bright prints, like children's 'scraps', of European ladies in low-cut dress. One smiled broadly while a pigeon posted a letter into her ear. There was a large coloured print of a big American city with overhead railways, buses and street cars.

"What place is this?" he asked the waiter who was bringing in the dishes.

"Jerusalem, saer."

"The New Jerusalem, I suppose."

"Saer?" the waiter frowned anxiously.

"Never mind, never mind," Lister took his seat. "Food's good."

"Arab food's bad for the inside," said Clark.

"My inside gave up long ago. I drink enough to keep it disinfected."

"Don't you want to survive this war?" asked Clark.

"No. What's going to happen to me in a post-war world? All my money was in Singapore. Don't expect to get it back. I'd rather die than earn an honest living."

"You're the worst kind of anti-social reactionary," said Clark.

"I am what I am. There used to be a place in the world for me—now," he shrugged his shoulders, "I can't change. I can but die out. But don't blame me for dying. If I don't get to bed soon I'll fall asleep in my chair."

They had just settled into their hard, narrow beds when there was an uproar outside.

"God!" Lister moaned, "the train has arrived. It comes only once a week—and it chooses the same night as we do!"

The whole hotel echoed with life. Voices shouted to the train and from the train. Feet tramped about the bare wooden floors. Half a dozen Arabs came to the bedroom, turned on the light, left their bundles and went away again. Geoffrey got out and turned off the light. Half an hour later they came back and got into bed. By midnight the hotel was quiet. Suddenly a lorry load of police arrived from Gaza on their way to Aquaba and the uproar started again. The police sounded drunk and one Cockney voice hammered away above the others. It seemed to go on all night, yet when the three were awakened at five next morning, the hotel was silent. The Arabs were asleep. The police had gone.

While they were eating breakfast a taxi arrived to take them to Wadi Musa. Geoffrey got into the back with Clark. Lister took the seat in front. They yawned and stared through swimming eyes at the village that was pale-coloured, clear-edged and deserted in the early light. Soon they were beyond it, passing into a region of immense rocks that shaded the car from the sun. In spite of the shaking from side to side, they slept as though doped. When they awoke they were passing a narrow terrace of fig-trees.

"Moya," said the Arab driver with pride. He pointed to a small, pure stream by the roadside, "Moya. Wadi Musa."

Geoffrey asked: "Is this the water Moses struck from the rock?"

"Eh? Eh?" Lister struggled upright in his seat to look at it. "Can it be?"

Geoffrey tried to question the driver in Arabic but it was obvious he would answer "yes" to anything.

"Wadi Musa," he pointed to the panorama that now opened before them. The road dropped suddenly down between the terraces of a great incurving hillside. Among the green fig-trees were small houses accumulating in the descent until there were more houses than fig-trees. Opposite the village was a desert valley, littered with rocks, that ran to the rock wall enclosing Petra.

The driver bent over the wheel, screwing up his eyes against the morning sun, and peered out: "Petra," he said.

They all bent to stare from the car at the distant rock wall—flat-looking in this light, the colour of plum bloom and spiny-edged as a dinosaur.

"Like a *chevaux de frise*," Lister whispered in a tone of almost agonised happiness.

The taxi skidded over the loose stones of the last stretch

of road and came to a stop before a building like a large prison. This was the police station.

"All on horses now," said the driver.

"Why can't we walk?" asked Clark.

The driver looked scandalised: "Not possible. I will arrange. Please stay and give policeman each one pound to enter Petra. Officers half price." He strolled over to a group of Arabs lounging against a wall. Salutations were exchanged and converse began. Twenty minutes later he was still gossiping.

Clark walked round and round, thumping his heels impatiently into the dust. Geoffrey leant over a low wall beside Lister, who gazed longingly down the valley towards the Petra hills. As the morning haze lifted, the light showed their surface wrinkled and dark as a prune. Geoffrey, from physical exhaustion, felt disembodied, but when he moved it was as though through a weight of water. When Lister spoke, Geoffrey made an effort and answered him, but all the time he was occupied with the foreboding that had been with him since he left Amman. He told himself he was anxious about the situation he must soon face in Cairo, yet when he considered it, it seemed unimportant. The issue now was between himself and his own failure. Whatever troubled him must relate to that—but he was too exhausted to care.

Suddenly Clark shouted: "For God's sake! Keeping us standing here in this heat. When the hell are we going to start?"

At this Lister remembered and became angry, too. He called to the driver. The driver at once waved an authoritative hand towards an Arab, who lumbered off slowly into the village; then, with an air of self-congratulation, he crossed to the officers and stood grinning before them. Lister had to turn away to hide his laughter. Clark gave a snort of disgust.

"I can't help it," said Lister. "He really does think he's achieved something." The driver grinned, convinced Lister was praising him. "It's not a bit of good losing your temper with him—he doesn't live in the same world as we do. He always thinks that to-morrow he'll find a bottle with a genie in it. They all do. That's how they tolerate this impossible existence."

"Better if they didn't tolerate it," said Clark.

"You'd have to tolerate it if you'd been born into this climate. You wait and see what it does to the European Jews in a few generations."

"Really! " began Clark, when Geoffrey, who had been watching the terraces, said "They're coming." Arabs on horseback appeared among the white houses and the olive trees. Aware of the eyes of the Englishmen, they were cantering gently, making their horses move like dancers so that manes and tails floated out on to the air.

Surrounded by a guide and an escort of armed youths that nothing would dissuade from coming, the officers started out at last. Clark and Geoffrey made an attempt to ride but in their hands the horses turned into old hacks, all spirit gone. Lister sat heavily in the saddle holding his horse by the mane, while a small Arab boy led him on a single rein. They left the houses behind and made their way down the valley among the rocks. Most of the rocks were carved and inscribed. When Lister noticed this he shouted to the boy to lead him closer to them but the guide ordered them on. "These are nothing," he said, "we will not waste our time."

A mile or so on they came to the cliff face of the mountains. "The Sîk," said the guide impressively and led them into a narrow alley, no more than a crack running through the thickness of the rock. The gunmen, bounding forward with screams, fired their guns so that the shots echoed and re-echoed up the high, pink, sandstone walls that bulged and curved and overhung the riders. The young men raced on, throwing up a haze of sand, and disappearing round bends in the sîk so that their cries came from the distance, answering one another and echoing from wall to wall. The Englishmen plodded after on their unwilling horses. Some of the young men turned back, as on a pivot, horses reared, and made another journey forward, shouting wildly but laughing at one another as though the whole thing were a joke.

"To frighten the evil spirits," explained the guide.

Lister nodded politely: "Are there many evil spirits?" he asked.

"This is the place for them," replied the guide.

With the cries of the young men almost out of hearing, the others, following slowly, felt come down on them an almost tangible quiet in this dim, confined air. The guide pointed to a trickle of water running in a gutter by the road.

"First apparition of the torrent," he said, "the torrent that fills the sîk in winter and makes inaccessible Petra!"

They turned a corner and the walls opened. Gazing out from the shadow they saw the great tomb called the Treasury. The sunlight, hazed with heat, struck on the pink rock that glowed as though the light came from within. To Geoffrey it seemed that this façade carved on the rock, massive yet seeming flimsy as gauze, had the quality of the super-real.

The horses had come to a stop. No one kicked them on. Lister sat upright, his lips trembling, and Clark stared at the façade with his brows tight in a frown.

Between the pillars a doorway opened on to a black interior.

"What is inside?" asked Lister.

"Nothing," said the guide, "no use to go inside. Just

big, square room cut in rock. Very mathematical, but nothing."

They noticed now that a pillar had fallen; the urn above the door was pitted with bullet holes and the statues—described by the sailors who first came upon the city after it had been lost for a thousand years—had gone down before Moslem zeal; but everything else was flawlessly preserved in this sheltered, breathless air. The Arab youths, who had been waiting at the top of the sîk, now made a flight into the valley and returned, startling the officers with their yells and turning their horses with great flourishes so that they glistened in the sunlight. The young men laughed towards their audience with pleasure at the pleasure this exhibition must arouse.

"Yes, you savages," said Clark angrily, "this would be perfect now if it weren't for you."

The guide began calling for attention: "El Khazneh," he announced, "or as you say 'The Treasury'." He pointed to the urn. "Up there is the treasure—so ignorant men believe, me not, of course, but many seek it."

As he spoke one of the young armed Arabs lifted his gun and fired at the urn. A flake of sandstone fell to the ground."

"Andak," shouted Clark, "majnoon." The young man looked round puzzled. "Stop it, bloody fool!" Clark's tone caused the youth to back his horse until he was hidden among his grinning companions.

"Bad men," said the guide, but when he turned he started to grin himself.

"You see what they're like," said Clark as they rode on down the valley that widened between the carved rock faces. "And when they've destroyed everything; when they've broken open every tomb, and stolen every treasure, and taken possession of every fertile piece of land and turned it into a desert with their damned goats, they'll be just as filthy, ignorant, empty-headed and half-starved as they are now! "

"Too hot," said Lister. He turned his gloomy eyes on Geoffrey as though seeking help in a necessary defence, but Geoffrey had nothing to say. He was shut off within his own personal problem, yet lifted into a sort of exalting despair as though a burden were about to fall from him. He shook his head helplessly and they all rode in silence. The valley opened on to the site of the ancient city. There remained now only a mound of rubble and potsherds, but on the surrounding cliffs were carved the vast façades of tombs and temples.

The heat concentrated in the enclosed valley was scarcely bearable. Lister took off his cap and covered his head with a handkerchief. They went at a tortoise pace.

"Come, come," the guide urged them, "here is water." He led them to a green stream among oleanders, the rocks around which had been used as a latrine by the Bedu. The horses drank but Clark insisted that one of the horsemen must go back to Wadi Musa for water for the men. When they dismounted, Lister slid down the flank of his horse and sat on the ground: "Can't move," he said. Clark took his hand and, with a jerk of the wrist, lifted him to his feet. They got their baggage into a cave where there were iron bedsteads left by a pre-war tourist company, and started at once for the high places of sacrifice.

Lister's gouty foot was aching. Large, wobbling on his stick, drenched with sweat, he climbed doggedly, missing nothing, skirting ravines, clinging to rock faces, arriving a little behind the others to stare at whatever was to be seen. Clark's hard, athletic body moved with a steady determination but Geoffrey, slight and agile, was always first. He felt driven on by a febrile uneasiness that might be explained to him round the next corner.

They descended into the valleys that ran off in every

direction. Here, in shadow, wading through sand that lay in patches of pink, yellow and slate-blue, they entered the dark, square-cut tombs. In some where the Bedu had camped the floors were covered with fleas.

"Fleas carry bubonic plague," said Clark.

Geoffrey returned to the light, and looking round at the rock, weathered here so that it seemed to be swelling out over the tombs like wax, stumbled towards the open city space.

"Hey," Lister called to him, "not that way. We're climbing up to the Deir."

He stopped and, looking round, saw Lister leaning on his stick, a knotted pink silk handkerchief on his head, and was reassured. Clark and the guide had gone on ahead. Geoffrey kept at the rear with Lister on the long climb up to the mountain edge of Petra. Here, facing the chasm of the Wadi Arabah, was cut the great grey façade of a Graeco-Roman temple.

Lister hobbled out to the verge of the chasm, then gazed back at the temple with his eyelids drooping from weariness over his eyes.

The guide shouted: "The Deir. In English, the Monastery."

"Why the Monastery?" asked Clark.

The guide shrugged his shoulders but after some moments' reflection he had an explanation: "Monks live on the tops of mountains."

"Some do, some don't."

A boy had followed them carrying bread and a tin of bully beef. He placed these at their feet and retired to sit a few yards away. They gazed over the rock edge and saw, some four thousand feet below, the valley lying in mist in the noonday sunlight. The mountains of Sinai and Palestine rose like shadows round the horizon. Lister sighed and sank down in the narrow shadow of the rock. He said weakly: "I can't look at anything more." Some moments later he opened his eyes and looked at the Deir: "It's the most extraordinary thing of all," he said.

"Why?" asked Clark.

"I don't know. Perhaps because it's grey. It looks like a bit of South Kensington. Just an isolated bit that someone's dumped down here in the desert."

Clark divided the bully beef into five and placed each portion on a round of Arab bread. The guide and boy received their shares, then retired again to squat opposite each other and eat in silence. This course finished, the guide produced from his ragged robe a handful of dried dates and offered them round ceremoniously. Then Lister brought out his flask, refilled at the hotel, to wash down the food. The Arabs expressed their thanks and smiled with pleasure, but would not drink. Almost in a moment everyone fell asleep. When they awoke they found themselves lying in shade. The colour of the light had changed. The Englishmen stirred painfully and sat up, desolated and ill from afternoon sleep. It must be nearly five o'clock.

"Thank God," said Lister, seeing that while they slept another Arab had arrived with a petrol can full of water from Wadi Musa. He drank deep: "Tastes of petrol," he said; "does all water taste like that?"

When they had drunk between them the whole can full of warm, sandy water, they began the long descent to the city level. In the Wadi at the bottom it was already evening. From somewhere in the distance came the sound of a goatherd's pipe.

The guide and the boys had gone on ahead to make a fire in the cave. The others followed slowly, walking soundlessly in the deep sand, all silent until Lister said to Geoffrey: "How do you feel?"

"A bit unreal, but hyperconscious."

Clark said: "We'll be plagued by mosquitoes to-night. I wonder if there's malaria here. Must look it up."

"This is the time," said Lister, "when the Nabateans would be coming out of their houses and climbing up to the high places and calling across to one another from the tops of the rocks. I imagine they were a likeable bunch of crooks—robbing everyone and enjoying themselves . . ."

"And spending their spare time hewing out tombs," interrupted Clark.

"Well, why not? The Egyptians were frivolous about everything but death."

"If they immigrated to Hebron—well, the Hebronites are as fanatical and ill-mannered a bunch as one would care to meet. When I was there I felt it was only the fact I had British protection that kept them from tearing me to pieces."

"Now," said Lister, "that's exactly how I feel when I visit a Jewish colony."

Clark said: "I don't think anyone could say I haven't a sense of humour, but . . ."

Geoffrey, who had dropped behind, could see Lister's shoulders shaking. He felt too remote from the pair of them to listen to their conversation. He walked very slowly so that they could get ahead, and when he looked towards them—two small, dark figures passing across the deserted valley—he saw them as though he were a bird gazing down from the reaches of the upper air. He hurried to the right, away from them. His sense of direction was acute and he made his way straight back to the valley entrance where the Treasury stood. He felt at once elated and nervous as though solitude in this place gave him an extra sense but no safeguard against what he might perceive. Through his whole body there was an indefinite ache of apprehension.

When he got back to the first tombs the sunlight, touching the upper rocks, was orange-coloured and heavy as treacle. In this light the carved façades had a bleak look as of long waiting. All the young horsemen with their cries and hoof-clattering had gone back to the village. No Bedu were camped in the tombs near the haunted sîk.

Geoffrey moved silently over the sand. The valley narrowed and the shadow enhanced the size of the tombs so that they had a quality at once brutal and desolate. He felt them staring at him and stopped, on guard, to stare back.

He knew that these cities, lost now in deserts, marking forgotten caravan routes, had hidden beneath their superficial air of civilisation all the hole-in-the-corner darkness of barbarous religions. Because he was alone he was unnerved by the menace of the place. It seemed to bring him to the verge of remembering something he had forgotten and he said in sudden desperation: "Now tell me everything," but his voice was too small. There was scarcely an echo.

He trudged on, looking for the Treasury, imagining it as he had seen it floating that morning through the sunshaft. When he reached it, it stood, like everything else, in heavy shadow. The empty tomb-chamber was filled with a swimming blackness. He went to it cautiously and, standing at the entrance, placed his face against the inner chill and whispered: "Death." The word met with no resistance until it touched the invisible inner walls, then it fell back with a hiss. He moved away quickly, glancing over his shoulder, but he was alone. He hurried over to the sîk—doing what he had planned to do—to look at the Treasury again from the point where he had first seen it. It was sunken into the shadow and discoloured. Now it was no more than a carving on rock and part of the natural substance around him. What else had he expected to find? What else was to be found here or in the rest of the world other than the bare reality on which the imagination must work for itself?

Now he could recognise even in his relationship with Viola the limitations of reality. It had been a natural, not a supernatural, thing. It had been subject, also, to Viola's nature and he had seen it only through his own. What had he expected? Only he could create for his own needs.

He did not glance at the Treasury again but turned and made his way back into the valley. The sun was hidden behind the crags. A premature twilight, like the summer twilight of northern countries, had come down over the valley.

Not wanting to see Lister and Clark before he need, he wandered slowly until he noticed a stairway cut roughly in a narrow pass between two rock faces. At the top, against the primrose of the sky, was a rough shape. Earlier in the day the guide had described it as a god called Dushara but had hurried them on, saying it was not worth the climb. Seen in silhouette now, it had the look of a woman holding a child in the crook of her arm.

Geoffrey started to ascend the steps. He was half-way up when he heard a shout from above him. Something—a shot or a sharply flung stone—struck the wall and glanced past him. Looking where the shot had chipped the rock, he saw an animal crouching on a ledge. He started running up to it and saw it was one of the Saluki dogs the Arabs keep as scavengers. Its coat was dusty, clotted with blood and flecked with foam. It strained back against the wall, quivering, with eyes thrown up and teeth showing. Instantly he felt the protective rage that possessed him when he saw animals ill-treated. He put out his hand gently to calm the creature and it snapped at him. Some part of its muzzle touched his palm as he jerked his hand away.

Two armed Bedu appeared against the light. They called a warning on a high, hysterical note that filled him with alarm. One of the men paused, took aim, and killed the dog. The other, chattering excitedly, came padding down the steps. He caught Geoffrey's hand and examined it carefully, back and front, then dropped it, laughing: "Quies," he said, "quies."

"Majnoon?" Geoffrey asked and the man nodded. Geoffrey felt his temperature drop suddenly. He had been bitten by a mad dog. He shivered with cold but he was astonished by his own calm.

The man was pointing dramatically up at the body of the dog and telling some story in Arabic which Geoffrey made no attempt to follow. Holding his hand and examining it with great thoroughness, Geoffrey could find no mark or scar, but the mound at the base of his second finger felt chilled as though wet. He looked at it closely; it was dry yet he was sure that something wet had touched him there.

He looked at the two Bedu. Something in his expression made them laugh. The older one touched his shoulder as though he were one of themselves and laughed reassuringly in his face. He scarcely noticed this. He was thinking that Clark was a doctor and he had better go to him. He turned and made off in the direction of the cave.

He could hear the Arabs laughing after him and there seemed to be malice in their laughter. He had no exact knowledge of what they feared but their warning had had a quality of primitive panic that had struck beyond his consciousness—and perhaps their reassurances had been to mislead him. He must get reassurance from Clark.

He arrived breathless at the cave. Clark and Lister were inside propped up peacefully against the baggage. They had made tea in a petrol can over an open fire. Lister was reading a novel and Clark his book on tropical diseases.

Geoffrey stopped and looked at them, startled by their

normality, before he announced: "I've just seen a mad dog."

Clark raised his head: "Not coming this way?"

"No. An Arab shot it. But it touched my hand."

"Did it indeed!" Clark rose in a businesslike way. Geoffrey put his hand out and Clark examined it.

"Where did it touch you?"

"Here. Something damp—its muzzle, a tooth, perhaps."

Clark peered at the spot then threw back his head and gave a roar of laughter.

Geoffrey asked in a flat voice: "It's a terrifying disease, isn't it?"

"Possibly the worst there is. Yes, I think the worst. You go mad with fear."

"And die?"

"Inevitably. Once it develops, you're doomed."

"But could I develop it?"

"Well!" Clark dragged out the word and sat down again with an air of elaborate reflectiveness, "one can be sure of nothing. There is a million-to-one chance that a speck of saliva has got in through some minute, almost invisible break in your skin. People have developed the disease who didn't remember having had any contact with a mad dog. Now you might think yourself safe, forget about it and in six months' time . . ."

Lister interrupted: "You're being ridiculous."

"And so is Lynd," said Clark scornfully. "What's the matter with you, Lynd? Pull yourself together."

Geoffrey turned from Clark to Lister then back to Clark. For a moment he looked oddly calculating, then he said quietly: "I'm interested, that's all."

Clark's face relaxed: "It's an interesting disease," he admitted. "For one thing, the incubation period can be so long. Usually only four to six weeks, of course, but it can be three, six, nine months—a year, even longer. In one known case it was two years. Two years! Most remarkable! A nice thing, when you think the danger's past, when you've forgotten all about it, finding yourself with a dose of rabies."

Geoffrey had seated himself next to Clark and gazed at him as though fascinated by every movement of his lips. He felt almost too sick to speak, yet managed to say in a tone of calm enquiry: "How does it start? I mean, how would one recognise it?"

"Let's consult Manson," Clark lifted up the book and flicked over the Indian-paper pages. "Here we are! First, anxiety and a desire to be alone; this gets worse until you're full of all sorts of sinister terrors. I've never seen a case—I must say I'd like to. Later the virus attacks the throat and you get those extraordinary spasms. I've been told they're so deep-seated no drug can affect them. Morphia's quite useless. Makes you worse, if anything. They come on if you try and drink—even the sight or sound of water can cause one. That's the hydrophobia idea. And all the time, of course, insane anxiety . . . Manson here describes it as the worst suffering known to humanity."

Lister said: "Why don't you shut up?"

"Lynd is interested," said Clark in reasonable tones. "Here you are, Lynd—there's two pages of pathology. Read it for yourself."

Geoffrey took the book. As he did so, Clark smiled directly at him for the first time since they had met. Geoffrey smiled back like a conspirator.

Part Two

When they reached Cairo, Geoffrey separated from his group of refugees at the station. They went off in their taxis with no more than a formal protest against his refusal to accompany them. Geoffrey was no longer popular. He had failed them and only longed to get rid of them. He smiled as they went, but when they passed out through the gates he stared after them blankly.

He waited for the ruckled surface of his consciousness to subside—but it did not subside. It seemed to him that everything about him cunningly contrived to irritate him. He could not think of Viola at all.

He looked for his porter and was furious to find the man was holding open a taxi door for him: "A gharry, a gharry," he shouted. The man blinked, bewildered by this display of temper, and peered through the tranquil Cairo evening at the string of old carriages standing with their drooping horses in the open square.

When he was in the gharry, his rage passed in a moment. He felt desolated by his behaviour as by a memory of ignominy. His instinct was as usual to fly from his own inadequacy into a compensating vision, but now he found himself thinking not of Viola but of Lister. The vacancy at his side was the absence of Lister. His return to Viola was like a journey to a stranger.

Cairo was unchanged. He thought that here he was back at last, but felt only anti-climax like someone who has arrived after a party is over. The gharry was moving at a gentle trot through the commercial area beyond the station.

He used to enjoy riding like this—intimate with the crowded street yet removed from it; feeling its currents and excitements, but himself making no effort. Now he perched on the edge of the seat, harried by a sense of insecurity among these people. He felt the street unsympathetic, even aggressively so. The traffic, the noisy, rattling tram-cars, the constant stream of strange faces, black, brown or white, hemmed him in painfully. He would have been glad of an excuse to escape his own mood by quarrelling with someone.

In the stifling air, in the late afternoon heat, the height of the buildings was oppressive. Jerusalem had been a small, stone town of low-built houses. Here everything straggled upwards in lath and plaster. Dust-caked and with paint peeling, the place seemed built of stage scenery. He imagined he had grown fond of Cairo. Now he found its heat, noise and tawdriness intolerable.

When the gharry crossed Fuad al Awal, some of the boys selling flowers at the street corner ran beside it. One of them held up a lily as big as a plate, its central petals tied shut with thread. When he said nothing, the older men abandoned him, but a small boy in a filthy scrap of a galabiah jumped on to the step and swung into his face a bunch of necklaces made of jasmine flowers. Geoffrey shouted and the boy jumped down laughing.

Again Geoffrey was disgusted with himself. The strong perfume of jasmine hung about him and he felt he had no right to breathe it. In a misery of disgust, he was conscious of an ache in the palm of his hand and he knew it had been there all the time. He gave himself up to examining it. He could not have said by what process he had decided exactly where the dog had touched him, but now he could put his finger on the spot. When he touched it, it was tender. There was no mark; not a scratch. Nothing to worry about—and yet it was always reminding him of what had happened.

He sighed and tried to take his mind off it. They were passing the fashionable shops of Kasr-el-Nil. Here the pavements were crowded with Levantine ladies in flowered silks, British officers returning to G.H.Q., and Egyptian government officials in the conventional fez, morning dress and brief-case. Neon lights were coming on although there would be another hour or two of daylight.

The driver swung into a side street to avoid the Midan Suleiman Pasha and they passed under plane trees. The dust hung like a mist in the air. Here the Egyptians were coming out on to their balconies—a man in striped pyjamas, scratching among the hairs on his chest; a fat woman rolling out of her yellow wrapper, gazing down through the dusty plane leaves at the traffic of the pavement. Some men were sitting on wooden chairs under the trees, swinging their little chaplets of amber beads and drinking coffee; some, cross-legged on the ground, were already eating their evening meal. Women in dusty black crêpe, veiled or unveiled as they wished, sat in separate groups; most of them fat, dirty and laughing, all shouting at one another with that riotous, gossiping gaiety that seemed peculiar to Cairene women. Occasionally a young beauty, gathering up the glances of the men, sat among them—always veiled but with a chiffon so fine it was a provocation rather than a disguise.

Why, Geoffrey wondered, were these women happier than the men? They were held by the western world to be uneducated and scandalously oppressed, but instead they seemed full of a confidant gaiety. They chattered with an endless vitality. Of course they had no responsibility. They knew they were the creators. Without them the world would come to an end—and what more should be expected of them than that they should be themselves?

They had a natural right in the world. Only their miserable men had to go about excusing themselves with a show of bravery, arrogance, vanity, wealth or talent. And if a man had none of those things, who would be the first to lacerate him with raillery? These shiftless women.

What did he, Geoffrey, expect of Viola, but that she be Viola? And what did she expect of him? Well, to-morrow he could return to his office, and remain there secure in the excuse of lack of time.

Round the next corner the road was in shadow. The houses, painted grey and blue, were in the French style with rickety wooden steps, coloured glass and, here and there, a conservatory crowded with foliage. The static air was heavy with the smell of Cairo—the old, distilled stench of urine overhanging odours of spice, dust and Oriental vegetation. At the end of the road were some tall city palms. The flexible, rubber-grey trunks were thrusting up a new growth of green from which rose the plumage crowns of leaves. Nursing his hand, Geoffrey watched the Cairo scene . . .

" . . . that I have not painted," he said, " that I have not attempted to paint."

Now they were coming into Garden City with its grey Italianate mansions and heavy foliage; the evening air was filled with the hiss of hoses and the smell of river water saturating parched lawns. He let the driver take him almost to the headquarters perimeter before he gave irritated directions. They had to turn and find among the winding streets a way to skirt the wire surround of the houses and blocks of flats in possession of the army. That added almost ten minutes to the journey—yet the end had to come. In five minutes, in three, in two, he must see Viola again. Facing that fact was like touching an exposed nerve in a tooth. He had to get out of the gharry at last.

Inside the gateway the boab, an old Soudanese in black

galabiah and white turban, was seated with two servants from another house, He rose, smiling, bowing, apparently delighted at Geoffrey's return. He raised his hand towards the open windows of the upper flat and said: "The sitt, a party! " his teeth white in his round, black face.

Geoffrey stood a moment listening to the sound of voices from the windows, then went slowly up the path to the door at the side of the house. He tip-toed up the creaking, wooden stairs and at the top stopped again. The hall was narrower and darker than he had remembered it. Unseen, he could look down it and see Viola's guests and, occasionally, Viola—her profile, then her face turned towards him, but she did not notice him. She was not still a moment.

He felt bitterly about the party. Unreasonably—yet he knew if he entered the room, he could not be polite. The bathroom was at his elbow. He went into it and turned on the bath-taps. If he were slow enough in bathing and dressing, these people might be gone before he was ready; but he could not be slow. He moved about jerkily, doing everything at the peak of impatience. Only as he lay in the tepid water, soaking from his skin the sand and sweat of the Sinai desert, he felt a short tranquillity. He felt deliciously the ease and softness of the Egyptian air. A fly-veil hung over the window; through it he could see the mango trees of the next garden richly dark in the rich golden light. From somewhere in the distance peacocks started to scream. This disturbed him at once, reminding him of the jackals he had heard yelping the night before on the plains near Rafah. The whining yelps had come together like the bells of a herd, turning in one direction and another so that he had felt the movements of the unseen creatures. Clark had told him that an Arab had been bitten by a mad jackal and had been brought in a taxi by his friends raving into Jerusalem.

"And that's been the only case here in years," Clark said, bored by then with Geoffrey's continual questioning.

One was enough. "That it exists," thought Geoffrey, "that it exists is enough." He got out of the bath at once and listened to the gulping of the water down the pipe.

He opened his suitcase and with an agonised nerviness scrambled among the things for a clean shirt and trousers. He had meant to please Viola by putting on his gabardine uniform, but now the effort was beyond him. His hands trembled so, he could scarcely do up the buttons of his shirt.

By going out through the spare bedroom he was able to get on to the balcony without entering the main room.

Old Doctor Tupman—doctor of music—was standing there very close to a girl. As Tupman greeted Geoffrey, the girl took the opportunity to slip back to the party.

"The exile returns," said Tupman, curved forward and bone-thin in his elegant white silk suit, his long head mummified by twenty years of Cairo, camel-poised on a neck like a stick of cinnamon. "A disagreeable journey, that across the Sinai desert. You need a drink."

"No. Please!" Geoffrey paused him. "Do you mind if we sit down? I'm a bit shagged."

"Sure you won't have a drink?"

Geoffrey shook his head. He had discovered that alcohol merely increased his unease.

They sat in deck-chairs facing the vast garden of the next-door house. Tupman, with his consciously old-world manner and his slight stutter, talked of a journey he had made on camel-back to Mount Sinai. Geoffrey, waiting, expected that at any moment Viola would come out and see him. She would be surprised, but what else? "Darling, why didn't you let me know you were here?" "Oh, I thought you were busy with your party." No, he wouldn't say that. Why shouldn't she have a party if she wished? She may have arranged it long before she knew he was coming back on that day.

"I remember," said Tupman, "that Cartwright the Arabist once made a memorable journey across Sinai, through Aquaba into the Hejaz. He told me of a curious experience he had. Indeed, he must have told me about it a dozen times. I always said he was in his anecdotage by then . . ."

Geoffrey gave half his attention to Tupman and the other half to the voices in the room. Once he heard Viola's voice near the door: "Yes, and think of eating bacon again . . . No, no, no, not bacon but ham, smoked gammon! Can you remember the taste of it?" Geoffrey knew that conversation. English food—what do you long to eat again? English apples, Devonshire cream, haddock cooked in milk . . .

"Have you never wanted to go back?" Geoffrey broke suddenly into Tupman's story.

"Where?" asked Tupman, surprised.

"To England, of course."

"But before the war I went back every summer. A very pleasant trip. We would get on the boat at Port Said and . . ."

Geoffrey thought of his own return and was afraid of it. When he first came to Cairo he had condemned Tupman and the rest of them for having sought and found here an easy fame. Here you could realise any ambition. Tupman, on the strength of a couple of monographs on Arabic music and a few mild jokes at parties, had become Cairo's wit and scholar. Nothing more was expected of him. He must have reached his zenith one day in the '20s, standing with a glass of sherry in his hand, the rest of the party giggling at one of his epigrams, and ever since he had gone round enveloped in the same aura of self-satisfaction, his hand lifted to hold the same glass of sherry . . . Geoffrey glanced sideways at Tupman's long, dry hand now holding a glass of gin and vermouth. He knew how much easier he, himself, would find it to remain here in this classical lotus land than to return to the struggle at home. Here he would have no rivals and no one would despise him if he never painted again. His whole problem would be solved. But what was his problem? He moved restlessly in his chair and sighed, and Tupman, offended by his inattention, murmured something about returning to the room. He got up creakily.

Geoffrey looked up at him and thought: "Impressive, but nothing beyond the grandeur of that façade." He towered there like the Petra tombs behind which there was only the square, dark, empty room and the word 'Death' echoing in nothingness.

Tupman frowned, disturbed by Geoffrey's extraordinary stare, and disappeared between the fly-net curtains into the room. He must have said something to Viola for almost at once she came out: "Darling, why didn't you let me know you were here?"

She looked an entirely different person from the one who had been in his imagination all these weeks. He thought: "This is how she looks to a stranger. When I've been with her a little while, I will cease to see her like this—yet this is what she is like."

Viola bent over him to kiss him, her green eyes puzzled: "Are you annoyed about the party? I wanted to have them in—for the last time."

Geoffrey knew he should say: "Why for the last time? You know you can have them when you like," but the thought of their return, the thought of the house always crowded with people as Viola would wish it, filled him with such horror, he could say nothing. He had not yet spoken to her.

She shook his shoulder: "What's the matter? Tupman thought you looked odd."

"Nothing. I'm tired."

"You look tired. I'll get you a drink."

"No," he caught her hand, but he knew she wanted to go back to the party. He could feel her pull away from him.

"Stay quietly here," she said. "They'll be going soon."

Her soft, smooth fingers slid from between his hands. She gave him a pat and hurried back to her guests. For a long time after she had gone he could feel her touch like a powder on his skin.

The sun had slid down behind the houses. The twilight, like smoke, was filling the garden below. The gardener, very thin, brown and naked except for a loin-cloth, was holding up the hose so that a shower of water rose in a great arc and splashed down on a distant flower-bed. He was lost in a dream, never moving. There was a large lawn, dry and bald-looking, and around it the dark, old mango and carob trees. Just below the balcony was a single banana palm. Geoffrey had looked down on it often before. Its pale green leaves were luminous in this light and its flower—that seemed always there, drooping but neither dying nor developing—was the size, shape and colour of a bullock's heart. One or two of the thick petals had curled back to show at the base of each an infant banana that never grew any bigger.

At one corner of the balcony, in a stone box that had once held the ashes of the dead, grew a grey, tuberous plant starred over with pink flowers. Now he recognised every wrinkle and nodule on its surface. He must have noted them a hundred times while he sat in a deck-chair waiting until it was time to return to the office. Then he had looked at them with apathy; now with an unaccountable impatience.

It was growing dark. He heard people saying good-bye.

The lights were switched on in the room and, screened by the fly-netting, he was able to look in without being seen. The party was guttering like a burnt-out candle. On the table stood empty bottles and glasses; sandwich plates covered with vine leaves and crumbs; a few rejected sandwiches already dry and curling at the corners like badly licked stamps. All the men had gone. Only a few of Viola's women friends remained. One, large and elderly with close-cropped hair and a flat, pale face wrinkled like tissue paper, wore a dark suit and collar and tie. She was rather drunk; she rocked on her heels and her eyelids drooped over her eyes.

They were listening to Viola with admiring intensity: "You can't tell me anything about life in London," Viola was saying. (She became excitedly talkative when she had had a few drinks.) "I can remember coming out of classes and standing about half an hour with the crowd on the kerb—head aching, feet aching, legs aching; bus after bus going by crowded. At last in desperation I'd go twenty-five yards up to the traffic lights and try to get on there. If the lights were green, I'd try and jump the bus. I can remember a little runt, an ugly little rat that had been kicked in the teeth until he was eaten up with malice—he jumped on in front of me and turned round and gave me a punch in the chest to try and knock me off. For no reason; there was room for both of us. The bus was going at full speed. My heels slipped off; I wrenched a muscle in my back, but I managed to hang on somehow. That's what life in London was like before the war—but I enjoyed it."

The elderly woman said: "There were plenty of taxis then."

"Yes, dozens of them. They used to crawl past the queues wanting to be hired. But if you had a taxi you had to go without your sandwich and coffee.

A girl in uniform said: "Now, in England, girls in mink

coats squeak 'Taxi, taxi', and even the empty ones don't stop."

Geoffrey, fascinated by this feminine conversation, forgot his impatience. These women, who must have had little enough before the war, now felt the world was theirs. The one in collar and tie said: "I got the sack when I published my 'Aspects of Politics'. The boss said 'Anyone who has time to write a book can't be giving her best to her job', and told me to take a month's notice. They'd been satisfied with my work before, but after the book they began to worry. They were afraid they weren't getting their money's worth. And I'm not the only one . . ."

"Far from it," said another woman. "I knew a girl that got sacked for publishing a novel. The excuse was that some passages in it weren't quite nice. The man she worked for was as hypocritical and dirty-minded a little trot as you'd find in a day's work."

"It wasn't fair to those poor little trots—a girl having a life of her own. It isn't fair to them now—a girl getting a decent wage. I can tell you, things have changed at home."

"Things have changed all right."

The conversation was failing, yet they stood together, smiling at one another. Geoffrey's irritation returned. He bit the edge of his thumb and whispered through his teeth: "Why the hell don't you go?"

"Life is much pleasanter here," said the elderly woman, her eyelids drooping, drooping so that she looked as though she would tumble down asleep: "Much pleasanter," she murmured, "much pleasanter, *much* pleasanter . . ." She touched Viola's hair: "How soft it is," she said, "just like silk." She put up both her hands and smoothed Viola's long, fair hair down as she would stroke a cat. The others smiled, lips parting. Viola, laughing, shining, cheeks pink, leant away from the caress but did not repudiate it. The older woman showed no consciousness of repulse. Viola shook back her hair so that it glistened under the electric light. " Just like silk," the woman repeated.

Viola jerked her head round suddenly and stared out at the balcony. Her manner stiffened. She said briskly: " Now girls, one last drink? "

" No, no," the atmosphere was shattered. They all remembered they were going on somewhere else. One had ordered a taxi. The others wanted to share it. The party was over.

When they went Geoffrey remained where he was, staring into the empty room. He had imagined that when the last of them had gone his nervous anxiety would subside—but there was still something wrong. Viola reappeared and he felt an intolerable agitation, so that all he wished was to get out of the house. He thought if he could walk along the embankment, he would find relief.

Viola called to him. He passed through the curtain into the room. They were alone at last but he made no attempt to touch her. She stood a little away from him almost as though on guard.

" Why are the lights so gloomy? " he asked.

She looked up at the chandelier, her fine, fair brows puckering: " Perhaps they are," she agreed vaguely. " We're going out to dinner. Do you mind? Joe Phillips is here just for one night and so much wanted to see you again."

" Oh! "

He grew cool and placid with relief as he was convinced that this was what he had been dreading. Even the evening he came back . . .

" Been seeing much of him? " he asked casually.

" No. He was wounded at Alamein. Didn't I write and tell you? "

"You only wrote once."

"Darling, you know I don't write much. Can you come straight away?"

"I've got to dress properly." He felt capable of going to any trouble now.

"Then I'd better go on. I said seven-thirty on the Continental roof and I've booked a table. Joe will be lost if we leave him there alone." She went into their bedroom and powdered her face: "Come on as soon as you can," she said and in a few minutes was gone.

He dressed slowly and carefully. He was completely at peace in his certainty. Remembering the incident at Petra, he paused to look at his hand. Even the ache was fading out and he said to himself: "That was all nonsense." It sank back into perspective and almost out of sight. He turned from it with indifference.

As he walked down the path to the gate he felt, for the first time for months, a sensuous consciousness of the world about him. The darkness was perfumed by lilies and soft as a veil. Although the street lamps were covered with blue paint, lights shone from the windows so that the pavements were mottled with light and dark.

The servants, with no meal to cook and serve, were sitting with the boab at the gate. Their white robes were a little lighter than the darkness; the crimson tips of their cigarettes swung in arcs through the air. Their gossiping and bursts of laughter were softened as they heard his approach. He hurried past them, not wishing to disturb them. He did not send the boab for a taxi, but wandered down to the river, where he hoped to pick one up. He stood for some minutes under the old banyan trees on the embankment and watched the luminous movement of the dark water. His unhappiness—he supposed it must be unhappiness—lightened him like despair. Every leaf and movement of the air had importance for him. He thought with dread of being again swept beyond life into the region of rushing, mazing terror—the region, which scarcely permitted consciousness of the visible world, in which he had been imprisoned since the incident at Petra.

He walked to the British Embassy and took the first taxi that stopped at the gate. As he drove towards the centre of the town he was distracted by the entertainment of the passing streets. After the sparse darkness of Jerusalem nights, Cairo seemed brilliant, crowded and vast. It filled him with an old mood—a nostalgia for things and people that, being unknown to him, might give him a response the known could not. He did not want to join Viola and Joe Phillips on the Continental roof; he felt a distaste for the intimacy he supposed existed between them. But there was nowhere else to go. He had often before experienced the rebuff of the unknown. Wherever he went, he must remain himself.

He looked out at the raffish quarter round the Esbekiah Gardens. Here more than anywhere else night gave to the faded, papery city depth, richness and mystery. The respectable offices and shops were sunken back into darkness, and buildings that were dust-dim and shuttered during the day now threw open their windows. Figures within moved through rooms ablaze with light and mirrors and noisy with music, where anything might happen. The old hotels that kept to the semi-black-out regulations stood up darkly among streets that were pied like a fairground with brilliant booths of light.

The front of the Continental was a rustle with movement. People were seated at tables on the dark terrace a few feet above street level. Waiters came in and out; light flashed from the revolving doors. As Geoffrey paid off his taxi, the dragomen who hung about the foot of the hotel steps—large men, usually half-Soudanese, with pressed fezzes, ivory-topped sticks, galabiahs of gabardine, and an air of insolent self-importance—peered at him, recognised him and let him go.

In the crowded hall of the hotel something scratched at his tranquillity. A number of faces were familiar to him but these people, unlike the dragomen, had already forgotten him. He knew that if Viola had been with him they would have remembered him at once—Viola's husband. Had he no longer any separate identity? If, indeed, he had not, for how long could he live alone? For how long could he remain self-sufficient?

He took the lift up to the roof. When he came out again into the open, he found the moon was rising behind the houses. The air up here was cooler. The desert wind was flipping at the thick, appliquéd curtains that screened two sides of the roof. The trellised jasmine and roses stirred and gave off their perfume. He stood where the lift had left him and looked for Viola. A plip-plop of music came from the orchestra. Soudanese waiters dripping sweat, balancing covers on crooked arms, brushed past him roughly.

The full brilliance of the moon was breaking in on the dimmed lantern lights, whitening the white, powdery arms of the women, giving their eyes depth in their blue-white moon faces, and touching here and there the facet of a diamond in a moving head. Geoffrey could not disintegrate the scene. He knew no one. No one. Viola was not there.

As he stood, he heard every word of a story a naval officer from Alexandria was telling with elaborate casualness at the next table: " . . . and we got 'em. A lucky shot. Down they came, one after another, the bloody wops, and floundered about in the sea. They looked pretty scared. They knew they'd asked for it. We put a boat out. They were all alive when we got 'em aboard. As a matter of fact, they were all more or less alive when we threw them back in again."

The girls yelped delight at this conclusion. One spilt her wine over her dress.

"Oh dear," the naval officer pulled out his handkerchief. "Mustn't spoil the pretty dress. Mustn't spoil the pretty dress," he repeated over and over again as he rubbed the girl's satin lap and she lay giggling helplessly.

Suddenly Geoffrey saw Viola waving to him. He must have looked at her a dozen times without seeing her. He made his way over to the table, not looking at her now, but at Joe Phillips, who had risen to meet him. Joe caught Geoffrey's hand in both of his. "Wonderful, wonderful," he said in a nervous, jerking tone, almost too warm, almost on the verge of hysterics, "I was afraid I might miss you again."

"He's off at dawn to-morrow," said Viola.

"To the desert?" asked Geoffrey.

"Not straight away. They're letting me have two weeks at Djebel Rest Camp."

Geoffrey took his seat at the table. He could not understand why Phillips was behaving as though in the past they had shared a deep, even an emotional, friendship.

Phillips asked excitedly: "Do you remember that morning in Jerusalem when we sat and had breakfast on the terrace?"

"Indeed I do."

"I was telling Viola about it."

Geoffrey glanced across at Viola and found she was staring at him in a troubled way as though they were entertaining someone on the verge of insanity.

"You were going up the desert then."

"Yes," Phillips laughed and lifted his glass; his hand shook violently, "Cairo was in turmoil when I got here. No need to tell you that. But the desert was as tranquil as the sky. It took me three days to find my unit," he gulped at the glass and put it down so that some of the wine splashed over the side. "My God, though! Our barrage! I kept thinking, 'This will make me screwy!' and then I thought: 'If it's like this here, what's it like at the receiving end?' That quite cheered me up!" He laughed wildly.

Viola said to Geoffrey: "I've ordered for you. I ordered jellied soup, prawns and creamed chicken. Is that all right?"

The soup arrived as she spoke. Geoffrey, keeping his eyes on it as he ate, let Viola and Phillips talk. He was disturbed by Phillips's state. He had forgotten that he had ever imagined they were lovers. He had, indeed, forgotten that he no longer knew how Viola regarded him. He was resentful that she had made him come here to meet Phillips when he himself was almost . . . He paused in his thought, and was disgusted with himself that he should resent this evening given to Phillips, who had experienced what he himself had not been asked to experience.

He smiled at the young man and started to speak but was silenced by a crash from the orchestra. A white limelight revealed a dancer with arms raised above her head, hands palm to palm, belly thrust forward. In the first breathless finger-tip taps of the drum, she began moving rhythmically from the waist downwards. There was a triangle of diamanté between her thighs and a star clipped on to each nipple; the rest of her body was so thickly powdered, the skin looked like white velvet. Beneath the velvet the muscles slid with a tense, slow smoothness like snakes in sleep. The rhythm quickened; the tapping grew to a hollow drumming and the thin wail of pipes broke in. The dancer remained as before, moving in sleep with a passionate slowness and jerking her hips forward like the thrust in an orgasm.

Some of the men sitting in the front began to clap to the

rhythm as they had seen Arabs do. The clapping grew throughout the audience, rousing a sensual excitement. Viola sat back in her chair, her eyes half closed, a smile round her lips; Phillips leant towards the dancer and began to clap with an edgy intensity. It seemed to Geoffrey that only he was apart from the excitement that bound the audience. He knew this was a much more accomplished performance than the one he had seen in Bethlehem, yet he saw it merely factitious where the other had had a genuine voluptuousness. He felt irritated. As though the next could bring relief, he was beset again by the old anxiety to get the present occupation—whatever it might be—completed. His appetite had gone in a moment. His food tasted like dust.

An officer from Viola's department came over to speak to her. He stood by the table, fluffing up the cavalry moustache he had grown to hide his civilian face and waving a fly whisk as he spoke: "Heard the latest?" he asked loudly, looking for glances from near-by tables: "Happened to go into the monitoring room before I left the office. The Germans are putting out half-hourly warnings in Arabic that they're going to bomb Cairo flat to-night." He laughed and looked up at the silver sky: "Full moon. Couldn't have a better night for it, could they?"

"They're always playing that trick," said Viola. "Even the Egyptians don't listen now."

Geoffrey stared in wonder at Viola's indifference. He had himself been immediately stricken by apprehension. The officer sat astride a chair and folded his arms on the back; he and Viola began to discuss some office business. Geoffrey turned away from them and glanced at Phillips. He realised that where he was afraid, Phillips was terrified. The young man was moving his glass about in an excess of nerves, rattling it against china and cutlery and staring at it as though it were about to cause his death. He raised terrified eyes and, meeting Geoffrey's, tried to laugh and pull himself together.

"I was thinking," he said, "what I would like to do—if you could bear it; if you and Vi could bear it—I'd like to get out of Cairo. I mean I'd like to go to Mena. I'd like to climb the Great Pyramid . . . I don't mean you should, of course, but I felt I'd like . . ."

"I'll come with you," said Geoffrey. "The din of this place gets on my nerves—and now this ass of an officer Viola's picked up . . ." He suddenly jerked his head round and said sharply: "Viola, we're going to Mena."

"Mena? Why?"

"Joe wants to go and it's his last night here."

The officer, acknowledging his dismissal, put his hands down flat on the table, raised himself to a standing position and glanced with an efficient movement of his head from Viola to Geoffrey to Phillips: "Well, be seeing you!" He went off, flicking his fly whisk round his knees.

As they drove out across the river and through the suburbs to the broad, moon-whitened Mena Road, Phillips kept staring from the car: "Funny thing," he burst out at last, "not having a proper black-out."

"People wouldn't co-operate," said Viola, "Besides, pilots say even this semi-black-out is nonsense. They've only got to follow the river."

"But all these lighted windows! Ten-storey blocks lit from top to bottom. Asking for it. Make me feel like ducking."

"They'll never bomb Cairo." Viola's assurance seemed to place her in a world apart from the two men.

The grotesque mansions on the Mena Road stood at intervals, black against the flat, moonlit fields. In the distance the pyramids began to appear, one sliding out from behind another as the taxi advanced. The desert wind, cold and pure after the Cairo stenches, blew through the car, sometimes carrying a perfume of bean flowers.

They swung in under the palms of Mena House. While Geoffrey settled with the driver, Viola caught Phillips's arm and walked him round the hotel towards the swimming pool. The palm shadows, like dark plumes, fell across the pair of them—Viola, fair-haired, brown-skinned, in a white dress, and the handsome young officer. "That," Geoffrey thought, "is something I have seen before, or imagined, or dreamed"; but where the dream, if it had been a dream, had had a classical clarity, the reality was like a gothic nightmare.

He shouted: "Not that way. Don't you want to go to the pyramids?"

Phillips swung round. In the full light of the moon he looked ten years older than he had done in Jerusalem.

"I'm bored with the pyramids," said Viola. "You two go, I'll see who's in the lounge."

When she left them, Phillips asked anxiously: "Will Viola be all right alone?"

"Good Lord, yes. She knows everyone. Put her down on the Antipodes she'd be surrounded by old friends within half an hour."

"She was always terrific," smiled Phillips. "I used to worship her when I was a kid."

They were walking up the curve towards the Great Pyramid that rose naked out of the flat sand . . .

"And quite inconsequential," murmured Geoffrey.

"What do you mean—inconsequential?"

"I don't know." Geoffrey was trying not to seem irritable. After a pause he said: "I meant the pyramid." They turned the corner to another facet that was grey in the moonlight. The way up, worn white by the feet of climbers, was marked at the corner. A few fellah 'guides', huddled together at the base, leapt up when they saw the two officers beginning to ascend alone. They shouted indignantly: "Not possible. Must have guide. Forbidden."

Phillips paused: "Is it forbidden?"

"Of course not. Nothing's forbidden here. Don't let them impose on you." Geoffrey threw down a handful of piastres and the Egyptians began to scuffle for them and laugh: "Quies," they shouted, and waved the Englishmen on.

The two started at a good pace, making their way by jumping up to sit on each huge block in turn and swinging their legs up after them. After some minutes, Geoffrey began to pant and at last had to sit and recover his breath. When he first arrived in Cairo, he had made this climb without a stop. Now his body trembled; he was drenched with sweat and when he glanced to the left and saw the knife-edge shadow of the pyramid lying across the sand, he felt sick.

Phillips was a long way above him. Geoffrey pulled himself up to the next step and began using cracks and breaks in the rock so that the climb became slower and easier. As he rose, greater stretches of desert became visible and the distances grew darker as though a shadow stretched from the horizon. In the distance were the pyramids of Saccara, some in ruins like mole-hills, some neat like little toys.

At last, shaken and exhausted, he reached the top. This was a platform formed by the removal of the apex blocks. Phillips, all his clothes flapping in the cold wind, was standing in the centre holding to the post that showed the pyramid's original height. Geoffrey, too tired to stand upright in this gale, sat on the edge and looked down the route up which they had come. Right beneath them was a hole hollowed in the rock on which the pyramid was built. This was now shown to be an intaglio of a ship's hull.

"What was it for?" asked Phillips, who had come to sit beside Geoffrey.

"The Ship of the Sun."

"The Ship of the Sun," whispered the young man, peering down at it. "The Ship of Death."

"What?" Geoffrey asked sharply.

Phillips laughed: "You know that poem?"

Geoffrey felt furious. For some minutes he could say nothing, then he made an effort to ask: "Do you want to get back to the desert?"

"Lord, yes."

"I envy you." Geoffrey held himself tense, trying not to appear to notice that all the time they were talking Phillips was tapping his shoe with a maddening monotony against the stone.

"Well, I don't know," said Phillips with hollow heartiness. "You wouldn't like it. You'd be bored stiff most of the time. Then when there's been a battle—the stink! Christ! You can't imagine what it's like—the wind blowing that awful stench at you. I helped bring in the dead once or twice. Remember coming on a gun emplacement where the whole crew'd been wiped out. One of them had printed on a piece of wood: 'In memory of a gallant comrade'—but they were all dead. No one knew which chap was which, the state they were in. It made me think—I know one shouldn't think such things—but it made me think: Well, what the hell good is it being brave or anything else?"

Phillips looked at Geoffrey and seemed, with his very young, careworn face, like a schoolboy afraid of a reprimand. Geoffrey shrugged his shoulders. He felt too remote from Phillips to say or do anything; he felt only resentful that he had to listen to this; and angry, as though he himself had failed in some way.

Phillips, his eyes frightened, gave one of his hysterical

brays of laughter. Geoffrey, wanting to escape from him as from a corpse, sprang to the step below and started to climb down. The down climb was easy. He jumped from stone to stone, yet Phillips was never more than a step behind. He hurried across the sand with Phillips clinging to his shadow; at the hotel gate he said: "Go in and get Viola. She'll have picked up a crowd and I don't feel like seeing them to-night."

Phillips went obediently, a self-conscious helpfulness in every movement of his muscles. When he had disappeared through the hotel door, Geoffrey ran to the taxi rank and ordered a driver to take him back to Cairo. He felt as though in escaping he had achieved something, but when he stood alone in the empty flat, the clear mood of his relief clouded over. He was shocked by what he had done.

He went out to the balcony and stood in the white light of the moon. The garden below was empty. Nobody moved in the street. The servants had gone to bed. At any moment Viola and Phillips might come in and ask for an explanation, but his mind was blank. He had no explanation to give.

The excitement of his action, like that of a drug, was wearing off, leaving him tattered, restless and nervous. He became, suddenly, appallingly conscious of the emptiness of the room behind him. The world was like a deserted world and he unprotected in it.

The air-raid warning went. The wheezy, squawking Cairo warning came like the voice of his anxiety and gave him relief as though he had yelled aloud. The warning ended. There was complete silence, then a car came from the distance, driven at great speed. It passed on towards Headquarters; silence again. A Cockney voice yelled in the street below: "Put out those lights." Lights in windows went out one by one. The houses became completely dark; the streets dark and deserted; the only thing that seemed to have awareness was the enormous moon.

He realised that Viola would be somewhere on the open road between Mena and Garden City. The thought was terrible. There was a thread-fine sound of a solitary plane passing at a great height. The Headquarters warning—a wailing English one—denoted that the plane was over the perimeter. When it died, the plane had passed and there was silence again. A long interval before the 'All Clear' sounded.

Geoffrey began to listen for Viola's return. After a short while his impatience became intolerable. He went to the telephone and rang the Mena House Hotel. Mrs. Lynd and a Captain Phillips—a lady with an officer! There must be a dozen couples like that. The Egyptian at the other end was irritated by the difficulty of the request. Where were they? Geoffrey did not know. Perhaps in the lounge, perhaps the bar, perhaps out in the garden looking for him. The Egyptian asked him to wait. The line went dead and he knew he might wait for ever. After five minutes he began rattling the telephone and shouting: "Hallo! hallo! hallo!" but there was no reply. He cut himself off and rang again but he could get only the engaged signal. He was sweating, frenzied and screaming at the telephone, while at the same time he watched himself dispassionately and thought that he was behaving like a maniac. While this was going on, he heard a key turn in the lock below. He put down the receiver and hurried to the sitting-room. He switched on the reading-lamp, and when Viola entered he appeared to be reading. She said nothing.

"Where's Joe Phillips?" asked Geoffrey.

"Gone back to his hotel."

"I suppose you're annoyed with me?"

"Well, it was rude. Joe said he was afraid he'd been getting on your nerves all evening. Still . . ."

"Was he hurt?"

"I suppose so. Apparently he'd said something about

not seeing much use for being brave; he was afraid he'd upset you. Poor kid! I told him not to worry. He came to the door with me, but he wouldn't come in."

"I'm sorry."

"He'd talked such a lot about you since you met in Jerusalem. He seemed to think you and he'd got on rather well."

"I'm sorry."

Viola went into the bedroom and started taking off her jewellery. Geoffrey waited for her to accuse him of being self-centred, indifferent to the feelings of others, a wretched egoist—they did not quarrel often but when they did it was usually on those lines. Now, too, she might remind him that he owed something to a young man broken up in desert warfare. She said nothing for a long time, then she was mildly rebuking as though uncertain of what might lie behind his behaviour.

"After all, even if you dislike him, he is an old friend of mine. I told you he had been wounded; you can see what a state he's in. I doubt if they would think of sending him up the line again if there weren't this shortage of experienced field officers."

No shortage of staff officers, of course! He sighed and let her voice slide out of his consciousness as though what she were saying had no application to him. He watched her face with its greenish, short-sighted eyes, rather too close together, her nose a little too short, her delicate skin and light hair; a face not wholly beautiful but with an expression of kindliness that gave it beauty. It was not vivacious now, but grave, mildly rebuking and bewildered. Remembering the sensuous warmth of their relationship when they had been in sympathy, he felt too deeply sunken into despair to speak. Because he was doomed, she was lost to him. He had forgotten now that their relationship had been spoilt long before. It seemed to him that only his inevitable and horrible death separated him from her. Moving through life, he had entered the aura of his own doom; he was like a man who had already started to fall from a sky-scraper. Because she was lost to him in this way, he was filled with despairing love for her.

He saw her lips moving as she talked. He closed his eyes so that he might shut in his private vision of her. He told himself that the comforting gentleness of her body had given him the only thing pleasant in his life. Beyond it there had been only struggle and chilly loneliness.

She put her hand on his shoulder and shook him. Her voice, changing its tone, broke in on him: "There's something the matter, isn't there?"

His resistance collapsed. He felt, like a drumming almost out of earshot, the throb of terror inside his body. Intent on it, he stared inwards at his own fear. The nerves tightened in his throat and his heart began to thud. He tried to decide whether he wanted Viola near him—whether he was not already skirting that first significant symptom: the desire to be alone.

"Geoffrey," there was an edge on her voice; she shook him again.

He made an effort to open his eyes and speak to her: "I must tell you something," he said, and then after a long pause: "You know, one goes mad with fear."

"What are you talking about?"

"At Petra, where we went, there was a mad dog . . ."

"You mean, you were bitten by one?"

"No, it didn't actually bite me. It touched me."

"Where?"

"Here on my hand. The place aches all the time."

"When did this happen?"

"About a week ago."

"Oh, don't be silly. If you were going to get rabies, you'd have had it by now."

"No I wouldn't." He was exasperated by her ignorance. "The incubation period's a month, or six weeks, even longer."

"Then it's too soon."

"No, there was one case when it was only a week. I read a book . . ."

"But if you were really getting it, you'd have a temperature."

He sat up and frowned helplessly like someone being worsted in an argument: "Clark didn't say anything about a temperature. He's a doctor."

"I'm sure if your system were struggling against anything like that you'd have a raging fever."

Relief flooded over him as he was convinced, then he fell against her bosom and burst into tears.

"Darling," she said, "how did you get like this? When did it start?"

"At Petra. There was a mad dog . . . it really was mad . . ."

"Are you sure? It might only have been frightened. You know these people are bloody to animals."

"Clark thought it must have been mad."

"Who is this Clark? He seems to have been a big help —and you say he's a doctor?"

"I asked him. He could only tell the truth."

"Well, if you're in any danger, you must go to the Pasteur Institute and be treated. Dozens of people go there. Two chaps from my office . . ."

"No. I can't. I'm not in danger. If I went to be treated, then I'd know I was mad."

"Oh dear!" Viola lifted his hand and peered at it under the lamp. "Where was it, exactly?"

He tried to show her the place but could not locate the pain: "Somewhere here," he said. "But my whole hand aches. It never stops. It keeps reminding me."

She stroked his hand gently. "You need a rest," she said. "Better get some leave."

"God, no. The one thing I need is to get back to work. I wasted weeks and weeks in Jerusalem."

"I suppose you didn't do any sketching?"

"How could I?" he turned on her in defence, "in that atmosphere, living in that hostel? And now my hand. I couldn't paint with my hand like this. I believe I'm going to be crippled," he held out his cupped hand. "I can scarcely open it."

Viola asked patiently: "Have you any sleeping-tablets?"

"Yes. And Clark gave me some sedatives. I take them at night so that I'm not afraid to sleep."

"Afraid to sleep?"

"Yes, I'm afraid if I go to sleep I'll wake up worse. I have to keep on guard. I'm afraid to close my eyes."

She said as though she could think of nothing else to say: "But you had your eyes closed a few minutes ago."

"Yes. *A few minutes ago.*"

She shook her head slightly as she watched him, then she said: "Take your sedatives and come to bed. Perhaps you'll feel better in the morning."

The heat still hung spongy in the air. In the mornings Viola was awakened by the flies dragging their feet over her damp skin. When she drew the sheet up to her neck and turned in her bed, she faced the sunlight stabbing through every crevice in the shutters.

In Europe it would be autumn—bonfires and a sweetness of apples. Here, where nothing changed, there was nothing to wait for but a drop in temperature.

She always lay awhile in her habitual tranquillity before she remembered Geoffrey—remembered, rather, the responsibility of Geoffrey who awakened each morning like a condemned man come a day nearer his execution by torture. He slept late now because of the sleeping-tablets. She would get up quietly and dress quietly, dreading the moment when his eyes opened and looked across at her, expressionless at first, then with a growing fear.

What could she do for him? In the morning she could behave as though he were normal. It was in the evenings, when he was at his worst, that she was at a loss. She adopted the bright, reassuring tone of a professional nurse, but got no nearer than that.

She was sorry for him, yet half-resentful. While he was away she had enjoyed independence, she had grown confident in her popularity, and she had determined that if he returned as selfish, demanding and petulant as he had been, then she would leave him. She had given that last party like a challenge—and there had been nothing to challenge. He had returned like this—like an invalid, or, perhaps, more like a child whom she could not blame because his demands did not impinge upon her adult world. And yet he was there. Helpless as he might be, he stood between her and the freedom she had anticipated.

She dressed quickly, hoping to get to the breakfast table before he awakened. She lived like that, in a hurry, always ahead of him so that he could expect no more than that she should throw a remark back at him over her shoulder. Before she could get away, he stirred and sat up.

She said: "Good morning, darling."

He did not reply. He was pressing his brow with the palm of his left hand. She said in a brighter, more urgent tone: "Tea at Groppi's?"

A pause, then he answered flatly: "All right."

"Must hurry." She made a get-away into the sitting-room and had gone off to the office before he had dressed.

That afternoon, seated in the enclosed warmth of Groppi's garden, she said in the same bright tone, demanding his attention by the same urgency:

"Darling, that party Peter Chuffley is giving in Bella Croup's house! He wants you to come."

Geoffrey's head was bent staring at the fine, cocoa-coloured sand on the café floor. When her question got through to him, he simply shook his head.

"You won't come? It might be good for you. Take your mind off . . ."

"I'll stay in the office. I have some work to do."

"Will you be all right?" Her freedom almost distressed her.

"Yes," he repeated vaguely, "I have work to do."

"When you come in, you'll take your sedatives? And go straight to bed?"

"Yes." He was impatient of these interruptions of his anxiety; he asked: "Do you want to stay here?"

"But I've just given an order."

He said nothing. Sitting there examining the palm of his hand, he seemed too remote to reach. She could only beg him: "Do be sensible, darling. You know as well as I do you're in no danger," but had no hope of the words penetrating the wall of fear around him. She sighed and looked about her for distraction.

The café garden was a garden inasmuch as it had no roof over it. The tables were set close together on the sand—a few striped umbrellas, a thin creeper trailing over a lattice, an occasional papery mauve flower carried out the garden idea. Tall houses enclosed the area on every side and on their colour-washed walls enamel plaques advertised Cinzano and Byrrh, and recent cardboard additions said that Egyptian whisky and 'In Memoriam' Gin were fifteen piastres a tot.

Wherever Viola looked she met the glances of men—

the respectful interest of British officers, the dark-eyed, deliberate offer of Levantine youths, and the mixture of caution and confidence in the stares of rich Egyptians. She returned them with amusement, and not without response. She had a habit of smiling slightly, almost with provocation, yet shifting the smile too quickly for any one to take it for himself.

Their tables had been in the shade when they sat down; now the sun had shifted. She felt it touch her shoulders and she gave a slight, sensual shudder of delectation. Having interested all the men around her, she suddenly disclaimed them and devoted herself to her husband:

"Egypt grows on one," she said, "it seems somehow to heighten the senses. Do you know what I mean?"

He lifted his head and listened to her with the look of a worry-distracted man trying to give his attention to something outside his own mind.

"You remember," she said, "when we first arrived—it disgusted me. It seemed so squalid and a-moral! The English residents seemed such a bunch of sex-mad neurasthenics! And yet it breaks down your resistance. At times I feel I'd like to spend my life here."

He twisted his lips slightly to one side, but made no comment. She put her long, creamy hands into the sunlight on the table. She was conscious of a nervous tingling, a new and voluptuous tenderness in contacts. The surface of her skin was delicately aware, the movements of her limbs significant and aware—aware . . . She stirred gently within the silk of her dress. She could smell the scorched smell of her own hair.

"Do you think," she said, "this is part of the process of becoming a Levantine? In England we're healthy, energetic and callow. Here we turn into sensualists. It's a demoralising process." As she spoke, she smiled, conscious of her own desirable body, conscious, as though by an extra sense, of the stares of the men. "There is something odd about the place," she chattered on. "The fellah women—they're not really dominated. They stand no nonsense from men and yet they maintain the humility of their position. They enjoy it. Have you noticed?"

"Yes. Yes, I have noticed something like that." He spoke with so much effort, with such a desolating patience, she was stricken. She tried to take his hand, but he withdrew it and she said: "Where is that wretched safragi?"

Almost at that moment their Soudanese waiter returned and slapped his tray on the table with all the insolence of the overworked. He threw off rapidly two cups, a pot of chocolate, two glasses of iced water and a plate of cakes. He stuck the price-chit on Geoffrey's plate and was gone.

"What will you have?" asked Viola. "These *mille feuilles* are good, and the strawberry and cream tarts . . ."

"I can't eat anything." He gulped down some water, then hid the glass behind the chocolate pot.

Viola pressed her fork through a *feuilles*. The white icing cracked, raspberry jam and cream oozed between the tissuey pastry. She said: "I bet you got nothing like this in Palestine."

"No. Very few cakes there." His preoccupied face disturbed her even as she ate with pleasure.

"What would you like to do?" she asked him.

He looked up again, his eyes cowed, and stared round him as though afflicted by enemies: "Anywhere," he said, "so one can move about. Let's get away from here. These walls are too close. Supposing one went mad here in front of all these people!"

She pretended to laugh: "You aren't going mad."

"It would be the indignity," he explained, then added:

"We might get a gharry and drive somewhere. The Muski, perhaps?"

"All right. If you like. I'll just finish my chocolate."

He relaxed as though beneath a weight of waiting. His eyes followed the curves of the iron table legs, the lines of his own brown suede shoes, of Viola's white sandals . . .

"Do hurry," he whispered.

"I'm ready." She rose, dusted crumbs from her skirt and walked through the café as though unaware of her audience. They ascended the steps into the darkened shop with its heavy, plummy smell of cakes and groceries. Geoffrey paid the bill, then they went through the bead curtain into the glitter of the street. There had been a slight hamseen, past now, but the sand still gritted on the pavement. A gharry was at the door. When they took their seats, it turned heavily so that they could feel the effort of the horse . . . At last they were under way, driving into the crowded, dusty, noisy, muddle of the Opera Square. Here the tram-cars, screaming round on a horse-shoe track, carried passengers bunched on the steps like bees swarming at a hive-mouth. This was the dentists' quarter and they hung out before their surgeries monstrous molars bloody at the roots. Viola noticed that Geoffrey was looking at these signs as though they had some peculiar horror for him.

"Aren't they funny!" she said like a mother distracting a child.

He did not answer. They passed round the square into the wide Sharia el Muski, where, among the dilapidated native houses, there still remained a few old mansions with delicately latticed meshrebeeyahs.

Viola said: "When we first arrived, we were always coming down here. I don't know why you couldn't find anything to paint."

He shrugged his shoulders: "I didn't want to be here."

"You set yourself against the place from the first. Because it wasn't Greece, that's all. I suppose I did, too, but now I love it. Supposing you started painting again?"

"Impossible. I haven't time."

"I looked at your paints this morning. They've dried up. There's a shop in the Midan . . ."

"No," Geoffrey half-shouted in his irritation. "For God's sake don't buy any."

Turning his back against her chatter, he became absorbed again in a game he had been playing since they got away from the nightmare teeth. On the pavement were men, throwing out their large feet from below striped, dirty galabiahs, and women, wrapped to the eyes in dusty black, shuffling in carpet slippers. He told himself: 'If among the next ten people there are more men than women, then I'll be all right.' 'If the next three are all men . . .' 'If the person nearest us down the next turning is a man . . .' For a long time, as though he had foresight, the conditions necessary for escape were fulfilled, but his satisfaction was never more than an instant's break in anxiety. He began to narrow upon himself the margin of safety: 'If among the next six people there are two women and four men . . .' and when there came instead a stream of six market women with baskets, and a dozen more women behind, he leant back in the carriage seat as though his strength had failed. He was doomed. Trembling, not only with terror but in a fury of self-hatred and bitterness, he demanded of himself: Was he trying to destroy himself?

Viola, noticing his haggard face, asked: "Do you feel ill?"

"No. Let's get out and walk."

The bazaar road turned off to the left, narrow and made narrower by the display of the little, open-fronted shops.

From the shadows of the crowded distance the old minarets lifted themselves sand-coloured into the blue.

"Everything here seems to be rotting," said Geoffrey.

Viola looked up to the traceries of the minarets and saw them clogged and coarsened by sand. She said: "Yes, it's all a bit tatty and too picturesque, but it's something more. If I were a painter, I think I could do something with it."

"Well, it means nothing to me."

When they reached the dim, roofed alleyways where tourists bought silks, jewellery, carpets and curios, Geoffrey came to a standstill. Viola took his hand. It was damp and corpse-cold: "What is it?" she asked.

"We're crazy to come here," he whispered. His other fear was jerked into insignificance before the menace of this crowd where anyone might be secreting leprosy or typhus lice or plague fleas: "Why on earth did we come here?" he asked.

"Darling," Viola's voice was growing weary, "we came because you wanted to come. Don't stand like that, everyone's looking at you." He let her lead him over to a shop where there were slippers made of coloured camel leather. She picked up a large pair, scarlet with turned-up toes, and held them up: "You need a pair. What about these?" She offered them to him but he would not take them. He kept his hands clenched in his pockets. She put the red slippers down and picked up others. With an anguished expression he watched her touching things and at last burst out: "Darling, don't touch things. You don't know who might have touched them before you."

"Why this sudden concern?" she did her best to laugh again, "we used to come down here a lot. You never worried before about picking things up." She went on examining the slippers and he watched her as he might watch an exhibition of crazy recklessness.

"Do let us go on."

She was startled by his tone: "All right," she said to quiet him.

As they strolled down the bazaar, she gently rubbed the touch of a fly from her face and pushed back her hair. Geoffrey said: "You're doing that to torture me, aren't you?"

"What?"

"Touching things, then touching your face? No one could be so criminally unaware."

"Really, Geoffrey! I know you've had some sort of a mental upset, but . . ."

He walked away to avoid hearing her. She sauntered after, behaving as though nothing unusual were happening. She stopped to examine a display of Turkish jewellery—rose diamonds set in a copper gold shaped like flowers and birds.

"Darling," she called, "how expensive everything is becoming. Do look at these things. They used to be quarter the price."

He paused in the middle of the road. When she did not come to him, he returned to her and pleaded in an undertone: "Darling, let's get away from here."

"Yes," she took his arm and gave the shopkeeper an indignant look, "let's go. The Muski's just a racket nowadays."

Driving back through Cairo to their offices in Garden City, Geoffrey said to Viola with a contrition that filled her with pain: "Please forgive me. I will get better. I can remember when I was a child there were times when things came out of the picture—I mean, they came too close and seemed monstrous and frightened me; but they always went back again. This will go back in the end."

She slid her arm through his, flooded by her old love

of him so that she could scarcely keep from tears. She thought: " Something must be done for him. He must be cured, must be made normal again."

" To-night," she said, " I won't stay late. If you feel bad, take your tablets and go to bed."

" Yes," he said like an obedient child.

" And don't worry about me."

" Worry about you! " He frowned in bewilderment. After a long pause, he said: " Yes, I remember I used to worry a lot about you; but now I feel everyone is safe but me. Compared with my danger, nothing that could happen to anyone else could mean much."

" A danger that doesn't even exist."

He did not reply; they drove the rest of the way in silence.

That evening she hurried back from the office to change into an evening dress. She twisted her hair on top of her head and put on some ear-rings of Yemenite gold that Geoffrey had brought her from Palestine. She was giving a lift to a couple of junior girls, Phyllis and Joan, from her office and had sent the taxi to pick them up first. When she was ready, she awaited impatiently the hooting of the taxi and was afraid Geoffrey might change his mind and return to the flat before she could escape. She listened for him with something like dread—but heard only the fretting of the palm leaves against the bedroom window.

She went out to the balcony. It was still warm enough to sit out of doors at night without a coat. She slipped her hands over her softly cushioned shoulders and breasts and felt delight in her own flesh. This warm air freed her from the exactions of reality. Considering this fact, she knew it was as though she had taken a step into fiction and now expected to live it. Her senses were heightened and soon she would demand experiences to gratify them. "And become just like the rest of the English here."

Her mood was disturbed at once, and when the taxi hooter sounded she was glad to run down to the distraction of company. Three girls and a young captain awaited her.

"Hello!" she said in surprise, "I wasn't expecting you, Bambi."

Bambi Mulhadi, a Levantine girl of mixed origin who spoke six languages imperfectly, chose when speaking English not to pronounce her *r*'s. She giggled and said: "Joan told me about the party so I wang up Peter and he said: 'Do come', and I said, 'Can I bwing my boy fwend' and he said, 'Bwing the whole bloody Bwitish army, if you like'. So I asked Joan to call for me."

"I hope it's O.K.," said the young captain in nervous, over-refined tones.

"Everything's all right here," said Viola dryly. She felt she had brought her disturbed mood into the car and, after a moment, smiled to reassure Bambi.

Bambi said: "I should have intwoduced Dewek. He took me to tea at Biget's this afternoon and when I said it was my birffday, he made me go to Circurel and bought me this." She held out an evening bag of *petit point*.

"What a lot of birthdays you do have," said Phyllis.

Joan leant forward and examined the bag in a businesslike way: "Genuine," she said. "Smashing gift. Now I picked up a meal-ticket the other day and he wasn't half mean. He wouldn't even go to Groppi's. We went to some other lousy little place he'd discovered, then he'd the cheek to think I'd see him again."

Bambi pulled down her little, fat mouth and shot Derek a complacent smile. Joan, intercepting it, was suddenly silent. Phyllis, a thin, bespectacled girl who had grown thinner in the Middle East, had been watching Bambi through narrowed eyes. Now she edged towards Derek and asked: "You just in from the desert?"

"Yes."

"Not much fun out there."

"Not much."

"Joan and I wouldn't mind showing you round a bit. I'm pretty booked up but I could give you an evening or two."

"Well . . ."

"You know there's a woman-shortage here."

"Well, thanks. We must fix something up."

The lights from the shops passed over Bambi's angry little face and exaggerated its crust of make-up.

"What about you, Joan?" Phyllis persisted, "I'm sure you wouldn't mind. What I always say is, when chaps come in from the blue what they want is a nice English girl."

"Is it?" Joan went into giggles as though Phyllis had made an improper joke.

"All this is so vulgar," Bambi said quietly and Derek gave her a relieved smile.

The taxi had started rocking about on a rough road. They had reached the outskirts of Cairo. Behind the neatly modelled mud houses was a dark fur of date palms. Here and there were vegetable stalls lit by flares and sometimes an open-fronted café ablaze with acetylene, where the men sat drinking thimblefuls of coffee and the wireless repeated long Arabic sagas.

"This is a rum place," said the young officer. "Where are we going?"

"This counts as the country," said Viola. "Some English officials built houses out here. One of them's let to a young couple called Croup. That's where we're going. He's one of the Long Range Desert Group."

"Is he, by Jove! And he's got his wife with him! How'd he manage that?"

"They met and got married out here. She used to work at the Embassy. They don't see much of one another, you know."

"Still . . ." Derek caught his breath, "to have a home and a wife! I'd give anything to have my wife out here."

"So would a lot of chaps," said Phyllis. "But there's not a hope in hell."

The taxi stopped. A safragi opened a white wooden gate and the taxi drew in under trees that blotted out like a cloud the closely-starred sky. The drive was full of cars; it was impossible to park nearer the house. When the women jumped out, the young man followed them slowly.

"You're tired," said Viola.

He looked at her seriously and respectfully: "I'm all right," he said.

The house, in an Edwardian style, surrounded by trees and an expanse of dry lawn, was as similar as anyone could get to an English country house. Every window was lighted. The front door stood open and near it stood a young man in tails.

"Oh!" cried Bambi. "There's darling Peter."

Peter Chuffley, noted for his wealth, was gripping by the arm a plump, sleepy-looking youth in battle-dress. He put his free hand on Bambi's bare shoulder: "Let me introduce Ronnie Kirkaldy."

Bambi, wriggling demurely under Peter's touch, said: "Oh, Mr. Kirkaldy, pleased to meet you."

Peter bent and, smiling round above her head, whispered for all to hear: "*Lord* Kirkaldy, darling. But call him Ronnie." He gave her a little shove that dismissed her into the crowded room.

Flushed and shaken, Bambi kept beside Viola for the next ten minutes. Viola took her over to the buffet where six roast turkeys were spaced down a table crowded with food and massive English silver. Between the turkeys stood bowls of strawberries and cream. Viola filled a plate for Bambi and picked on an elderly lieutenant-colonel to get drinks for both of them.

A door at the end of the room opened and Bella Croup, in a green satin dressing-gown, examined the room. When she saw Viola, she called to her: "Arthur's back," she said, "I just opened the front door this afternoon and there he was, coated with grime. No warning. Such a wonderful surprise." Bella's young, strained face looked like the face of a child exhausted with excitement. Tears came into her eyes.

"Is anything the matter?" Viola asked.

"No, no, it's wonderful," the word shook in her throat. "But Peter would have his party and Arthur wants to clear them all out. Some hope of that! He's got a beard. They told him at G.H.Q. to take it off at once, but he's still got it. Have you met Ronnie Kirkaldy?"

"In a way. Peter told us who he is."

"Yes, Peter's got hold of him but he wants to go to bed. He arrived with Arthur. They're both worn out. How's Geoffrey?"

"The same."

"Do come and talk to Arthur. You know he's devoted to you."

The room beyond was probably known as the library for the walls were pasted with the spines of books. A heavy baize-covered door shut out the sound of the party. Within were twenty people sitting round a roulette table. Viola had seen the roulette crowd often enough before—old, grey-faced pashas poured like ectoplasm into their chairs; grey-skinned, skeleton women, hung with jewellery; Levantine business men that might have been modelled from lard; middle-aged women with the eyes of thyroid patients; all with the look of creatures that never saw daylight—but not one had ever looked up and seen her. Now, only Strachey, a young Englishman with ruffled hair and loosened collar, who held the bank at the head of the table, raised his long, thin head and watched Bella and Viola with an impatient expression.

"All right, all right," said Bella passing on tip-toe. Strachey sighed, looked away, and the game went on.

Arthur Croup, also in a dressing-gown, sat in a long chair. His skin was burnt an orange-brown but the creases round his eyes were white. A large cat lay on his lap.

"Here's Viola," said Bella.

"Hello, Viola," Arthur did not move. He smiled indulgently into the eyes of the cat. The two girls seated themselves on the rug at his feet: "Now, look! " he said, "watch her! "

"Darling," said Bella, "do put that cat down."

He made a thin, scarcely audible noise somewhere high in his head and the cat began to wriggle forward as though drawn by the noise. Chirruping in its throat, paws opening and shutting, it drew itself up the lapels of his dressing-gown until its nose was buried in his reddish beard. There it gave a loud squawk.

One or two of the players clicked their tongues with annoyance. Bella said in a small voice: "Darling, she's ruining that dressing-gown."

"Never mind," said Arthur, "I love my cat more than my dressing-gown." He looked directly at Bella and gave her a provoking smile. She turned her head away and said to Viola: "Darling, you look depressed. Are you? "

"A bit, perhaps. I've just been thinking about the effect this place has on people. A horrid effect, really! "

"On whom? For instance? "

"Everyone. Take Phyllis and Joan . . ."

"Oh! " Bella interrupted, "I wouldn't worry about that

pair. At home no one would look at them. Here they're as much in demand as a couple of reigning beauties."

"Yes, but at home they were nice girls; too nice, probably, even to have learnt discretion. Here—even Bambi can get away with calling them vulgar."

"It's not the place; it's the opportunity. Now, tell me about Geoffrey."

Before Viola could answer, Arthur, who had not been listening to their conversation, said: "Have you noticed? There are certain cats in Egypt much bigger and more muscular than other cats. Like small panthers. I believe they're descended from the ancient sacred cats. And they're ver-ee, clev-er cats, aren't they, Pusser?"

"Darling," murmured Bella, begging attention, "ever since we got up, you've been playing with that damned cat."

"Now! Watch her, now!" Arthur pulled the cat down to his knee, turned it over and began stroking its large creamy front with a twitching movement, so that each time he reached its lower belly it curled into a ball. He began laughing, his teeth gleaming in his beard, his delight infecting the two women so that they had to laugh, too.

Strachey, from the table, said peevishly: "I say, Arthur!"

Arthur swung round in his chair, his body trembling in a sudden, nervous rage: "If you don't like it—clear out! And take that bunch with you!"

"Keep your hair on," said Strachey. None of the Egyptians spoke, but one or two gasped in indignant protest.

Arthur smiled again, absorbed again in the cat. Bella and the cat watched him with an equal intentness.

"One day," Bella said quietly, "when you come back, that cat won't be here."

Arthur laughed pleasantly: "Then perhaps I'll have no reason for coming back."

There was a long silence, then Bella sighed and said: "Darling, would you love me if I were a cat?"

"Perhaps."

She stretched herself on the hearthrug and, pulling out the sash of her dressing-gown, put it down behind the curve of her backside: "Look, darling. Look."

He glanced at her.

"I'm a cat." She snuggled into the fur rug and flicked the sash up and down. All the time she gazed up at Arthur with round, green, unhappy eyes.

"Really!" he fidgeted in his seat. "Do get up."

She kept her gaze on him, slowly moving the sash, until he threw the cat off his knees and poked at her with his toe: "Get up, you idiot, and get us a drink."

She sprang to her feet: "Have you had anything to eat?" she asked Viola. "No? Then I'll get you something. And I know where Peter's hidden some champagne."

The cat had sat where it landed and was stabbing its soft belly with its tongue. As soon as Bella had gone Arthur picked it up again and whispered: "You are my own good cat!"

Viola said: "You must be a long way East now?"

After a pause he answered: "Yes. I got a lift in a plane."

"Things are changing, aren't they? The strain's lifting here. We used to feel in the thick of it so that personal considerations meant nothing. Now the danger seems to be over and we're all free to worry again about our own little problems."

"Yes," Arthur agreed slowly. "And I'll soon be superfluous."

"I suppose the war has to end some time."

"How's Geoffrey?"

"Bella's told you about him?"

"Well, she said he'd got a bit neurotic."

"I'm not sure he isn't going mad," said Viola. "I don't really know what's wrong with him. I know he used to feel frustrated because he couldn't be out with you boys."

"I'd go crazy myself if I were under the heel of one of the little power groups. The only thing is—they were nothing before the war and they'll be nothing after it." He paused, then added sombrely, "I could say the same thing about myself. The reverse is true for Geoffrey. We take our turns."

"If only he could realise that."

The door fell open and Bella returned with a safragi carrying a tray of food. She held a champagne bottle under either arm. Arthur took one from her: "Not that Syrian stuff, I hope? No, Mercier. Better than nothing. Are these all?"

"No. I left two."

"Get them and we'll drink the lot. That'll teach him."

Bella said: "It takes four to make a party. We need a man for Viola. Who shall we get?"

"She must choose for herself. The opposite sex divides for all of us into the possible and the impossible."

Bella and Viola went to the door together. To Viola it seemed that while she had been shut up in the library, the party had somehow gone insane.

"What are they drinking?" she asked.

"Two gallons of medicinal alcohol. I had it for cleaning the baths and Peter poured it into the cocktail mixture."

It was as though a pin had been pulled from a piece of machinery so that some parts had fallen out, static, while others whirred without meaning in eccentric circles. Joan was lying senseless on the hearthrug while Lord Kirkaldy and a young round-faced Egyptian in a fez, talking with earnest intensity, walked up and down the length of the rug.

Every time they came to Joan they stepped over her as though she were a prickly hedge. Bambi, her powder smeared, her skin violet and puffy, was sitting on the knee of the old lieutenant-colonel and striking at him with a vicious anger as he tried to snatch her hands. Phyllis had taken off most of her clothes but only one or two unsteady young men were conscious of the fact. Others were sleeping or talking in corners or dancing unhappily on their own. A colonial officer was shouting abuse over the uproar of a wireless and a gramophone, playing different tunes.

"Chaos!" said Viola.

A few people stood apart, on the rim of chaos, sober and lost. One was a tall man, a major, with a muscular body and a long, brown, even-featured face.

"What about that one?" asked Bella. She shouted to him: "Hey, you!"

"I don't know . . ." Viola began, but as he crossed to them he smiled so that the two women felt come out from him an unusual warmth and pleasure in their femininity. Involuntarily they both smiled back.

"But he's a doctor," said Bella uncertainly.

"He'll do," said Viola.

Half an hour later Bella and Arthur were lying together in the chair. Bella, with her eyes fixed on the ceiling, held Arthur asleep in her arms. At times she moved her head to look at him, to touch his hair or to shift the dressing-gown tenderly from his face as a mother moves the shawl that might smother her infant. Once when Viola looked at her she was holding Arthur's hand to her mouth and dragging her lips along the hairs on the surface of his skin. After that Viola did not look again.

She and the major, sitting on the hearthrug with the last bottle of champagne between them, talked seriously about the war. The conversation passed to Palestine, from which he had just come.

"You don't, I suppose, know a doctor there named Clark?" asked Viola.

"My name is Nicholas Clark," said the major.

"Oh, is it!" Viola sat up accusingly. "The Clark who went to Petra with my husband? With Geoffrey Lynd?"

"Yes."

"But what have you done to him? He's going crazy."

"Isn't he any better? I'm sorry . . ." In spite of himself Clark started laughing. At the sight of Viola's serious face, he said again, still laughing: "I'm sorry. But he's in no danger. His skin was unbroken. I looked at his hand myself. Even if the dog was mad—and it probably wasn't—it couldn't have infected him."

"But he believes . . ."

"I know, I know. He's developed a neurosis. You needn't be frightened; he's not going crazy. If anything, he's saved himself from any possibility of going crazy. He's felt the situation too much for him but before it could overcome him, he's bolted away from it into this cul-de-sac."

"But what's caused it?"

"Strain of some sort, I suppose. No telling what. Don't worry. He'll get over it. Neurosis is a sort of occupational disease of war." Clark refilled her glass from the bottle. "It's you I feel sorry for."

Viola drank from her glass in sips; she gazed vacantly before her. She had reached a pleasant state of drunkenness when, detached from discretion, she could talk about anything. She said slowly: "Geoffrey died on me here. In Greece he was another person. He was amusing; even brilliant, at times. He had a sort of self-sufficiency that made him seem stronger than most people. But here he just became a drag and a nuisance. He couldn't enjoy himself and didn't want me to go anywhere either with him or without him. And now . . ." She shrugged her shoulders.

"Obviously you've had the worst of it all along the line."

"Perhaps. I must admit that when he went to Palestine I was pretty relieved. I'd begun to think I was the one who'd go crazy."

"Look," said Clark as though on an impulse, "we must have a talk about this. Would you meet me for tea one afternoon?"

"Yes," Viola agreed, "you ought to see him."

"I don't want to see him. We didn't get on very well. If he's really bad, he'll have to be treated. There are some excellent chaps at Ismailia."

"He wouldn't go," said Viola. "I told him he should take leave and he said the only thing he wanted was to go back to work. You couldn't get him into a hospital. He seems to think the office couldn't get on without him."

"Well, he might see Kristel, a friend of mine; a good psychiatrist. I'll arrange it if you like, but don't tell him I'm here. It would only upset him. He's got an idea I'm a sort of enemy—all part of the neurosis. But come and have tea with me to-morrow. Let's talk quietly somewhere."

It was his very persuasiveness that made her hesitate: "All right," she agreed at last, uncertainly, and for the first time since her marriage she felt that here was a relationship that might prove a dangerous one. In reaction, she stood up, saying: "I must get back now. I don't like leaving him alone."

"Don't worry," said Clark, "people in that state never do themselves any harm. They don't really believe in it all, you know. It's just a game."

"Still, I must go. I promised I'd be back early."

"Then I'll drive you to Cairo."

Bella and Arthur were both asleep. Viola and Clark left quietly. When they came within sight of her flat, Viola looked up and saw a light in the bedroom window.

"He's still awake," she said.

"You will turn up at Groppi's, won't you?"

"I said I would," she answered almost angrily and jumped from the car.

Geoffrey was sitting up in bed, a book open in his hand, but she was sure he had not been reading. He was staring at the bedroom door as she entered. His expression was desolating and she could only treat him like a child.

"You haven't taken your sedatives?" she said.

"I saved them up," he replied.

"Then you can't be so bad, after all."

"But I saved them," he repeated childishly. "I saved them to take when you came. I'll take one now."

While she undressed, she watched him in the mirror. He was holding the phial of tablets in his hand. She had no faith in his ultimate sanity and was afraid that if she insisted on his taking the tablets, some awful obstinacy would come over him. She said quietly and reasonably: "You remember, darling, last night and the night before—you felt exactly as you do now. Then you took two sedative tablets, and then your sleeping pills; and when you woke up next morning, you were no worse than you ever are in the mornings. Can't you reason with yourself?" He did not answer, and after a long interval she added: "Can't you tell yourself that what happened last night is happening again to-night, and will go on happening until you jump out of it?"

"But it's always different," he argued. "It's not the same as last night. I never recognise it. It's always new, always different."

She said, annoyed: "You argue as though you wanted to believe the worst."

"I don't," he seemed suddenly on the point of tears, "I long to be convinced I'm all right. I long to be . . ."

Feeling the situation beyond her, she said: "Now, no more indulging in misery. I want you to take those tablets."

He obediently shook two pellets on to the table and put one of the green sleeping cachets beside them.

"Where's the water?" she asked.

His mouth twitched at the word so she wondered if he had been afraid to drink. "Here," he whispered. He leant over the edge of the bed and brought the water-bottle and glass from under the bedside table.

She made no comment but watched him until he had swallowed the sedatives. She felt herself divided now between her warm awareness of herself as a sensuous animal and this nightmare of Geoffrey's mental sickness. She might in a moment have slipped away from consciousness of him, but, instead, she forced herself by an effort of will to be a little over-aware of what he said and did. When she got into her bed and opened a book, he smiled across at her in the mild, almost idiotic, good humour that came after release from fear. He took the sleeping cachet.

"Why didn't you take them before?" she asked.

"I don't know. Why do you tolerate me? You could simply leave me. I wouldn't blame you."

"Why should I? I'm used to you."

"Not as I am now—a sort of semi-lunatic."

"You're ill, that's all. You'll get better. You wouldn't expect me to desert you if you developed jaundice or appendicitis?"

"I don't mean only because of this; I mean because I've changed as a person."

She laughed, surprised at his self-perception: "How silly!" she said. "If we've stayed married, more or less happily, for as long as we have, we're likely to go on. I know all your faults. Anyone else I married would probably have different ones, but just as many and perhaps worse. I accept yours."

"You mean, you don't think you'll ever leave me?"

"No, I don't think I will," she said, and wondered if she were speaking the truth.

He sighed and, without saying anything more, settled down in his bed, turned his face into his pillow, and slept.

Geoffrey was not told that Clark was in Cairo but an appointment was made for him with Clark's psychiatrist friend Kristel. Viola had no great difficulty in persuading him to keep it.

"You only have to talk, darling, that's all. You can go and see him in the afternoon. It won't interfere with your work."

Geoffrey grunted, keeping up a front of reluctance that came from a shame-faced knowledge that he wanted to do nothing more than talk about his anxiety. He was relieved that Viola had arranged this interview, that someone was doing something for him. What he wanted was reassurance; a continually repeated reassurance—not by Viola, who did not know what she was talking about, but by a doctor who knew more about the disease than he did himself.

"You will go, won't you?" she insisted before she left that morning for her office. She would not be back for luncheon and did not trust him to keep the appointment without her influence. Waiting for her question to penetrate the mist of his continual preoccupation, she went to the window. He, looking up, saw her like a shadow against the milky iridescence of the morning gardens. The elements of his febrile anxiety disintegrated suddenly and reformed themselves into a hope that was like exaltation.

He saw beyond the trivial, temporary situation that was destroying him into consciousness of himself as a creator that had a quality of eternity.

Viola, glancing round and meeting his brilliant eyes, smiled, took a step towards him, then stopped. The brilliance had gone like a light switched out. He bent his head on to his hands and sighed as from the depths of despair.

She crossed the room and sat on the bed beside him. She sighed herself: "I wish I knew what was the matter with you." She put her arm round his shoulder and he shook it off as though its weight were intolerable.

He said: "The same thing, I suppose, that's the matter with everyone. It's because we're pent up on this wretched planet with all its idiocy. There's no hope of getting away from it. Someone or other said God was a necessity, and it's true. Every race has discovered it. We can't just be trapped inside our bodies like this. When we realise we're trapped—just hopelessly trapped—we turn on ourselves and go crazy like an animal trying to bite its way through steel. That's what I'm doing. I want to escape into space and all I can do is shuffle round inside my own miserable mind and chew at myself with this neurosis."

Viola said, mildly, reasonably: "I didn't know anyone worried about God these days. There are other things more important than the salvation of our little souls."

"It's no good," he shouted, "that's not my business. You can't force me to it. You may find that social consciousness helps you to feel like Jesus Christ, but it doesn't work with me. I hate people. I must be left in peace. I must be free to . . ." he stopped and looked round as though he had forgotten what he was going to say.

"Darling, try and explain," she glanced at her wrist-watch.

"I can't. I can't. I can't," Geoffrey jumped up in a restlessness of nerves.

"All right. You can tell the psychiatrist all about it. I must go."

Geoffrey paused, then said tremulously: "I must ask him about my hand, why it keeps aching. It must be a symptom."

"That's all imagination. Like stigmata."

"It's there, anyway. I shall never be able to paint if this goes on. Look!"

"It's cramp. You think too much about it and hold the muscles taut. Kristel will explain. Now I must hurry."

When Geoffrey came back to the flat to eat luncheon alone, he began to feel nervous of the psychiatrist. Since Viola first spoke of Kristel, Geoffrey had carried around a vision of a man who looked exactly like Lister, but now there had come clearly to him the knowledge that the psychiatrist would almost certainly not look like Lister. The empty shape became a container for fear.

The sun was coming on to the verandah. While Geoffrey ate his meal, the boy Hassan closed the shutters and pulled the curtains. His feet slid about inside an enormous pair of white and tan shoes, his galabiah was not over-clean and he carried about with him an aura of garlic. Geoffrey, suddenly on edge with fury, shouted for the safragi Mohammed.

"Why the hell has the boy to be in here while I'm eating?"

Mohammed frowned darkly at the boy, pretending to take the matter seriously: "Very bad boy," he announced, "very lazy. Always forget." He ordered the boy to go, and the boy, grinning vacantly, went.

"And who the devil's this?" asked Geoffrey, looking at a dark and dirty figure in the pantry doorway.

"Dhobi man. Bring washing. Want money."

Geoffrey threw down a pound note and shouted: "Now

leave me alone." Before he could recover himself Mohammed was back holding a sheet.

"Mislyn sheet lost. Can't find. Dhobi man say this sheet very good."

Geoffrey looked at it helplessly, knowing no means of telling whether the sheet was good or bad. He took it, to give an impression of caution, and noticed the name 'Coningham-Carr' on a name tape.

"But this belongs to Colonel Coningham-Carr!"

"All right. Just as good as Mislyn sheet."

"But it belongs to someone else," Geoffrey could scarcely speak for exasperation. "It—is—the—sheet—of—Colonel Coningham-Carr."

"Colnel Conincarr gone away."

That was true. Coningham-Carr had been posted to Iraq six months before.

"I don't know. Don't ask me. Ask Mrs. Lynd. Now, go away! Yallah!"

Mohammed, puzzled by Geoffrey's bad temper, ambled off, flat-footed, with an air of good-humoured consciousness of his own sense and reason. The pantry door closed. There was silence.

Geoffrey's anger was gone in a moment, leaving him ashamed and desolated. He looked round the room with its peculiar dinginess that came when the curtains were drawn in daylight, and felt his own solitude. There was no one and nothing here he could blame for his inadequacy and, looking in on himself, he saw nothing but his own fear.

He had to get out into the open. His appointment was not until 3 o'clock, but he left the flat as soon as he had had a shower and changed his shirt and underwear.

The heat was losing its intensity but the afternoons were, as always, brilliant and shadowless. The gardener was hosing the strip of earth in which the palm trees grew. The first thing Geoffrey saw when he left the house was the crystal snake of water hissing across his path. The sound of it caught him in a spasm of horror, but in a moment he remembered a reason for legitimate anger with the man. Hadn't Viola told him a dozen times not to water the ground while the sun was on it? The man smiled, puzzled as Mohammed had been, and shut off the hose. Geoffrey knew that as soon as he was out of sight, it would be turned on again.

When he reached the high, ornamental gate-way of the house, he saw a dog standing with its nose against the bars. It was large and sand-coloured, one of the half-wild dogs with jackal blood that skirted human life here. It backed timidly as he put his hand to the gate and he saw in its movement the whole of its wretched, vagrant life in a Moslem world that looked on dogs with disgust. He opened the gate and reached to pat it, but it backed from him, alert to flee. There was a blood-caked, dusty cut over one of its eyes; fleas moved through the hairs on its nose.

"Good dog! Good old boy!" said Geoffrey. It advanced a little—then he remembered and pushed the gate shut against the creature's muzzle. It waved its tail uncertainly. Geoffrey looked round for the boab and saw him lying, knees under chin, arm over eyes, asleep on the seat by the wall. The gardener had gone behind the house. Geoffrey stood like a prisoner inside the gate, unwilling to make a fool of himself by calling to either man for help, and the dog watched him. He felt he hated it. Suddenly he shouted in an unnatural voice: "Yallah, yallah, yallah!"

The dog dodged and ran as from a blow. It kept ahead of him as he walked through Garden City. Once or twice it paused at some gutter refuge, then, scenting his approach, ran on. He watched it in a wretchedness of compassion for it; he felt pity for the dog and pity for himself that he should be cut off from animals in this way. Like someone weakened by a long illness, he could have broken down there in the street and wept.

The dog led him down to the embankment, where he paused under the banyan trees to let it get away. It sat for a while on the pavement a few yards from him, then when he did not move, it ran off towards the English Bridge. Relieved to get rid of it, he leant on the parapet and looked across the glittering, grey Nile to where the opposite bank lay hazed and colourless in the sun. He could just make out the tidied shore of the sailing club—a terrace and sun umbrellas. The yachts, whitely dotted over the pearl-coloured distance, were making a good pace towards the island of Zamalek that lay in mid-river like a vast, boat-shaped basket of ferns. From among the island's edging of palms and flowering trees rose blocks of flats—cream, cream-pink and brick-pink. The atmosphere hazed everything. It washed out all richness of colour and left flat earth-greens, umbers and fawns, so that the scene was like an early water-colour. He thought: "It has beauty. If I lived, I might remember it with emotion—but now I merely acknowledge it with my head. That's what the war's done for me." Again, as he was overwhelmed by pity of his own destruction, he was almost in tears. It was not a narrow pity; he was conscious, vaguely, that it embraced the whole suffering world, but himself was dominant in his mind, a symbol of the destroyed. He saw himself harassed now by fears. He thought of his short walk from the flat to the river as it had been—beset by the appalling significance of symbols—and knew it beyond bearing. If he could be cured, he must be cured.

He found a taxi and drove to the centre of the town where the psychiatrist lived in a large, old-fashioned block of flats. There were shops on the ground floor, offices above and on top, neighboured by Egyptian and Indian doctors, Kristel's flat. Viola had said Kristel was a European refugee of some sort and Geoffrey, picturing a man suffering and reduced to poverty, expected to feel in sympathy with him. His immediate hope on seeing Kristel was that this might be the wrong man.

"Dr. Kristel?" he asked resentfully.

"Sit down, please. I am Dr. Kristel."

Kristel spoke English correctly and, instead of the intimate manner of most foreign doctors, had the restrained self-assurance of a Harley Street specialist. He was a tall man with a square, sallow face and black hair. His spectacles were rimmed heavily in black horn and his small, dark eyes were scarcely visible behind the heavy lenses.

Geoffrey, unable to hide his antagonism, was agitated, but Kristel behaved as though unaware of it. He started talking at once, easily, with a patronising kindliness: "You are an artist, I believe, Major Lynd? Tell me, now. What do you think of my Kaugermann? I have been told it is an exceptionally fine example of his work."

Geoffrey moved over to a large picture that was fitted against the wall among the cupboards, book-cases and filing cabinets of pale, polished woods. As he followed the complex composition of angles and curves, he could find no fault in it and yet he was convinced of its dishonesty. Could he have believed in it, it would have comforted him, but as it was, he was certain that Kristel showed it to him to comment on his own failure, to insist on his inferiority. He said nothing, but turned to look at the room in which every article fitted like the parts of a jig-saw puzzle, leaving the maximum of space and light. This functionalism was something Geoffrey had always disliked.

Kristel said: "Are you admiring my room? It was designed for me by a brilliant young German Jewish architect who came here as a refugee and died of typhoid. I do not think there is one line out of place, do you? People tell me his work in Berlin was excellent. All destroyed now, of course. This is his memorial."

Geoffrey observed the enormous, vacant window, the fawn carpet with its few blue-grey and chocolate lines, and Kristel's enormous desk, and said nothing.

"Sit down here," said Kristel, "and put your feet up."

Geoffrey faced the window and Kristel settled himself behind the desk: "Now! Your wife tells me you have developed a morbid fear of hydrophobia. That is not an uncommon neurosis; others have suffered it before. I think we can disperse it. It may take some time, but . . . Anyway, this afternoon I just want to have a little talk and ask a few questions. Don't regard this as a treatment. Just tell me anything you can."

Kristel paused as though expecting Geoffrey to start talking at once. When Geoffrey said nothing, he added: "Let yourself relax. Just tell me anything you think I should know . . ."

Geoffrey found it difficult to listen to what Kristel was saying. He had nothing to say himself; his mind was empty. He felt miserably exposed here in the middle of this large, bright room facing the naked blue of the sky. From the couch on which he sat he could see nothing but the curving movements of the kites that floated unceasingly over the city as on a bowl of air . . . Kristel's voice faded from him, but he was startled into complete consciousness by a faint cry that came from somewhere behind the desk. He swung round and asked: "What was that?"

Kristel frowned at this interruption of his talk, then, regaining placidity, he said: "Only a kitten."

"A kitten! Really! But where is it?"

"Here," Kristel glanced over his shoulder. "It is shut in a basket. Someone is calling for it."

Geoffrey jumped up: "Let me see it."

"I think we should not disturb it," Kristel frowned again. "It came on approval, and now its owner will take it away."

"I would like to see it," Geoffrey insisted like a child that cannot bear to be denied. He was trembling, his whole will set on the kitten as though through it he could escape from his discomfort in this room.

"Very well," Kristel reached behind him. He fidgeted with a basket clasp then lifted on to the desk a cream-coloured kitten, very small and thin, with brown points and clear ice-blue eyes.

"A Siamese kitten," Geoffrey crossed to the desk and putting out his trembling hands, lifted the tiny, nervous animal to his breast, sick with his own tenderness like someone deprived of love for a lifetime. "It isn't yours?" he asked.

"No. A lady heard I wanted one and brought it for me to see. It is a nice little thing, but . . ." Kristel shrugged his shoulders, "not a perfect specimen. You see," he leant forward and casually fingered the kitten's tail, "there is no knot in the tail. A knot is essential."

"I don't think so," said Geoffrey eagerly. "There are two kinds of Siamese cats—one with a knot, one without. He is perfectly all right."

"I must have the knot," said Kristel irritably, "it is essential."

"But what does it matter?" began Geoffrey, then he found the kitten was licking his hand. He dropped it on the desk. He felt the colour pass from his face almost before he was aware of his fear: "God," he whispered, "it licked me."

"Yes," Kristel said dryly, and he put the kitten back in its basket. He had been pressing the bell on his desk. A servant entered. Kristel gave an order and the man took the basket from the room. When Geoffrey looked up the kitten had gone, but he did not care. He went back weakly to his couch, his whole body seeming to sink in upon him in fear of all the fear to which the moment of handling the kitten must give rise. His antagonism against Kristel had passed. Staring round, seeing Kristel sitting impassive behind the desk, Geoffrey felt in his helplessness that his only hope of salvation might be through Kristel.

"It was the same hand," he said as though that fact must have for Kristel a significance as terrible as it had for him.

"You are fond of animals?" asked Kristel.

"Yes. Yes, I used to be."

"But not of human beings?"

"Human beings? I don't know. It's not that I dislike them, but that they dislike me."

Kristel grunted and made a note. "Now," he said in a sing-song tone of encouragement, "tell me what happened at Petra."

Geoffrey did his best to tell the story of the Petra visit clearly and carefully, omitting nothing.

"And when did you begin to feel so anxious?"

"Not at once. I felt rather empty and nervous, but not actually afraid. I couldn't get it out of my head but I thought it would pass. We went back to Jerusalem and a few days later, when I was preparing to come to Egypt, I realised I was worse. I realised I . . ." he paused, then said calmly: "I was terrified."

"Yes."

"I could scarcely face the journey. I was obsessed by the idea I would go mad on the train—make a ghastly exhibition of myself. I don't know what I would have done, but Clark gave me some sedatives."

"Now," said Kristel, looking up, "what do you think yourself was the significance of this terror? What do you think lay behind it?"

"So hideous a death . . ."

"But there are many hideous deaths," said Kristel.

"Yes," Geoffrey agreed. Kristel waited and, after a minute, Geoffrey, his face flushed, his voice high in a sort of exaltation of discovery, said: "That is it, of course. One comes into life to create. One comes ready and eager, one's whole will eager, wanting perfection . . . The most perfect and beautiful world. And there they are waiting to leap on you—hideous deaths, madness and agony. The ghastly hideousness of a thing like leprosy . . ." his voice broke, "I can't bear it. Whatever you say—it breaks down the basis of morality. Almost everything else could be explained away as some sort of flouting of good—either your own fault or someone else's. Reasonable; part of the mathematical formula of morality. But this—you are walking in the evening (you know the tranquillity and beauty of desert evenings?), and you see a wretched little dog, driven and terrified, perhaps persecuted . . . You put out your hand to it, it bites you out of fear, and you die in what Manson describes as the most frightful agony known to humanity."

"But it didn't bite you," said Kristel.

"No," said Geoffrey impatiently, "but that has nothing to do with it."

"Have you ever been a religious man?"

"No."

"But you believe in God?"

"No. Of course I don't."

"Do you believe in anything?"

"In reason."

"Why should you believe in reason if not in God?"

"I suppose because one can't accept chaos. Yet that, of course, is exactly what we have to accept."

"I see."

Geoffrey made an agitated movement, then he sprang

up and started wandering round the room: "Are peopl like me to exist any more? It's all right for you and every one else—you've all got such a grip on life to-day. Look a you in this room with every angle right, and this picture You're justified. You belong. Yet, in a way, you're lik the Elizabethans. This medieval horror is part of life an you can take it. It is unbearable for me that such thing exist. Hydrophobia exists, leprosy exists, tetanus exists Belsen exists. It is the fact they exist."

"You are sorry for the persecuted?"

"No. I can do nothing for them."

"So you hate them?"

"No. Yes. I suppose so. They hate me. I can do nothin for them. It is unbearable to be so helpless."

"Why do you suppose that you, more than anyone else should have to do anything for them?"

Geoffrey shook his head: "I don't know," he sai vaguely, "I suppose everyone feels the same."

"Why have you such a horror of these diseases in partic ular? Have you any idea?"

Geoffrey stared at his feet and frowned, then he starte speaking quickly, almost incoherently: "They're part o the medieval world that used to terrify me when I was child. I forgot about it when I got older, but I remembe it now. Other children were excited by it, but it used t terrify me. My aunt had that book—Foxe's *Book o Martyrs*; it made me sick—the humiliating horror of th tortures people were made to suffer then. The humiliatio that one's fellow men could do it to one. I hated them. couldn't bear the existence of such cruelty. I used to pla how I could have some safeguard—a means of dyin quickly. I've been told the Jews in Germany did the same.

Kristel nodded.

Geoffrey went on: "One used to have the sense of tim between oneself and those horrors—but now they're co temporary. Now I keep thinking if I could get enough sleeping-tablets so that when I knew—*knew for certain*—it was starting, I could escape it. But sleeping-tablets are no good. There's always some busybody who finds you and calls in help and brings you back to life. Imagine returning to find yourself . . . But what else can one do?" Geoffrey, the force gone from his voice, dropped back on the couch and said helplessly, "If you are afraid of water, how can you commit suicide?"

Kristel glanced at Geoffrey's revolver holster and set his lips: "No doubt there are ways," he said as though the matter were of no importance, then his voice took on new interest. "You mentioned your aunt. Was she kind to you?"

"Yes. Kind enough."

"What about your mother?"

"She died when I was six. She wasn't married. I didn't know this, of course, until I was twenty-one and inherited some money she left me. I was brought up by my aunt, my mother's sister. She was married and had three children of her own. Everyone knew I wasn't her child—I looked so different from the others. They never let me forget I was different, either. I can remember being brought down with the other children to be shown to a visitor—and seeing the visitor catch my aunt's eyes, and my aunt's significant nods—and feeling there was something odd about me. I'd be playing with my cousins and all the time I'd be trying to hear something being said about me. I imagined that everything they said was slighting and mysterious, and I began to feel a sort of guilt that set me apart . . ." Geoffrey looked at Kristel, expecting him to draw some pertinent conclusion from that, but Kristel merely nodded and said: "Yes?"

Geoffrey, resentful, said: "But that means nothing. I don't want to speak about it. There are other things more important."

"Such as?"

"This pain in my hand. It's there all the time. It won't leave me alone, so I can't take my mind off it. And, worse than that—my hand is becoming crippled so I can't paint. You'll say that's an excuse for not painting, but it's much more complex than that."

"Of course," said Kristel. "Now, what about your life in the army? Are you reasonably contented?"

"I'm glad to have my job. I'd go mad, I think, if I hadn't got a job now—but I'd rather do something more active."

"Could you give me some idea of what you do? Not, of course, what your work's all about—that's probably secret. But just the sort of work it is?"

"The usual army office work. I get trays full of files and papers. I go through them; answer questions; make notes; say 'Yes' or 'No' to things."

"You think it's important?"

"No. Yes. I suppose it's important in a way."

"Now what, do you think, made you pick on hydrophobia?"

"Because I was bitten . . ."

"You know you weren't bitten. There's no mark at all on your hand. If you'd been normal you'd have forgotten the incident in half an hour."

"That's the danger, of course. People have died of it who couldn't remember having had any contact with a mad animal. They didn't know their danger. It was just able to overtake them."

"Would there be any advantage in knowing?"

Geoffrey reflected, then said reasonably: "If you knew, of course, you could take precautions. You could have these injections at the Pasteur Institute. They work in ninety-nine cases out of a hundred."

"You don't want to have the injections?"

"They're very painful."

"But if you were in serious danger, surely you would prefer to have the injections?"

"I don't know. If you don't have the injections and the disease develops—well, it develops within six weeks or so. But if you have them, they're not one hundred per cent certain. They may only delay it. There is the case of the man who developed it two years after he was bitten. Imagine two years of uncertainty! One would go mad."

"You seem to know a lot about it."

"I read it first in Manson—afterwards I read all the medical books I could find. I was looking for a loophole, but it fitted exactly . . ."

"Fitted what?"

Geoffrey shook his head.

"Do you dream about it?" asked Kristel.

"No."

"Before this developed, did you worry much about things?"

"Yes, I worried about my wife. I was always frightened of something happening to her."

"Did she interfere with your painting in any way?"

"No," Geoffrey became angry, "no. On the contrary. I suppose you're going to tell me I wanted her to die?"

Kristel smiled: "Everyone's becoming an amateur psychiatrist these days." He settled more comfortably into his chair: "Well," he said, "we may say that all hypochondriacal ideas result from fear of self-injury sustained through sexual relationships. You can easily see for yourself how your wish to destroy your wife might project itself into a wish to destroy yourself. The skeleton of the neurosis, of course, is usually clear enough. It is the structure and the hidden basis that we want to reveal . . ."

While Kristel talked, Geoffrey stared from the window. He had gone up close to the sill where a row of small, grey cacti plants stood in white pots. There he could see the roofs of Cairo, thousands of them, flat and square, all the same buff colour, stretching away into the haze at the desert's edge. Kristel was talking steadily. Above the roofs the kites floated in placid curves. As they turned, catching sunlight on their plumage, Geoffrey could see they were not brown but bronze. That bronze colour was right, of course . . . His aunt, who had travelled in her girlhood, had a lot of faded sepia photographs of Eastern cities. He must have seen a photograph of Cairo among them, for from the first it had belonged to the frightening past. The birds, too, belonged. They were watchers, scavengers. When he first arrived someone had said as a joke: "They're waiting for the air-raids," and from then he had felt a horror of them.

Kristel was still expounding some theory of the neurosis. Geoffrey was not listening but for moments his attention would flit on to Kristel's voice so that, like someone glimpsing a landscape through patches of mist, he would hear him breaking all fear down to the bare bones of analytical principles. Geoffrey thought: "This disgusts me."

" . . . then," came Kristel's voice, " we must ask why you are obsessed by this disease in particular? "

"Because . . ." Geoffrey broke in quickly, then paused, baffled, "I don't know. Perhaps because one is infected by an animal—a dog or cat, or a jackal. It is worse still if you are bitten by a wolf."

"I suppose wolves symbolise medievalism to you? It's as though wolves roamed England, perhaps? "

Geoffrey felt angry at this suggestion. It seemed unrelated to all he had been trying to explain—not only unrelated but absurd. Kristel had no understanding of the subtlety of this fear. As Geoffrey considered this fact, he became furious that his neurosis, his creation, should be broken down by a process that seemed to him like shying balls at a cocoanut. He said: "It's no good. You only make me feel worse—more hopeless and helpless. I feel I need to be built up, not broken down."

"Yes," Kristel was not upset, "everyone feels resentful at first, but we must go through the breaking down process before we can rebuild."

"I don't think you could rebuild. I don't think you have any idea of what I'm talking about. You are so occupied with breaking my neurosis down to some formula of your own, you miss the point altogether. I know the formula as well as you do, but the structure that has grown up round it is more important than the formula."

"I understand how you feel, but . . ."

"Let me ask you some questions." Geoffrey's anger was like a stimulant, enabling him to put aside his fear as he might put down some object he held in his hand. "Why did you become a psychiatrist?"

Kristel smiled indulgently: "I have always been interested in the workings of the mind."

"You seem to me quite the wrong sort of person. You have no imagination."

"I'm a scientist. Imagination is the disease I'm combating."

"*Disease!*"

"It is imagination that keeps you maladjusted. You turn from life to find an ideal instead of facing a reality. You expect life to adjust itself to you—to become a sort of imaginative fantasy like a novel, but life isn't a well-constructed novel, is it? That's your quarrel with it."

"I've always known that," said Geoffrey weakly. "Knowing it doesn't make me accept life as it is. On the contrary, I only hate it more for being unalterable."

"Exactly," Kristel threw down his pencil—a gold pencil with a ring in the top—and Geoffrey watched it roll along the length of the desk. He noticed also that Kristel's hands were long, narrow and very white, and wondered if the psychiatrist ever went out into the sunlight. Geoffrey stood at the desk like a schoolboy waiting for a master to speak, but when the silence went on he began to think he must meet Kristel half-way. If he remained critical, obstinate and unresponsive, he might be abandoned. He began trembling at the thought.

He said: "You know, if there were one person (a qualified person, of course) on whom I could rely to give me chloroform when the thing started . . . I mean, not someone who'd wait for more certain symptoms, or wait out of curiosity because they'd never seen a case before, but someone I could trust—then I wouldn't be so afraid."

"Lie down on the couch again," said Kristel quietly.

Geoffrey obeyed: "You don't really believe you can cure me?" he said.

"I can promise nothing. It is easier to diagnose a case than cure it."

"But if you try, how long might it take?"

"A year, eighteen months—a little longer, perhaps."

"Good God! Are you serious?"

"If I cured you within a year, it would be remarkably quick."

Geoffrey lay on the couch because he felt too weak to sit upright: "And then—when I was cured—there'd be no danger of my becoming normal, would there? I mean, no longer a painter?"

"Well," Kristel stood up and crossed to the window, "there's always the danger of an artist losing something. It is a danger I should try and avoid. But I've been told the trouble is that you no longer paint."

"That's true, of course. If I became normal—then I'd be at home in the world like other people?"

"You'd have to adjust yourself to present-day life. It wouldn't be easy."

"I see. You're admitting your limitations. But there are other treatments, aren't there? Narcosis and shock?"

"Nothing I'd recommend in your case."

"But they're treating men every day."

"I know they are. Indiscriminately. Half of these army psychiatrists have no idea what they're doing. They put every type of case into the machine for shock treatment and often get some sort of temporary cure. That's all they want—but it may be disastrous to the patient. No, I would not recommend it. You are not ill enough to justify it. Your condition is not anti-social. You don't rave or make a nuisance of yourself."

"No," Geoffrey sighed, "I did not realise it would be so difficult. When my wife said that something would be done for me—I thought she meant at once."

"A miracle?" Kristel laughed. He swung round from the window, his attitude now one of complete confidence. "I've treated cases worse than yours with good results. Now! To-morrow afternoon at the same time—and we'll start getting down to things."

Geoffrey rose automatically and let Kristel grip his hand with a force in which he had no faith.

"Good-bye then," said Kristel and Geoffrey murmured: "Good-bye."

When the door shut behind him, he stood on the landing like someone turned adrift. He began very slowly to make a descent of the stairs. As he made his way down the six stone flights, sliding his hand heavily on the banister, he felt stupefied by desolation and slighted as an individual. Why had Viola sent him to this Kristel who would thrust him, as though he were a pig in a canning factory, through a process that would destroy him? A bitter resentment flooded up through him; his eyes filled with tears, and leaning, half-sobbing in the darkness of the hall, he whispered: 'The poor little kitten! The poor little kitten!"

Out in the street he did not know where to go. The sunlight stupefied him. The afternoons were still too hot for walking. He was drawn towards Groppi's garden because Viola might be there. When he stepped out from the shop to the terrace, the first person he saw was Lister sitting alone at a little table overlooking the café.

Geoffrey's pleasure was so great, every other thought went from his mind. There was Lister—like a great baby propped, cigar in mouth, on the little iron seat—with his usual air, the ridiculous air of the plutocrat. Geoffrey could have embraced him. Lister, looking up and seeing him, flushed pink and started to grin.

"How long have you been in Cairo?" Geoffrey asked as he sat down.

"Oh!" Lister took out the cigar and stared at it. "Only a few days."

"But why didn't you let me know? You had my telephone number!"

Lister stared and stared at his cigar, a fat man deflated by embarrassment, his cheeks growing more pink, and Geoffrey knew at once that Lister had not wanted to see him. He knew that to Lister, as to everyone else, he was a man set apart by a mental sickness; he was a nuisance; he required special consideration and Lister would not discommodate himself to the extent of giving it. Although his smiling friendliness and air of sensitive good-nature had so long denied it, Lister was at the core a self-protecting egoist. All that was suddenly as clear to Geoffrey as if Lister had spoken it.

From long practice in such discoveries, Geoffrey was able to adjust himself in a moment: "Did you come alone?" he asked. "Didn't Clark come with you?"

"We came together; he brought his car. I'm on leave but he's been posted here, lucky devil. No Palestine winter for him. You'll see quite a lot of him."

"I doubt it."

There was a difficult silence. Geoffrey, making no effort to talk, looked at Lister's hands and, for the first time, saw them separate from the rest of Lister. They were small as a woman's hands, pale pink and satiny. The softly padded palms were circular and from each the five small fingers tapered as smooth as china. Lister wriggled in his chair. Geoffrey felt his uneasiness and wondered: "What does he want? If I expect nothing, I'm less of a nuisance. Do people prefer you to expect what they're not prepared to give?"

Lister appeared to pull himself together. He sat upright, smiling with an air of mischief that was rather too elaborate. He said confidentially: "I was looking for Clark when I came here this afternoon. I found him, as usual, with a lady," his eyes slid round to survey the sunlit expanse of the garden café below. "I did not intrude."

Geoffrey, looking where Lister was looking, saw Clark sitting with Viola. He became red and hot like a man in a fever; then his mind and nerves were stilled in a calm that was like a death cutting him off from the agitations of the living. He was soon able to say composedly: "I've never understood his attraction for women."

"Neither have I, but, then, we're not expected to. It's something he doesn't switch on for us."

"And how is Jerusalem?"

"Wet and cold. I envy Clark getting away. Winter in Cairo, summer in Jerusalem—that's what I'd like if I could work it."

Now that the first calm of shock was wearing off, Geoffrey's throat seemed to have fallen in on itself. When the safragi came, he could scarcely give his order, but he was determined not to let Lister know of his state. He drank some water from a glass on the table and managed to ask: "What hope of your getting posted here?"

While Lister grumbled, Geoffrey allowed himself to

glance again at Viola and Clark. They had their backs to the terrace and he could see them both in profile. Clark, smiling, was leaning towards Viola. Viola lolled in her chair, her whole attitude languorous and yet—so it seemed to Geoffrey—inviting. Her face had a bloom, a glow of youthfulness . . . Geoffrey remembered that years ago, when she had first been in love with him, she had looked like that. "I am jealous," he thought, "I am sick with jealousy."

"How are you now?" Lister was asking.

"All right," Geoffrey dragged his attention from the couple down in the café.

"Before you left you weren't—I mean, you had a bit of a breakdown."

"Yes."

"You know," said Lister with the heartiness that Geoffrey seemed to be meeting everywhere, "I don't think there was much wrong with that dog. You know what Arabs are like!"

"Yes, I know what they're like. They won't take life if they can help it. Nothing would have induced them to shoot that dog if it hadn't been . . ." he paused. Listening to his own talk, he heard himself—a man obsessed on to his own obsession—and tried to excuse himself: "I shall never forget when I was in Damascus a few years before the war, I was going round that little mosque with the domes—what was it called?"

"I know the one you mean."

"There was a cat—terribly mutilated. It must have been run over or something, and somehow survived. It was dragging itself across the courtyard and there were half a dozen Arabs sitting on the rim of the fountain watching it. They were completely indifferent. I know there's no excuse for me. I could have done something about it—killed it, or something. I don't know. I did nothing."

"Just as well you didn't," said Lister. "In the precinct of a mosque, my God!"

"I didn't think of that. I simply hadn't the courage to make myself conspicuous."

"Who has?"

While he was talking, Geoffrey had been acutely conscious of the two behind him in the garden but when he looked down again, they were no longer there. He stared, bewildered—they must have gone out by the back entrance.

"Clark's gone," said Lister. "Went off with his cutie a minute ago. She's a nice, comfortable-looking piece."

Geoffrey said: "I've been seeing a psychiatrist called Kristel."

"Oh! Clark's friend?"

"Clark's friend!" Geoffrey echoed, stunned by what he believed was a revelation of a plot against him. He turned pale, but Lister noticed nothing, having been distracted by a small boy standing beside their table.

"Who's this little horror?" he said.

Geoffrey made an effort to turn and observe the boy. He recognised him at once—a small figure, more like a dwarf than a child, who stood by one's table, silent, unmoving, waiting to be given something. In a town filled with whining, persistent beggars, this approach was noticeable and, apparently, effective. The boy had a flat, pale, Slavonic face with mature eyes and an expression of confident cunning.

"Repellent little beast!" commented Lister. "He can't be an Egyptian—he's too horrible."

Three years before this boy had worn a dirty galabiah like all beggar children, now, though not much taller, he had become sturdy and dressed himself in an European pin-stripe suit. He looked like a child about to do an act on the stage. His calculating, ancient stare was unchanged.

"Here you are!" Geoffrey gave him a five-piastre piece,

feeling the silent, waiting presence an unbearable irritant. The boy took the money, saluted smartly, but did not move. He, turned his stare on to Lister. Lister, looking at him with loathing, said: "You've had enough. Yallah."

The boy did not move.

"Clear off, damn you," shouted Lister.

"Thank you, sir," said the child and, with dignity and decision, moved off to a group of American officers.

Lister smiled uncomfortably at Geoffrey: "To part with money is to die a little," he laughed; "That brat will be a millionaire one day."

Geoffrey knew that Lister was joking when he made the remark about parting with money, yet he felt repelled by it. It was as though he had now taken a step away from Lister and, seeing all his characteristics newly focused, disliked him. Geoffrey glanced at his wrist-watch and stood up. Lister watched him with unhappy eyes, his large face smiling uncertainly and with something like guilt.

Geoffrey made no mention of seeing Lister again and, giving Lister no encouragement to mention it, said: "Must get back to my office," and went.

Out in the street, he called a taxi. For the first time he felt through his own fear a curious detachment from life. The fear had become more important than life and gave him a sort of satisfaction. He thought of Viola and of Lister and lumped them with all those claims of his life that he could regard with contempt. They had all sunk back secondary to this preoccupation. Everything that had had power to hurt him was now defeated.

The knowledge flashed on him like a revelation, then he turned upon it, denying it, and his old anguish descended upon him again.

A chill crept into the evening air. In the cool mornings a haze, increasing in some way the brilliance and purity of the light, hung over the trees and buildings by the river. On a few days, so rare that visitors were fortunate to experience one, the haze deepened into a mist that obscured the sun and coloured the sky like a pearl. In the unusual light, the greens of the public parks became like candy. If rain fell, which might happen once in a year although many years were rainless, the papers stated the fact in headlines and published photographs of girls running and businessmen protecting their tarbooshes with handkerchiefs. If it fell in the desert—a rare occurrence indeed—the sand would lie sodden in sculptured folds and age-old seeds would sprout and put forth flowers in miniature. This was the Egyptian winter.

Viola found it pleasant at night to sleep under a blanket. During the day she enjoyed the comfortable weight of her flannel suit.

There was something adventurous in the change of the light as the gharry carried her past the little Esbekiah Gardens towards Shepheard's. The air had a thunderous look although thunderstorms were unknown here, so the tall palms and trees of the gardens, shut in by railings, seemed to stand apart from one another and have the alert intensity of captive animals. These gardens contained a camp of Nubian troops, a group of whom stood shadowy at the gate, faces lifted to the sky, dark skin ashen in the violet light.

The cement of buildings looked peculiarly livid; the blocks of flats bleak and spotted. This was a summer city unfitted for gloom. Shepheard's façade fell back darkly behind dark, dusty palms, and lights were coming on in the windows.

A few drops of rain touched Viola's hands as she paid the gharry. People darted into the hotel from the terrace. Newspapers left behind on tables flapped chalky in the twilight. Viola was safely inside when the deluge descended and hit the glass dome of the lounge with a roar. People started talking excitedly; some went to watch the phenomenon.

Clark, sitting with Viola on a divan against the wall, behaved as though nothing were happening. Viola was irritated by his indifference. She found herself constantly irritated by something overbearing in his masculinity and now she broke into whatever he was saying to say: "You're not impressed by our storm?"

He looked up, surprised, and listened for a moment to the rain on the glass: "Of course," he said, "this *is* unusual, isn't it? I'd forgotten—in Jerusalem we'd been getting it every day before I left." He was obviously so innocent of affectation, she warmed to him because she had misjudged him: "Would you like to go and look?" he asked, noticing that other people were moving to the hall.

"No," she reassured him, pandering now to his masculinity. And here, she thought, was where their relationship had, after nearly a month, come to a standstill. It had come to a standstill because she refused to develop it further. Almost his every movement filled her with irritation. His large, long hands, the hairs on his fingers, the unyielding hardness of his arms when he brushed against her, the fact that he smoked a pipe, and an assurance in his movements—all repelled her; not only repelled but filled her with irritation; yet she could not bring the relationship to an end.

Clark asked the habitual question: "How is Geoffrey?"

"More remote, if anything. I keep telling him what you say—even if he had been bitten, he's past the danger period, but he doesn't listen. Besides, you told him there was a case of a man developing rabies two years after he was bitten."

"I know," Clark smiled to himself, "but those very long incubation periods only occur in cases who've had injections."

"I'll tell him that, but I'm not sure he even wants to listen."

Clark said: "He's playing a little game with himself now. It's easier to be a mental invalid than to return to normal life."

Viola was annoyed as always by Clark's contempt for Geoffrey's condition: "He doesn't let it interfere with his job," she said.

"In time he will. Let's talk of something else." Clark bent slightly towards Viola as though to divert her attention, but she would not look at him. She wondered why she went on meeting him. All they did was get on one another's nerves.

As he leant towards her, she stared coldly over his shoulder at the large, circular lounge. Shaded lights flattered the squalor of the ancient Egyptian *décor*. A couple of Australian privates were wandering self-consciously up and down the centre aisle. One was wearing a waste-paper basket on his head and the other was bowing and waving a palm leaf before him. The waiters and every officer in the room kept backs rigidly turned against this display.

"You're not listening to a word I say," said Clark.

"Sorry. I was watching those Australians."

Clark glanced at them, then away quickly: "They're drunk. Don't look at them or we'll have them making trouble over here. If no one takes any notice, they'll begin to feel sorry for themselves and crumple up. Viola, look at me! Why do you go on seeing me?"

"I don't know. I don't want to—and you aren't even very easy to talk to. To tell you the truth," she raised her voice slightly in irritation, "I can't think of anything to say to you at all." She frowned over her shoulder, keeping her eyes away from him, and started biting the side of her thumb-nail.

"Well," he said humbly, "I can't think of anything much to say to you either." He drew in his breath sharply, then added: "But you know why, don't you?"

She would not look at him or try to answer him. The voluptuous glow that had made Clark's attention so pleasant during their first meetings was gone now. She felt only restlessness and an impatience with him that kept her on edge in his presence.

He caught her arm and shook it a little: "Viola," he said with a pleading she found intolerable, "Viola, darling! Are you to go on leading this abnormal existence because of your crazy husband?"

"That question's becoming a habit with you," she said, still staring into the lounge. The Australians had wandered off but Viola's attention was fixed on a fat man—whom, she remembered, she had seen somewhere before—sidling along the other end of the lounge, apparently watching them and avoiding them at the same time.

"Who is that man?" she asked.

"Where? Oh, Lister."

"Lister! So that's Lister. Geoffrey was very attached to him in Jerusalem."

"They got on all right. He's had a month's leave—going back in a day or two."

"He's watching us. I've seen him doing it before."

"I suppose he thinks it's funny. Anything he doesn't understand is a joke to him. He's a cynic—thank goodness his leave's up to-morrow."

Lister, seeing they were looking towards him, moved off quickly. Clark seemed to forget him at once but there remained with Viola a sharp image of Lister's avoidance of them. She was sure he knew who she was and she knew he supposed her to be Clark's mistress. Had it been true, she would have been discomforted enough; because it was untrue, she felt shamed.

She felt nothing but a shamed chill when Clark said suddenly with miserable anger: "We can't be expected to stand any more of this. I'm going up to my room. I've moved to 198—got a room to myself now. You must come up there to me. If you don't—then we don't meet again."

What he said might have agitated her a few days before; as she watched him striding across the lounge to the lift, she felt nothing. He had to stand for some time waiting for the lift to descend. She sat dispassionately watching his handsome male body—the long legs, the wide shoulders, the narrow waist held by a leather belt. Although he was only a doctor he looked more like a soldier than most of them. Having seen men of all shapes and sizes appearing in the accoutrements of fighting men, she had found nothing to excite her in the dress. Now, watching Clark, she saw it anew. Something stirred in her, her lips parted and she raised her eyebrows—at that moment the lift door opened and he went inside. She shook off this new consciousness of him and told herself with annoyance that he was sure of her. He went, confident she would follow—and he was a fool.

She finished her tea leisurely and went at leisure and at peace towards the hall. A number of people were standing round the door and when they realised she wanted to go out, they seemed surprised, but made way for her. She had forgotten the rain. It had stopped; the sun was cutting through the mist; the street was a river. There were no drains in the gutters and the water had accumulated until it covered the lower steps that led up to the terrace. All traffic had stopped. A few Egyptian boys had bound up their galabiahs and were wading about for the fun of the thing. The jewellery shops opposite had barricaded their doors and windows to keep out the flood. People, leaning from the upper windows, shouted enquiries to the boys. A cry of delight went up when an old man appeared floating in a tin slipper-bath with the two Australians, up to their waists in water, one still wearing the waste-paper basket, zig-zagging him about the centre of the stream. Seeing Viola standing uncertainly at the top of the steps, they shouted that they would carry her home. As they plunged towards her, she fled back to the hotel.

"How long will this last?" she asked one of the porters.

"Perhaps one hour; perhaps two hours; perhaps one day. Who knows?"

She went to ring her office and found a queue of people at the telephone before her. When she at last got through, she was told by the switchboard girl that all the offices were empty. Everyone was trapped somewhere in the same way. It was then she remembered Geoffrey alone in the flat surrounded by a waste of water. She was troubled for him. She wandered back to the door, thinking she should ring him and wondering what she could say if she did. Because of her helplessness with regard to him, she was unwilling to get into touch with him and her old resentment returned. It became clear to her that because she could do nothing for him, she suffered through him in reaction from this knowledge: she thought of Nicholas Clark and wanted him.

She went to the cloakroom and powdered her face. Her reflection in the mirror, with a glow about the cheeks and an unusual brightness in the eyes, watched her guiltily. Everyone must notice her excitement; they must guess that she, with her senses heightened by celebacy, longed for passion. She hurried away in a nausea of excitement.

In the hall she lit a cigarette. She supposed that even when she seemed indifferent, she had all the time known what she would do; she had held to uncertainty to prolong an entertainment in which she was both actor and audience. When she came to the end of her cigarette, she stubbed it out slowly. She walked slowly down the hall between the little tables where every seat was taken. The stairway was at the end and everyone knew it led only to the bedrooms. She imagined it would be less conspicuous to run up the first exposed flight than to wait in the hall for the lift. She glanced brightly at the tables nearest the stairs—no one whom she knew. If she went confidently enough, she might go unnoticed.

Clark was lying on his bed in a dressing-gown. He lifted his head as she entered and when he saw her, his face was lit by its smile. He said: "I knew you would come."

She frowned as he said that, but when he put his arms round her, her frown faded in delight of him.

Geoffrey spent that afternoon, as he was beginning to spend most of them, in his office. At one o'clock he sent his sergeant to get him a sandwich and a whisky from the bar. After he had eaten and drunk, he settled down again at his desk, pretending to himself that a few hours extra work might bring him to the end of the stream of papers that passed through his hands.

He studied the folder of the top file: "Please give your comments." Above that Major Johnstone, late of the British Council, had written his: "Brekkekek Ko-ax, Ko-ax." Geoffrey reflected that two years ago, even a year ago, he might have dared to do that himself; now he took everything seriously. He began to go through the thick coating of paper that had grown like scar-tissue round someone's failure to do something. He noticed he had had the file in once before. He did not care. It helped to give him something to do.

Geoffrey's office was in a large house that had been, before it was requisitioned, the mansion of a wealthy Italian. The rooms were empty now except for trestle-tables. On Geoffrey's wall a sectional map of North Africa had been pieced together to show the road from El Alamein along which the Germans were retreating out of Africa. There was nothing else to distract him. His hand ached but with a steady effort of will he was able to keep his thoughts from it as he might keep his eyes from an object at his elbow—but he knew it was there all the time.

Between three and four o'clock, Henderson, the sergeant, strolled in, hands in pockets, cigarette hanging from lip. When he saw Geoffrey he whipped out the cigarette and, standing to attention, kept it hidden behind the seam of his trousers.

"Didn't know you was in, sir."

"Just getting a few things cleared up."

The sergeant, not taking this out-of-hours work seriously, relaxed and showed inclination to talk. He was newly appointed to this office and Geoffrey, unsure how to deal with him, said weakly: "No end to this bumf."

"That's right, sir. Worse and worse every day, and where's it come from? New chaps everywhere, too, and when 'Winnie' came here to have a dekko, you should've seen the bowler hats he handed out. Makes you wonder."

"When I came back from Palestine, nothing seemed changed."

"Nor was it, neither, not so as you'd notice. And I don't believe it ever will change. You'll find this lot going on just the same ten years after the war's over. To tell you the truth, sir, when I first came here—I'd been in the desert, see—I thought I was so blooming lucky, I was pissing m'self to do a bit extra to show I deserved it, but I soon saw nothing mattered but whether we could cook things so's to get another chap on the staff so's we'd all go up one. I saw my bloke in VKO, name of Tapley—you know him?—little dark moustache!—I saw him go up from captain to lieutenant-colonel in nine months, and it'd've made no difference to anyone if him and his blank, blank establishment had been blown to b—— blazes overnight.

All last year when I was in VKO I spent my time making a duplicate filing system just in case the other one got lost, and when the Germans got to Sollum we burnt both of them, and who cares? I've seen brass hats come here and look around and get raging mad, but in the end it just buries them—they can't do nothing. It's too big for them."

"I suppose it is."

"Now take VKO. I was there eighteen months and . . ."

While the man talked, Geoffrey watched his face—a long, narrow face, red, blue-eyed, long nose, long, heavy chin and folds from nostrils to chin enclosing a small, full mouth. He thought: "This man's pleased with himself. He's happy enough; he's alive and well. If a dog came up to him, he'd probably make a fuss of it just as if he were in England. He doesn't know. If I hadn't gone to Petra, I'd be as happy as he is. I would know nothing about it—instead, I think of nothing else."

The sergeant, to avoid Geoffrey's stare, was looking from the window as he talked. His cigarette was burning out behind his back but he did not attempt to smoke it. He broke off in the middle of a word to say: "What d'you think! We're going to have rain."

"Surely not." Geoffrey looked out at the unfamiliar darkness of the sky. A dusty wind was flipping up the leaves of the bougainvillæa on the house opposite. Detonated by something sinister in this gloom, the symptoms of terror, familiar yet always unfamiliar, began to grow in him. He said quickly: "You can go now, Henderson. See I'm not disturbed."

When he was alone, he hurried to the window. A laden camel with its driver was passing in a slow rattle of bells. The red and yellow of its trappings flashed in the strange light. The beast was straining from the lead, on the verge of hysteria, while its driver, almost as frightened, shouted wildly and tugged at it in the rage Arabs could display towards animals. The rain fell to earth and the camel, tearing away its lead, bolted with the driver after it.

A greenish darkness blotted out the room. Geoffrey went back to his desk and sat with his hands over his ears. He could scarcely breathe from the sense of swelling in his throat and could not swallow his own saliva. The rain, quivering past the window like a bead curtain, shut out sight and light. He could hear in his covered ears his heart thumping at an abnormal speed; a nausea and a stifling heat crept over him so that the sweat broke out on his brow . . . Now he knew, he knew it had come at last. He had told the sergeant to leave him because he wanted to be alone; he was possessed by an insane anxiety; his throat was swelling and at the sound of water a spasm would contort his body . . . He uncovered his ears and listened, but the roar of the rain was as continuous as silence. He got up and tip-toed out to the landing. The house seemed to be empty; it was dark and cold. A marble staircase, made squalid by army use, swept in a curve down to the front door. On the white walls were bands of grime, shoulder-high.

Geoffrey leant over the banister and saw Henderson standing in the porch talking to the sentry. There was no one else in the building. Doors lay open all down the corridors. Geoffrey tip-toed to a position from which he could see into the colonel's empty room. During the moments of his exploration, the symptoms of his neurosis were at a standstill. Now he knew he had the place to himself, he could safely release them. He stood and listened. The whole house seemed to be awash and dripping. From the front door came the rattle of rain breaking through leaves; from the gutters, a crystal trickle of the most fatal significance. He waited, his consciousness concentrated upon himself, his body trembling, each instant expecting worse, yet scarcely knowing if he were worse or not. Suddenly he remembered—it was curious how often he forgot—he had his sedatives in his pocket. He went to the bathroom and swallowed two with some water. He returned to his desk and waited for them to smooth his nerves back into place. His heart-beat began to slow; the nausea and fever receded gently until a normal calm overlay his immovable fear. In his relief, he felt affable and eager for companionship. Hearing Henderson come up the stairs he went to the door and looked out: "Never seen anything like it," he said.

"It's clearing a bit now, sir," said Henderson, "but outside's just like a lake. You'd need a boat to get about."

At six o'clock Viola rang him to ask if he were all right. She was, she said, at Shepheard's, trapped by the flood, but hoped to be back for supper. Detached, he noted in her voice an excited warmth and knew its cause exactly. He erred only in thinking her affair with Clark had started long before. Then he put down the receiver, he felt indifferent. Viola had become in his mind two distinct persons—one remained with him like a symbol of sweetness to which he no longer had right; the other was free to prefer Clark if she chose. He made no claim on her. He did not care. That evening when he returned to the flat, the streets were almost dry. Viola was home, crouched over the small cow-cake fire that filled the room with smoke. After three summers here, she felt the cold intensely, and began complaining about it as soon as he entered. He knew that her complaints and her nervous attention to the fire were meant to disguise any betraying vivacity in her manner. She broke off in what she was saying and pointed to a parcel on the mantelpiece:

"See what I've bought for you."

He unwrapped a large sketching book and a box of conté crayons.

"I couldn't get paints," she talked quickly with a slight,

unfamiliar blurr in her tone, "they've gone off the market. They had a few tubes of burnt sienna and Payne's grey but nothing worth buying, so I got the conté."

"What am I to do with these?" he asked.

"Start drawing again. Draw, or write. Get it out of your system somehow. If you won't talk about it to Kristel, then write about it. Write to me, if you like."

"Why to you?" he asked coldly.

"Well, there must be someone . . ."

"But why to you?" he repeated, looking at her with dislike, almost hatred.

She looked back at him, unnerved and bewildered by his manner: "If not me, who then?" she asked.

He had nothing to say. He was conscious, as of a gap before him, of the vacancy of his life. For a moment of insight, he thought that he was to blame; then his mind clouded over and he was lost in a muddle of recriminations. He saw himself as deserted, cuckolded, driven into madness—then this all dwindled to a life-size grievance that Viola, who could desert him now, was trying to fob him off with a sketch-book and crayons. He threw the parcel down angrily.

Viola sighed: "What are we going to do with you?"

He turned on her: "It's not your fault, is it? If you've failed me, it's not your fault."

"How have I failed you? I only asked you to start drawing again. I think the trouble is that you've given it up. Do try again. To please me . . ."

He broke in in a wild exasperation at her and accusation of himself: "I can't."

"Then write," she said, irritated because she was helpless and guilty, "write, write, write."

"I can't," he shouted, "it's like asking me to massage an open wound. I can't write about it. It frightens me too much."

"But you are always thinking about it. You think of nothing else."

He knew that last sentence, too casual as it was, was bait to bring to the surface any suspicion he might have of her. He answered her unspoken question: "Nothing else matters. I can't be afraid of anything else. Nothing else is important."

She seemed relieved and went back to her earlier point: "Well, if you'd only try and draw again, you'd probably find you could, and . . ."

"I can't. I can't give my mind to anything but being afraid. Besides, it isn't worth it."

"What do you mean—it isn't worth it?"

"I've lost the sense of the future. You can't do anything without that. You can't paint. You can't write."

"I don't really understand you, Geoffrey. I thought artists were so wrapped up in their work, they'd go on doing it if the heavens were falling."

"One needs peace and security. I've longed for peace and security. What I seem to have lost is the feeling of being protected. You know how you grow up thinking nothing really dreadful can happen to you. In spite of all the people who've died before you, you still think you'll never die. But if some disaster shakes that—then you lose the sense of being protected. Once you've lost that, you're done for. Anything can happen to you—the mischance in a million is waiting for you, the awful coincidence, the rare disease . . ."

"Really, Geoffrey, you know how unlikely . . ."

"Unlikely, but not impossible."

She picked up the sketching block and opened it: "Beautiful paper," she said.

"Yes. Whatman's."

"Well," she said lightly, bringing to a close an unsatisfactory interview, "promise me you'll try, just once."

"All right," he said.

A few afternoons later he took the block and crayons up to the roof of the house. He had never been there before. The roofs belonged to the servants and it was unusual for an English employer to intrude on them. His going there was in some way part of the effort to draw. He had to go up a winding iron staircase that led from the pantry. He was nervous of the servants' surprise that might even be resentment, but there was no one in the kitchen. He had heard and seen so much of Egyptian dirt, he had always supposed the kitchen better left unvisited. He found it very hot—in summer it would be intolerably so—but large, clean and surprisingly like an English kitchen. The luncheon dishes had been washed and were placed in order on the dresser. A fire burnt in the iron cooking-range. The tea things were placed ready on a tray and on the kitchen-table were spread vegetables for the evening meal. Geoffrey picked up a large aubergine and examined the way in which the top rosette of leaves joined the swelling, purple satin fruit. He was touched by the order behind his daily life. The muddled speech and actions of the servants in his presence had convinced him of chaos. Now he was touched that before they went to their afternoon sleep, the dishes were washed and put away, the tray was laid so that when he rang the bell tea might appear in a moment. The sink was clean, the table scrubbed, the floor swept. Though, no doubt, at night the place, like all kitchens in hot climates, would heave with the movements of cockroaches, black beetles and ants, at the moment there was order. The sense of this as a place where work was done, simple and essential, filled him with tranquillity. He looked out through the door to the roof that was brilliantly white beneath the winter sky. The servants were lying on their mats in a protected corner that held the warmth of the sun.

He went out quietly. He did not approach them but

looked at them as they lay, their dark feet bare and showing the pink, tender-looking soles. Mohammed and the boy had covered their faces with their arms, but the Soudanese cook, Osman, was on his back, snoring heavily, his turban fallen back and his whole round head, with its close-clipped curls, glistening in the sun; his open mouth exposed the inner lip and gums and tongue, pink like a part of the body too intimate for exposure.

Geoffrey thought: "Wonderful to paint, that skin! But difficult—the glow under the dark."

He leant for a long time in the sun against the kitchen lintel, absorbed by these men. His fear was not forgotten but it had stepped back a little, like something not needing immediate attention, and for the first time for weeks he felt an interest beyond it. He thought of the lives of these men in as far as he knew anything of them. They slept here at night in huts on the roof, taking the heat and cold of the seasons. A blanket was wealth—he knew, for he had once given one to Mohammed—and what else did they possess? Almost nothing. Before he awoke, they cleaned the sitting-rooms and made breakfast. Osman had his wrangling in the markets—the price he was willing to pay for meat or vegetables indicated to the outside world the status of his employers—he had the satisfaction of making a few millemes on every deal; he had, possibly, savings hidden somewhere and would one day make the journey to Mecca. He was a superior—but what had the others beyond their work and sleep and hope of paradise? In the evenings before dinner and after, they would gossip, vivaciously, with much laughter—but about what? What was the real content of their lives? He knew nothing. He could not imagine that any man was so simple that this daily life revealed him, and yet these men were as simple as that. He remembered how, when they first moved from a pension into the flat, Viola had given Mohammed twenty piastres and said: "Buy flowers for sitting-room." Mohammed made no protest but a little later the twenty piastres reappeared on Viola's dressing-table as an indication that the commission was beyond him. Another time, Geoffrey complained to Viola that whenever he rang the bell and got no answer, he would open the pantry-door to find Mohammed down on his face in prayer. He had believed the servants were fooling him; they were beyond him, a mystery—but now he felt close to them as though he were as simple as they. Thinking of the stories he had heard about their occasional outbreaks—the savagery of sex resulting from long frustration, their hashish-taking and the violent murders that could flash out from their laughter and good-nature—he knew that this moment of apparent contact was illusion. Their simplicity was beyond him; he was part of another world.

An uneasiness began to creep back on him. He looked at the block in his hand and remembered why he had come here. He went to the edge of the roof from which he could look over other roofs to the Mokattam Hills. He studied them unenthusiastically. Once they had edged an ancient sea that covered the whole Delta; now, burnt-looking and lifeless, they stood like cliffs against the creamy surf of Cairo. He stared around him, not knowing what to draw and feeling no reason for drawing anything. Everything was coloured by its patina of sand. Towards the hills the minarets of old Cairo rose with the rising land, one above the other until they reached the foot of the Citadel.

Geoffrey started sketching the Citadel mosque but felt only a distaste for what he drew. He had always disliked Oriental architecture and the design of the mosque with its flattened cupolas and its exaggerated minarets like sharpened pencils irritated him by its romanticism. In a few minutes the conté broke. He let it fall. His mind seemed empty and stale and would not stay on what he was doing.

He felt only boredom and discontent with what he was trying to do. He shut the book and went over to the other side of the roof where the trees and the houses hid the river. When he looked directly over the parapet he saw for the first time that there was a little garden behind the house—a triangle of dry grass at the apex of which was an old carob tree, the leaves washed glossy by yesterday's rain. He could look down on to the tree as on to a dark head and he remembered that Mohammed had told him carobs housed evil spirits. In the centre of the grass there was an ornamental pond. Surprised and interested, he supposed all this must have been arranged by Selim Bey, who lived with his large family in the lower flat.

When he thought he could go down into the garden, he was filled with a sense of purpose and adventure. He hurried from the roof and down the back stairs.

The garden, enclosed in high shrubs, was very warm. Selim Bey's kitchen door gave off a smell of stale grease but beyond the range of this there was only a faint, dry perfume from the tree. When he reached the pond, he saw a flicker of goldfish frightened by his shadow. He seated himself on the rim in the sun and waited for them to appear again. It was very quiet—the middle of the afternoon and of siesta time. He scarcely breathed until the three fish came out of the dark rocks, twitching a little like actors displaying indifference to an audience. He sat for a long time gazing down into the murky, ill-kept water with its few strands of weed, absorbed by the perfection of the movements of the fish, satisfied by their self-sufficiency, oddly drawn by them out of his own nightmare into reality. Like someone returning to life after a long illness, he saw every detail of the natural world with an abnormal clarity. When he looked at a spiny plant creeping flat and neat over the rim of the pond, he was hyperconscious of its red-tipped thorns and the glow of its berries, and felt as though he were part of it, the careful placing of its leaves so that each was in the sunlight. He felt, as though upon himself, the process of an insect down its brittle stem. He felt with the plant not in a world or a universe, but in space, and, for the first time in his life, he could comprehend limitless space without bewilderment or terror.

As though melted into the heat and silence of the garden, he lost awareness of his own outline; then a twitch in the grass touched his nerves. He looked down and saw a snake slide between the coarse, yellow grass roots towards his foot. It was a small snake, black, very poisonous, but he did not move. For an instant it was as though he were himself the snake sliding between monstrous grasses, feeling beneath his belly the Delta mud—then in a flash it had disappeared into a crack at the base of the pond, and he shuddered, jerked by loss of it into consciousness of himself.

He looked round the garden and, seeing it shrunken, parched and neglected, he knew he was irretrievably lost. He could not make an effort to move. As he sat on by the pond, feeling the concentrated heat, smelling the odour of kitchen grease that seemed now to be all around him, he was overpowered by a memory of the past as of a time of supernatural beauty and happiness.

He saw his doom with the poignancy of a drama upon the stage and could scarcely bear to contemplate it. He remembered Viola's love for him as though it were now beyond the grave and he was filled with tenderness for her. Looking back on the normal quietude of his past, he felt such desire for it, he said aloud: "If I could return to it, I should never be unhappy again."

He rose like a man weighted by hopelessness and, returning to the flat, he felt about him, as he might a touch of extreme softness, his vision of Viola. He thought he would be alone to concentrate it about him, but when he went into their bedroom he found the real Viola lying on her bed with a book in her hands. He frowned at her in disgust.

She said with too much interest: "What have you been drawing?"

He threw the block down beside her. She opened it and he, with distaste, watched her examine his paltry and meaningless scribble of the mosque.

"Well," she said, "a beginning! A beginning!"

He wondered why she had to be there. She was an intruder—she ought to be out with Clark, as she usually was. Keeping his back to her, he sat on the side of his bed and noticed the water-bottle on his bedside table. He began to tremble slightly; he could feel, like the remote intimations of a tidal wave, a bout of terror coming up upon him. He felt for his sedative tablets and swallowed two of them. As his nerves relaxed, he sank inwardly with the exhaustion of despair. He drew his feet up on to the bed, let his head drop to the pillow and was at once asleep.

Viola had lunched with Clark but he had had to spend the afternoon at G.H.Q. He had driven her back to Garden City and promised her that he would try and see Colonel Bagshot and advise him to order Geoffrey to take leave.

She held, as to a convention, to her concern for Geoffrey—but it was all meaningless. She talked about him, urged Clark to do something for him, and knew that between herself and Geoffrey there was now an empty space. She never really thought of him at all. She never thought of anyone but Nicholas Clark. At night she lay on her bed and stared at the ceiling, intensely awake, her nerves trembling with consciousness of him and desire. When he had first kissed her, her restraint had collapsed. Before, she had played with all sorts of moral considerations—her marriage, her loyalty to Geoffrey, the fact she had never been unfaithful to him and felt this no time to start. After, everything had dwindled before the onslaught of her physical passion for Clark.

When he left her that afternoon at the flat, she had no idea what to do with herself. She had been deprived of her occupation and nothing remained. When she came on a book she had left half unread weeks before, she took it to her room but did not read it. She lay on her bed, staring again at the ceiling, seeing nothing, obsessed by memory of Clark's physical strength, his virility, his confidence and his arrogance. Everything else was meaningless. No other consideration could distract her. Geoffrey meant nothing. If she were never to see him again, never to see any of her friends, it would not matter because to-morrow she would again see Clark. She saw before her very clearly the shape of his eyes and the expression in them . . . It seemed to her that for the first time in her life every instant had depth and meaning and she was alive with sensation. This, she knew, was the peak of her desire and she dreaded descent. Change must come, and she might lose him. No sensation could last for long, and he was too good-looking and women meant too much to him.

She sighed and buried her face in her hands and felt, in the midst of her own ecstasy, a diffused wretchedness because nothing could last. Then, for the first time since she became obsessed by Clark, she began to think of Geoffrey.

She thought of her marriage as of a relationship finished and done with; she went back in her mind over its early days and was able to rouse in herself resentment. Geoffrey had patronised her. Although she had been young when she married and had done nothing more adventurous than study in London, she had been an intelligent woman, an embryo personality that had had to struggle for development against, yes, against actual discouragement. If their coming to Egypt had destroyed Geoffrey, it had, at the same time, made her. For what, indeed, had she been in

Greece as Geoffrey's wife? Trailing round, bored, from island to island, meeting no one but Greek peasants and a few English eccentrics, with no occasion for dressing up, for being seen or admired. Geoffrey's art may have been everything to him, but it had not been everything to her. And he was not—here she smiled in to herself—a man of much physical vigour. She knew now he had never satisfied her.

By the time he returned to the flat and opened the bedroom door, she had built so strong a defence against him she looked at him with active dislike. She did not see his disgust of her. He seemed to look at her blankly from the great distance of his withdrawal out of normal life. She wondered if he even recognised her and it passed through her mind that he was insane. Seeing the sketchbook in his hand, she was able to speak of it. When she looked at the few lines he had drawn, she felt compassion for him. She kept her eyes down, showing nothing: "A beginning," she said brightly, feeling it an end.

When she noticed him again, he had fallen asleep on his bed. The telephone started ringing in the hall. She hurried out to it so that the noise would not disturb him. It was, as she expected, Clark ringing from somewhere in the perimeter. Her compassion for Geoffrey had taken her a step away from her lover and she heard with irritation his confident, possessive voice. His news surprised her. His appointment had been changed; he was not to go to the hospital outside Cairo but to one in Alexandria. She felt a chill of disappointment and was surprised that she felt nothing more. It was as though she were to be deprived of a diversion.

"When will you have to go?" she asked.

"Within a week. What I want to ask you is—are you coming, too?"

The question puzzled her before she realised he meant

was she going with him to Alexandria. Worried by the urgency of his tone, she answered: "But it's impossible. You know it's impossible. I couldn't leave Geoffrey as he is."

Clark said: "What good are you doing him? He'll have to give in sooner or later. He'll have to go somewhere to be treated."

She said, playing for time: "But are you sure he can be treated?"

"Yes, of course he can. They're treating cases like his every day. If he'd been reasonable he could have gone quietly to Kristel and no one would have known anything about it. As it is, he'll have to go into the machine like the rest of them."

"Hm!" Viola brooded on the telephone. She traced a letter on the dust of the telephone ledge and saw the letter was *G*. "I don't really like the idea," she said. "He's not an ordinary man."

Clark laughed grimly: "There are no ordinary men these days. If the psychiatrists had to give up months and years to analysing every neurotic in the British army, they'd be at it till Doomsday. We've had to use quicker methods in this war. Kill or cure methods."

"I see. So it might be kill."

"Don't be silly," Clark spoke with the first impatience he had shown towards her. "He'll be all right. Come out of it good as new. But this doesn't answer my question."

She watched a strip of orange sunlight that lay over the shabby woodwork at her feet: "There's my job," she said.

"That's no longer very important, and you're a civilian. You're free to leave if you like."

"And be evacuated next day as an unemployed army wife."

"Not much risk of that now. Anyway, there are plenty of useful jobs you could do in Alex."

She knew that was true. She was at a loss what to say next. There was a long silence through which he broke upon the tangle of her uncertainty to say: "Look! I don't expect you to decide at once. It was just to let you know I've got to go and I want . . ."

"Yes," she agreed quickly, "let me think about it. I'm very worried about Geoffrey."

"I'm going to see Bagshot now," said Clark—the voice of the man in control. "I'm meeting him at the Turf Club for a drink."

When she put down the receiver, she wandered out to the balcony with Clark's proposal like an irritant in her mind. She could not seriously consider the possibility of leaving Geoffrey. Parallel with Clark's physical attractiveness, she saw the qualities that would make him intolerable to her when the attraction failed. His self-confidence excited her yet at the same time piqued her. The impatience she had heard in his voice was the first hint of the irritation that could grow between them. She knew him to be humourless and she wondered if she respected him; she wondered whether she even liked him. She knew, as by a sort of clairvoyance that functioned through all the force of her emotions, that he would one day bore her.

The air was pink with sunset. She was late for the office but could not leave Geoffrey sleeping there to wake alone in the flat. She felt a complex of irritations with herself, with Clark and with Geoffrey. Acting out of them, she went into their bedroom and shook Geoffrey's shoulder. He moved on to his back and when she saw the thinness of his neck and jaw, her irritation failed. She touched his cheek. He lifted his hand and with great tenderness, covered hers; then he opened his eyes. There seemed to be a haze over their darkness. It passed. He withdrew his hand from hers and shifting away from her touch, sat up: "I thought you were my mother," he said.

"But your mother died while you were a small child."

"Yes," he pressed his wrists against his eyelids, "she escaped everything."

Viola tried to embrace him but he shook her off impatiently: "Must go to the office," he said. He jumped up and walked unsteadily to the dressing-table and started brushing his hair. The twilight was deepening rapidly and he could scarcely see in the mirror.

Viola said as though on an impulse: "Do you know that Nicholas Clark is in Cairo?"

"Yes. I've seen you with him."

"Have you? You didn't mention it."

"Neither did you. It doesn't matter."

"He's been posted to Alexandria. He asked me to go with him."

There was a long pause before Geoffrey asked in an expressionless voice: "Are you going?"

"Do you want me to go?"

He shrugged his shoulders. At that moment he believed he did want her to go. Her presence interfered with the necessary solitude of his suffering. There was nothing he wanted more than to feel himself freed by her desertion from his last tie to reality.

"It never entered my head to go," she crossed the room and switched on the light.

He picked up his cap and stood holding it by the peak. He seemed unable to speak and she felt there had come upon him one of his instantaneous changes from calm to panic.

She said: "I have no intention of going."

He still said nothing but he raised his head and she saw his face grown old with strain and fear, his eyes cowed under apprehension.

"Must go," he said and hurried away.

Outside there was still a glimmer in the air but by the

time he reached his office it was completely dark. All the windows were alight except his own. As soon as he entered his room, Henderson appeared to tell him: "C.O.'s been looking for you, sir. Rang through twice."

"Is he in his room now?"

"No. He rang from outside. Didn't say where."

"Then I can't do anything about it," Geoffrey spoke with an indifference that startled Henderson, who began: "Well, sir . . ." when the telephone rang again. Geoffrey lifted the receiver and heard Bagshot's tired, old voice: he noted in a remote way without applying it to himself, the almost cunning kindliness of the tone:

"Ah, Lynd, there you are! You haven't got much on hand at the moment, have you? Wondered if you'd come along to the club for a drink? Like to have a chat with you."

"Yes, sir. I'll come straight away."

"Like me to get you a taxi, sir?" Henderson asked eagerly and with curiosity.

Geoffrey himself, sunk into a desolation that was like tranquillity, did not consider the C.O.'s invitation as unusual. He did not consider it at all. He obeyed automatically. In the taxi, staring out blankly at the flashes of neon, the lighted windows of curio shops that stayed open half the night, the crowd on the pavements and the stream of expensive cars, he was scarcely aware of where he was going. He was absorbed by the thought that now he was utterly deserted. He had not listened to Viola's protestations that she did not intend to leave him; he had not wanted to hear them. He saw Clark now as monstrously powerful and working with monstrous power to destroy him. Viola might not intend to go with him, but go she must. Geoffrey did not question that but felt only the vacancy of her loss. He was grateful that when madness and death overtook him he would be alone. He had dreaded more than anything else the destruction of his control by pain and terror, and the unspeakable humility of losing control before his enemies. As for his enemies—now he saw enmity behind every face he met.

When the taxi drew up in the centre of the town, Geoffrey did not stir. The driver turned and bawled: "You want club; Officers' Club, yes?"

"All right," he was harassed by the need to move. He adjusted his sight with difficulty to the outside world.

The club, with its dim lighting, its shabby discoloured armchairs and bead curtains, was almost empty. It would not begin filling up until the offices closed at eight o'clock. Geoffrey wandered round in a dazed way, wondering if he had come to the right place. At last he brought himself to ask one of the safragis if Colonel Bagshot had been there. Yes, yes, Colonel Bagshot was there. The man hurried ahead to throw open a door and Geoffrey, on the threshold, saw Bagshot with Clark and the psychiatrist Kristel.

"Come in, Lynd; come in, come in," said the colonel as to a diffident child. "Shut the door. I thought it would be pleasanter in here. A small room to ourselves."

Geoffrey stood still looking at each of the three men in turn. He smiled in a deliberate way. Bagshot, of whom he had always been fond, was simple and well-meaning. It was the other two with whom he would have to deal.

The colonel patted the seat of the chair beside him: "Come in, Lynd. Come in and shut the door. Sit down."

Geoffrey obeyed these orders exactly. As he did so he kept his eyes on Clark. He felt like an actor on a stage, his every movement significant, and he was completely in control of himself. He had been forewarned about Clark—and about Kristel, too, because he was an ally of Clark—and he believed them to be at his mercy rather than he at theirs.

"I've ordered you a whisky," said Bagshot, "but if you'd rather have something else . . ."

"Thank you, sir. Whisky for me," Geoffrey still stared at Clark.

Clark said: "You aren't surprised to see me?"

"No, I've seen you a number of times. You've been in Cairo about a month."

Clark grunted and made no comment.

Geoffrey was satisfied by his own self-control but he was careful to do nothing on his own initiative. He had made a point against Clark, but he did not try to follow it up. He waited for the attack.

Kristel was polishing his spectacles. His naked eyes looked weak and shrunken, so that his personality lost half its force. He seemed to be making a great business of going round each lens carefully with his tussore handkerchief. Clark, who sat directly under the standard lamp, was looking into his glass. His wide, thin mouth was caught up in an uncomfortable smile.

Geoffrey began to think in a dispassionate way of Clark making love to Viola. He could not imagine it. Clark had become a monster for him and this extraordinary attraction for women made him seem less rather than more human. Then Clark stretched out his arm and put down his glass—a muscle turned against his sleeve and in that movement Geoffrey saw like a vision the lovers in an embrace. His sudden jealousy was agony, yet he scarcely knew if he were jealous of Viola's passion for Clark, or Clark's for Viola. He did not want to look at Clark again.

Clark murmured something to Kristel. Kristel coughed slightly but did not speak. Now they had got Geoffrey there they did not know what to do with him. Geoffrey sat quietly sipping his whisky. He knew they had expected him to betray himself at once and he was not going to betray himself. Bagshot, who had been awaiting a lead from the others and did not get it, leant forward and cleared his throat: "Well," he said, "er . . . er . . ."

Geoffrey looked up politely at the weathered, wrinkled face behind its grey moustache. Bagshot was preparing to skim happily over this situation as over a thousand others: "Major Clark here seems to think you should take a little holiday!"

The corners of Clark's mouth turned down; his straight brows met over his long, straight nose.

"What makes him think that?" asked Geoffrey.

Clark shuffled in his seat; he gave the old man an exasperated look but Bagshot, not seeing it, smiled charmingly: "Well, he . . ."

Clark interrupted: "Before Major Lynd left Palestine he was far from well."

"That was over two months ago," said Geoffrey.

Clark looked at Kristel. Kristel put on his glasses and wiped his lips and fingers before putting his handkerchief away. He cleared his throat and said: "You came to see me less than three weeks ago."

"Yes."

"You did not come back. I rang up your wife and she said you weren't better, you were worse."

Geoffrey said nothing. Clark emptied his glass, then said with decision: "Dr. Kristel is the only English-speaking civilian psychiatrist in the Middle East. If you refuse to let him treat you, then you'll have to take what the army has to offer. You know we've no time for anything very elaborate."

"I'm against short-cut treatments," said Kristel, "especially for a neurosis."

"They work," said Clark. "I've had a talk with the medical specialist here and he says results are satisfactory."

"Even so," Kristel persisted, but nervously, "a neurosis! And when dealing with an artist . . ."

Clark interrupted, raising his voice: "My dear fellow, do remember there's a war on."

Geoffrey smiled into himself at the change in Kristel. Clark dominated Kristel, he dominated Bagshot, but he did not dominate Geoffrey.

Kristel was silenced; he took off his glasses and started polishing them again. There was a difficult pause, then the door opened and a safragi brought in another round of drinks. The colonel paid. Geoffrey, sitting with downcast eyes, heard Clark fill a glass from a soda siphon and he looked up sharply. His muscles tautened and, feeling the first intimation of terror, he put his hand in his pocket for his sedatives. He had left them on his bed-side table.

"I must go," he said.

"No," Bagshot caught his arm and said with the authority of rank. "No, Lynd. I want you to stay. Sit down."

Geoffrey fell back in his chair. He knew he was lost.

Clark and Kristel exchanged significant glances.

Bagshot said kindly: "All right now. Take it easy Only want to have a little chat. Your friend here, Major Clark, tells me he felt uneasy about you when you left Palestine; and Doctor Kristel—I believe he's what the lads call a 'trick-cyclist', isn't that it?—well, Doctor Kristel says you consulted him after you got back. They're both of the opinion you need a rest. You probably think they've no right to interfere but they were given authority by your wife, and I must say I'm grateful for their advice. You musn't forget I've got an important office to run and I want my men up to the mark."

"Has there been anything wrong with my work, sir?" In Geoffrey's voice the effort of control was too obvious to make it effective.

"Well, no. I can't say I've noticed anything wrong, but I'm a busy man, Lynd, y'know! I can't keep a special eye on everyone. I did think you weren't looking yourself lately."

Bagshot glanced at Clark and Clark said casually, not moving: "Perhaps you'd like us to go?"

"No, no," Bagshot sounded alarmed, "I'd much rather you stayed. I don't know much about these things. I've heard of fellows being broken up in this way, of course—we even had some funny cases in the first war—but it's not my line at all."

Kristel pulled himself together and spoke with all the weight of his professional manner: "We understand what's the matter. When a situation becomes intolerable, the mind has to find an escape . . ."

"Intolerable," interrupted Bagshot. "But Lynd is doing a safe job. I doubt if he's even heard a gun go off."

"Well," said Kristel, "you have to consider the man with whom you are dealing—in this case, a man who in private life is a painter."

"A painter! Is Lynd a painter? You mean a chap who paints pictures, of course?"

"Yes. Now, I always say . . ."

Geoffrey, slumped back in his chair, ceased to listen. He had put his glass on the table and was rubbing the spot on his palm with concentrated attention. He was, as they felt him to be, outside the circle. In the midst of Kristel's exposition on what he called the 'mystery of the mind', Geoffrey suddenly sat upright, face flushed, eyes moving in terror, and cried: "But I must go. I must get into the air."

Clark whispered to Bagshot: "He is safer here."

Bagshot held to Geoffrey, saying: "My dear fellow, don't get upset. Stay here with us. We'll see you're all right. I'm only trying to find out what would be best for you."

Geoffrey took no notice of Bagshot but stared again across at Clark. Clark's face had a look of professional concern. Geoffrey knew that that look put them on different levels. Clark could afford to drop his ironical guard now for Geoffrey was no longer a rival, no longer even an acquaintance; he had descended to the level of a patient.

Bagshot stubbed out his cigarette and, giving a chuckle, said: "You know, I was bitten by a mad dog once."

Kristel said: "I wouldn't . . ."

Bagshot blundered on: "It was while I was at Ismailia—a little black bitch came into the mess. I thought she looked a bit odd: 'Here,' I said, 'what's the matter with you?' and I bent to pat her and she just sprung at me and got me here," he tapped his forearm. "The M.O. shoved the dog into a sack and put her in a pen for a couple of days—she'd got rabies, all right. I had to come into Cairo and get injections at the Pasteur Institute. Did me no harm at all."

Geoffrey, who had been watching Bagshot intently, asked: "How long ago was that?"

"Three years. I remember I got talking to the chap at the Institute—wog, of course—and what do you think? He said they had a film showing a case of hydrophobia—that's what it's called when human beings get it, of course, hydrophobia; apparently they're scared of water. He offered to run it through for me. 'No thank you,' I said, 'I'm not nervous but I don't believe in being morbid.'" Bagshot chuckled quietly to himself as he lit another cigarette.

"I'd like to see that film," said Clark.

Geoffrey, white-faced, said incredulously: "You mean they let someone suffer that disease through to the end so that they could make a film?"

"Why!" Bagshot became disconcerted. "Only some poor wog, y'know—one of these fellahin."

Geoffrey could not believe it and yet he knew it was true.

A film unwound itself in his brain—old fashioned, grey and jerky; a bare hospital ward; nurses in old-fashioned clothes; the patient, a young peasant, in striped hospital night-shirt, flinging himself, mad with fear, from the bed; foam at his lips, his body contorting wildly . . .

Geoffrey said: "You must be crazy to tell me that."

"My dear fellow, I didn't mean to upset you. Clark mentioned, before you came—just casually, of course—that you were a bit nervous about . . . and I . . ."

"They let him suffer to make a film. They would let anyone suffer. I hate doctors. I hate every sort of accursed . . ."

"My dear fellow," broke in Bagshot. "My dear fellow! *Please!*"

Kristel became animated: "I remember asking you . . ."

Geoffrey broke in wildly: "Cruelty and wars. Here we are, caught in this dreary interminable war—a war for the second-rate who seize authority. It imprisons people like me, makes life shabby, so that I'd be glad to die."

Bagshot leant towards Geoffrey and Geoffrey flung himself away, sobbing. Bagshot clicked his tongue: "Poor fellow," he said, "poor fellow."

"It's a classical case," said Kristel with satisfaction.

"Y'know," Bagshot lowered his voice, "it's a good thing he didn't break down like this in the office. Been a bad show—very bad show."

Geoffrey shouted: "Why should my life be destroyed in this way?" His voice trembled and as he broke off to control himself, Clark said quietly:

"Before the war I had a good practice in Leeds. I had a wife. She went off with a Polish officer. No one's enjoying this war—but we've got to give up our private happiness for something more important."

"But it's not important," Geoffrey spoke wildly, almost in tears: "To me it's not important. This is only another trade war, the second trade war, a patch of blight on life . . ."

"Really!" Bagshot was becoming flustered. "I didn't realise he was so bad. I always thought him a queer chap but not . . . not a *complete outsider*."

"He isn't normally like this," Clark said impatiently. "The balance of his brain is disturbed. He doesn't know what he's saying."

"I do. I'm not mad. I know what I'm saying. If you prevent me from being a painter, then I'm less than a man. I've become mean, possessive, grudging, resentful; I hate your war. I only want peace. I only want to do my own work. Because I can't do it, I'd be glad to die."

"You won't die," said Bagshot reassuringly.

"I will," Geoffrey insisted, "I must. I'm doomed."

Bagshot 'tut-tutted' at Kristel, who said: "If he'd only returned to me, he need never have reached this stage."

Clark broke in, impatient and businesslike: "Too late to discuss that now. He'll have go into the machine. I'd better telephone his wife."

Geoffrey twisted furiously in his chair and spat out at Clark: "Tell her you've destroyed me. That's what you meant to do. You made me read that medical book. The page infected me." For emphasis, he was trying to use the most melodramatic phraseology he knew. He wanted to talk like someone on the cinema screen.

"Now, now! No one wants to harm you." Bagshot pressed Geoffrey's arm, but Geoffrey, with insane force, threw off his hand and screamed:

"He wants my wife. I tell you he was determined to destroy me."

"What nonsense!" Clark was breathless with indignation.

"It's true. You go and telephone her. Tell her she's free. She's free to go to Alexandria with you."

"I suppose she always was free," said Clark coldly.

"She didn't think she was. She thought she ought to stay with me—but now you're getting rid of me and she can do what she likes."

There was a knock on the door. Bagshot bustled forward, opened it a little and spoke importantly to someone outside, then shut the door sharply: "Must get him out of here," he said. "Chaps are wondering what the row's about."

"I won't go," Geoffrey screamed.

Clark picked up a leather case from under the table: "I'll give him an injection. Better get him quiet before taking him through that room. I suggest, sir, you ring the Scottish General. They're expecting a call."

"Yes, yes," breathed Bagshot looking round him with shaking head, "I'll ring at once." He stood for some moments as though the telephone might appear in the room, then went to look for it.

Geoffrey had collapsed into his chair and grown suddenly calm. At last responsibility was being taken from him. No more effort was required of him. He had become an invalid. He made no move or protest as Clark prepared the injection and drove the needle into his arm.

"There!" Clark wiped over the place and said cheerfully: "All right in a minute."

Bagshot returned from the telephone: "Everything's arranged," he said, as cheerful as Clark. "Ambulance coming directly."

Geoffrey felt oblivion cloud over him.

After Geoffrey was moved from the Scottish General to a hospital on the Syrian coast, Viola saw nothing of him for nearly three months. During that time she remained in her job in Cairo but, whenever it amused her to do so, she visited Clark at Alexandria.

The war had moved to Europe and things had become

so slack at G.H.Q. that Viola could occasionally catch an early train on Saturday morning.

She was content with her life at this period. She liked living alone in her flat in Cairo and being free to go to Clark, or not go, as she wished. Her first obsession with him had stabilised now to a manageable affection. Actually she had stabilised it by an effort of will. Her instinct had been against him from the first—or so she believed. She had questioned him until he admitted he had not been faithful to his wife, then she decided he could not be faithful to anyone. She felt safer in the situation now she was in control.

Travelling up one morning through the Delta in the tranquil morning light, she looked at her face in her pocket mirror and thought: " A placid woman, a pleasant woman! " Emotion was too exhausting. She could not be bothered with it.

She reflected that as a young girl she had been impressed by violence of feeling and temper in others. She had been attracted by Geoffrey by a sense of depths in him not in herself, but now she was an individual in her own right and she chose tranquillity as she would, if choice were offered, choose this flat and tranquil delta country.

She began to wonder why Geoffrey could not paint it. She thought of him, not as he was in the Middle East—wretched, ill-at-ease in uniform, wearing a revolver he couldn't fire, becoming a nonentity—but as he had been in Greece, simple, self-possessed and natural, a man justified by his art.

She was convinced he had stopped painting from some suicidal obstinacy, like those negroes who make up their minds to die, and die. She saw no reason why he could not catch the quality of these fields detailed over, as they were now, in the crystalline morning air. They were divided into squares by water channels and chequered in the various greens of vegetables, maize or cotton. Over the whole vast chequer-board were the pieces—a white mosque, a palace painted pink, a village sliced neatly from mud as from milk chocolate, water-buffaloes treading water wheels, wells with their long, balanced poles, women upright under water-pots or the innumerable little figures that moved between the vegetable rows. Had she been a painter she would have chosen to paint this scene a dozen times—in the sharp-edged morning, or the heat-greyed noon-day, or mist-green in the evening mist. Why had Geoffrey, after a first interest, refused to look at it?

When they left the dockside at Alexandria on their arrival from Greece, he had watched excitedly from the window of the Cairo train and pointed things out to her: Look! A buffalo, a camel, a cemetery, a well! At Tanta they had bought bananas—a fruit unobtainable in Greece—and as they ate, he had scribbled a note on a newspaper: "Small, green-skinned, pink-fleshed, tasting of flowers!" They had never tasted of flowers a second time. She had found another note somewhere: "The south side of the Mediterranean—camels, bananas, tawdry cardboard towns, pyramids, bones and mummy-cloth buried in the sand; a new place, a new light," and yet he had done nothing. At first there had been no time and then, when there were occasional free days, he seemed to have lost the habit of painting. This had surprised and troubled her. She had been told that the force that made an artist must break through every obstacle like those sprouting seeds that split rocks. Because his art had been so easily discouraged, she began to think the less of him. In that she knew she was right, for he became a nonentity, and an unreasonable nonentity at that.

Now, reaching Alexandria, she rose out of memories as out of a long gentle dream, and looked from the window, already smiling, to see if Clark had been able to meet her.

Finding he was not there, she was not disconcerted, but went, as she often did, to the flat he had taken in Cherif Pasha and bathed and changed her dress. By the time she was ready, he had arrived to take her to luncheon at Pastroudi's. This was her favourite Alexandria restaurant; it reminded her of the Soho restaurants to which she had been taken during her life in London. The whole situation had for her the charm of the freedom she had known for the first time in her student days.

Clark made his formal enquiry: "How is Geoffrey?"

"Improving. But, apparently, he still has some bad moods."

"That's usual. He'll get over them."

"But when he's cured, will he be permanently cured?"

"Why not? He's got no mental disease."

"Some people seem to think this treatment isn't permanent."

"Well, he may have a relapse. Just have to take that risk. When you're analysed everything's brought to the surface. You're forced to remember; but that's not the end of it. Then you've got to readjust yourself to life. That's where analysis breaks down in times like these. Geoffrey, for instance, collapsed because he can't face the life we have to lead. Most of these fancies are just funk holes. Chaps like Geoffrey bolt down them. Thinking he's going to get hyrophobia with not even a scratch—just a funk hole. Now what happens if you spend months digging him out of it? He takes a look round, doesn't like life any better (why should he?), and bolts down another funk hole. See what I mean? Well, this other treatment is a reverse process—makes you forget."

"Like driving a boil back into the system?"

"If you like; but it works. Quick and effective and the chap is made usable again. Don't mean he's one hundred per cent efficient—far from it. More like a re-tread tyre. All part of the war effort."

"And after the war?"

"I don't know. I expect he'll be all right."

"And when they let him out what will he be like?"

"Quite normal. Probably vague and forgetful at first, and a bit depressed. It's a lowering treatment—but all that wears off."

Clark always talked of Geoffrey with a show of great patience and changed the subject as soon as possible: "What shall we do to-night?"

"What do you suggest?" Viola seemed more interested in the young officers who always filled Pastroudi's at meal times, lolling on red plush seats, giving occasional glances at their own faces in the mirrors, their buttons glinting in the light from the chandeliers that blazed day and night. When she exchanged a look with one of them there was always a half-smile in her eyes.

"Would it be fun," asked Clark, not for the first time, "to eat at the flat and stay in this evening, and be alone?"

"I don't think so," she stretched herself a little, not ceasing to smile.

"Perfectly charming," commented Clark, "and quite inflexible! You don't even pretend you come up here for my sake."

"Then why do I come?"

"Because it amuses you. It's a sort of game."

His insight surprised her because she had scarcely yet realised herself that this affair was a sort of game.

She laughed: "Well, you're a necessary partner."

"But not the only possible one."

"Perhaps not. Let's go for our walk."

They walked, as usual, along the Corniche with the grey blocks of flats on one side and the deserted winter beach on the other. Twilight fell as they returned. The

Mediterranean, dark and chilly, lapped in on the pale, crumbling rock, and the palms shook in the evening wind. When they reached the centre of the town they went to one of the Greek tea-shops.

"I suppose," said Clark, "you think you could replace me easily? But I'm not sure there are many chaps would tolerate this state of affairs."

"Nonsense. This is just the state of affairs most men prefer. You are the one who would have some difficulty in finding someone like me who makes no demands, asks no questions and tells no lies."

"I'm not sure. Alex is full of Waafs and Wrens eager to oblige."

Viola looked over her shoulder at a group of buxom, creamy-skinned Wrens and met the curious glance of one of them. She wondered.

"I hope you find them obliging," she said.

"That's rather indecent."

Viola laughed: "You've had quite a few affairs, haven't you?"

"Perhaps a few."

"And is this the first time you have not had the upper hand?"

When he grasped what she meant, a hurt expression came into his eyes and she saw him as vulnerable. For all his confidence, and perhaps because of it, he had been the loser before. She said, not relaxing: "Do you know the blonde girl behind me—one of those Wren officers?"

"Yes. She goes to the Union."

"She seems interested in you."

"Does she?"

"Is that why you are not interested in her?"

"Possibly."

"I wonder why you and Geoffrey did not like one another?"

After a pause Clark said: "I can't bear that sort of weakness."

"But Geoffrey wasn't weak."

"He expected to be privileged because he was a painter. I've no use for that. A man's got to take what comes to him."

After a day or two of Alexandria and of Clark's company, she felt a gloom come down over the wealthy streets. The showers depressed her—so unused had she become to rain—and the wet skies gave her claustrophobia. All this, she knew, symbolised her boredom with Clark, and he, knowing their relationship merely superficial, would question her:

"When will you be back?"

"I don't know for sure. I shall have to work next Sunday."

"That's ridiculous. Surely they don't still expect you to work on Sundays?"

"They do. But I'll let you know. I'll send a wire," and so at last she would get away.

In February, she heard that Geoffrey had been moved to a rest camp on the coast a few miles west of Alexandria. She applied for permission to visit him and received it for a week-end she had promised to Clark. When she telephoned him with the news, she was amused by his disgust.

"After all," she said, "he is my husband."

"Well, exactly what do you intend to do when he comes back?"

That was the first time he had asked this question and she, smiling into the telephone receiver, said: "How can I tell until he does come back?"

"I see. You'll look him over, then choose between us."

"Exactly. Anyway, I've got to go and see him. Will you let me have the car?"

"Yes. I'll come with you."

"No. No, I don't think that would be a good idea, but I promise you I'll be back by dinner-time."

She caught an early train to Alexandria and found Clark's car waiting for her at the station. As she drove out through the Egyptian quarter of the town towards the desert coast, the light had still its morning delicacy. It was a grey day in which colours burnt richly. The Arab quarter through which she passed had been bombed. The roll-down doors of the little shops were buckled by blast, the cement walls pitted with shrapnel and the people in the streets looked blackly at the army car.

"Don't half make a fuss here when a bit of sh—— stuff, I mean, comes down," said the driver. "Talk about a panic," he drew in his breath so that it whistled. "They'd scare you more than the bombs."

At the end of the road the sea became visible in its jewel-dark layers of blue and green. A frill of foam moved at the edge. A few yards out were the masts and funnels of two sunken ships: "Copped it a year ago," said the driver.

All along the coast road were the cement-covered summer houses, some painted in the Greek manner with washes of pink or yellow, and all standing in tangled gardens. Here, where the Delta soil was washing out thinner and thinner into the desert, and the desert sand was blown into the Delta, the fields were sparse and grey. Soon they petered out altogether and the road cut into the limestone desert of the ancient anchorites where the oddly shaped rocks glimmered like salt. Here were the mineral lakes, jade green, raspberry pink, curded over with a scum like cream and distorting into monstrosity the reflection of rocks and birds.

When the car got out into the sandy desert, the mists dissolved and the sky grew bright. A few miles along the coast was the oasis and village; outside it, standing among jacquaranda trees, was a palace in the Turkish style, its stone indented by cannon-balls. This had been a dressing-station during the El Alamein battle and was now a rest camp.

When Viola arrived, Geoffrey was in his room. It was a square stone room designed to catch every draught and keep out the summer heat. It was furnished with a hospital bed, two chairs, and a striped Arab rug that matched the narrow curtains. An oil-stove gave off a comfortable smell but the air was cold. Two tall, arched windows, built side by side to overlook the sea, formed recesses in walls a yard thick. Geoffrey sat in one recess making, in the sketch-book which Viola had sent him, small drawings of the jacquaranda blossoms spread beneath him. When the car stopped in the drive below, he looked down, saw Viola alight, and went on working as though she had nothing to do with him.

When he first arrived the trees had seemed to be dead. He supposed they had been blasted during the raids. One morning he awoke to find them covered with a violet vapour. When he went to the window he found the vapour was flowers. He stood for so long in his pyjamas gazing at the trees, that his orderly found him shivering with cold.

He felt now, as he did then, startled and unwilling to return to conscious life. When Viola entered the room, he sat still, looking at her. She crossed to him. He knew who she was but he found it difficult to relate her to himself.

"But, Geoffrey," she said, "surely you know me?"

"Yes, you're Viola," he got up slowly and held out his hand. "How are you?"

She took his hand and raised her face to him, but she had to reach up and kiss his lips herself. He looked embarrassed, as though a stranger had behaved impertinently.

"Shall I get you a chair?" he asked. He brought one over to the window and sat himself on the sill again.

"You're working?"

"Yes," he said politely. "I'll show you what I've been doing. Now I'm making some sketches of the jacquaranda trees. Do you know what the Egyptians call them? Examination trees. That sums up effendi life, doesn't it?"

He laughed but she barely smiled. She and Geoffrey had called the jacquarandas by their nick-name ever since first hearing it.

"Have you done any painting?" she asked.

"Some. I haven't got an easel so it's difficult to keep a canvas propped up." He went over to the alcove where his clothes hung and brought out a small board. It was a sketch of flat, pebbled sand over which loomed a vast structure of clouds, blue-black, grey and brilliant pearl white.

"Winter day in the desert," he said. "What do you think of it?"

She answered truthfully: "You can still paint. Nothing to worry about."

He seemed pleased: "I thought it was all right," he said. He showed her a pencil drawing of the jacquaranda flowers. He had made them look transparent at the edges where air and flowers met.

"I like that," she said.

He smiled for the first time since she entered. He was about to speak but a bell sounded below for luncheon and he took her down with the courtesy of a new acquaintance. She was relieved to get into the dining-room where thirty or so young officers, mostly fighting men, were taking their seats at tables. Everyone appeared normal. Geoffrey introduced her to the three with whom he shared a table, then, forgetting her, joined eagerly in a conversation that was exclusively about food.

"For crying out loud, lamb again!" said the man on Viola's left and that started a survey of everything they had eaten during the week.

Viola noticed that Geoffrey spoke exactly as the others did—intonations, slang and complaints were the same. He was enjoying himself. He was at home. Bored by the food topic, she gazed out over the room at the sunburnt young men, all talking, some laughing, all seeming as sane as herself until one, about to put a fork-full of food to his mouth, suddenly let the fork fall and burst into tears. A male nurse who had been standing by the wall, went to him at once and led him from the room. The others noticed nothing. Viola, sobered, turned her attention to her own circle and listened to the conversation. No one asked her a question about the outside world from which she had come. No one, indeed, addressed any remark to her. When the meal was over she followed Geoffrey out to the hall and it was only there that he seemed to remember she was with him: "Would you like to go down to the shore?" he asked.

"Yes," she moved out of the house at once, as glad to get away from these men who ignored her as she had been to see them at first.

They walked down over the rough, sandy earth to the break in the cactus hedge that led to the shore. It was a still, deserted noon-day full of passive sweetness that was like a narcotic.

Geoffrey walked to the water's edge and stood watching the waved undersea sand that was visible for a hundred yards out. The horizon was hidden in mist. The sea, broken here and there by dark, spiny rocks, was flat as stretched silk. Three men came down from the rest home and pushed out a boat. Their voices seemed muted by the air and as they rowed, their boat moved with scarcely a ripple, as silently as a sailing-boat.

"Geoffrey," Viola touched his arm. He turned, startled, and after a second, his eyes showed awareness of her.

"Shall we walk to the point?" he said.

They went along the firm sand of the shore that was decorated with nothing but a fluted tide line of pink and cream shells. It was as untrodden as the shore of a deserted island. Half a mile beyond the palace, there was an outcurve of rock, yellowish and full of holes like cheese. When they reached the farthest point Geoffrey made to sit down.

"For goodness sake!" Viola caught his arm. "There'll be scorpions there, and those horrible white spiders."

Geoffrey gave the rock a dazed look: "But I often sit there," he said.

"Then don't do it again," she scolded him, glad of an excuse to do any natural thing, and led him to the sand below the tide line. Geoffrey laughed, but as he sat, chin on knees, and looked towards the village, he became lost in silence. The sand, a white dazzle in the afternoon sun, rose like a collar round the little oasis with its greenery and white houses beside the scintillating sea.

Viola said: "Geoffrey," and when he did not turn, more loudly: "Geoffrey, are you better?"

"Better?" he considered the question for a long time: "Do you mean, am I frightened any more? Not as I used to be—but I haven't forgotten what I was afraid of. It's never out of sight."

"Oh!" she had picked up a handful of shells and now shook them about nervously, "but you'll get over that."

"I don't know. At the moment it seems to me, I can't get over it. I've overcome everything else—rationalised everything; pulled my imagination off things I feared the way you pull a dog off a dead rat—but I can't get it off that. It's not a thing one can rationalise out of existence. It exists—and it blots out the possibility of God."

She said helplessly: "I wonder what it symbolises for you?"

"I don't know. And I'd be too frightened to find out. I don't want to find out. Perhaps it symbolises everything I've turned my back on."

"But what sort of things?"

"Things I hate. I don't know. They've risen against me in this form. I've managed somehow to hit on the worst thing in the world. I know too much about it. It stands between me and the sun."

"Yet you're quite calm now," she said hopefully.

"Yes, I am quite calm. But there's a darkness over the light."

"A *physical* darkness?"

"Yes, it seems to me I can see it; and it hangs over me."

"Yet you paint."

"Yes. That's quite separate."

"Well, that's something."

There was a long silence before he said: "I can paint because nothing stands in my way any more. You don't stand in my way."

She stared in a shocked way: "What on earth do you mean?"

"Only that now I'm alone. I was never so completely alone."

"I thought you were getting on so well with the other men."

He did not answer that but said: "I'm so alone, I'm nothing—so I can become anything: a fish or a snake or a leaf on a tree, and when I become them, I paint them."

"And hydrophobia?"

"That's the outside world."

While he spoke, she watched him, but he did not look

at her. She thought he was looking unusually well. He was sunburnt and his hair, that had not been cut for several weeks, was curling as she liked it best. She reached over and touched it as she used to do; he smiled politely but without any response. His eyes, wherever they turned, seemed to her to be looking in rather than out, yet he had regained some of his old force. Where, before, she had seen this force as part of herself, now she knew it to be separate. He was not hers for the taking. She feared he was not hers at all.

She said: "Why do you say I don't stand in your way? Did I ever stand in your way?"

"If it hadn't been for you, I would never have left Greece, or joined the army, or stopped painting."

"This is absurd! If you'd stayed in Greece, what do you think would have happened to you?"

"I don't know and I don't care. I only wanted to paint."

"You'd have pretended to be a Greek, I suppose, and lived under the Nazis? How could you think of such a thing?"

"I didn't even want to know the Nazis existed."

"But they do exist—that's the point. They exist just as hydrophobia exists," she caught her breath. She'd mentioned it again!

A flicker of awareness came into his eyes and she urged her point quickly: "You can't turn your back on realities like that."

"I must, if I'm to survive."

"Then I don't see why you should . . . I mean, how can you survive?"

He said without interest: "I know you don't."

"But, really," she protested, "there must be some better solution of your problem."

"Can you think of one?"

"Not at the moment, but . . . This attitude is ridiculous.

It's scarcely sane. Is there nothing I can do for you?"

"It seems to me that the world is scarcely sane. Bring it back to its senses and you won't think me mad. But why should you worry! You're justified, whatever I may be. You are superficial, not very clever and you're rather insensitive—and yet you're more use in the world to-day than I am. You are what is wanted."

"Geoffrey, this is pure spite. And your ideas seem to me not only unreasonable, but vicious. You are saying that intelligence and sensitivity are useless."

"I'm saying they can't survive."

She felt indignant and at the same time vulnerable and deserted: "But what are you going to do?" she insisted against her own judgment. "Don't you want to live with me again?"

"I don't know. I've no sense of the future at all."

"Well!" she stood up and brushed the sand off her skirt. "You'd better think about it. If you want to leave me . . . I won't try and stop you."

She hoped he would protest, but he said nothing. She felt that by his very silence he was being—as he always had been in his way—kind to her. He could not answer. He did not know.

"This is so unfair to me," she was conscious of her own pettishness yet had to speak.

"I'm sorry. If I said definitely that I was not coming back—would that make it easier?"

"No. No, don't say that. I'm sure you don't mean it. I must start if I'm to get to Alex before dark."

"I'll write to you," Geoffrey got to his feet. They walked back to the car and he went to find the driver.

Geoffrey kissed Viola lightly before she got into the car and then he watched her departure with expressionless eyes.

"Don't forget to write to me," she called to him. He nodded but she knew he had no sense of obligation towards her. When she glanced back, she saw he was already walking away in the other direction.

Out in the desert, a hamseen was blowing up. She watched the wind running under the surface of the sand as under a carpet, then the first sand curling up into the air. The air turned red as the sunset was blotted out and there was nothing to see. Shut into the confines of the car, she thought of everything Geoffrey had said. It seemed to her he was completely and hopelessly mad and yet, in spite of that, she wanted him to want to return to her. In fact, she wanted him to return. For Clark she was beginning to feel something like contempt.

Viola heard nothing of Geoffrey for several weeks. She asked Clark to write to the neurologist at the home and the reply came that Geoffrey had had a relapse. He had been permitted to go into Alexandria and when he returned, he broke down completely. Geoffrey, apparently, had supposed himself cured but the neurologist had known from the first that his condition had not been normal. Contact with the outside world had proved too much for him.

"Owing to the fact that we have so many men suffering in this way," wrote the neurologist, "cases tend to be discharged prematurely. Lynd's relapse is probably the best thing for himself. We can now continue treatment and this time there will be every hope of a complete recovery."

When Geoffrey returned to Cairo the summer was advanced. In the suburbs the flamboyants, their toothed greenery heavy with dust, held out plates of blossom like tomato soup. It seemed to Geoffrey that their irritating colour hung over him for hours as they drove along the glittering, sandy roads. His memory was not very good and time could be for him oddly elongated or telescoped. He had in his mind a picture of the house in which he lived, but he was uncertain how to get there. Fortunately the driver knew the way.

The river, colourless and brilliant in the hot light, was crowded with the white sails of feluccas. When the car crossed the bridge, Geoffrey's sense of the geography of the place clarified. He said to the driver: "Nearly there." The man smiled reassuringly. When they reached the house, Geoffrey saw it was not as he remembered it; but he supposed that this, not his memory, must be the real house.

"Here we are, sir," said the driver. "You'll be all right now."

"Yes, thank you; I'm all right." Geoffrey had his key and let himself in. He had only a small bag with shirts and some underwear Viola had sent him; he had left his paintings and painting materials at the rest home. He went through the empty, echoing flat like someone feeling out a way through mist. As he stood in the sitting-room, not knowing what to do next, Mohammed came out from the pantry and greeted him delightedly. Geoffrey asked where was Viola and Mohammed ran to a side-table and picked up a note.

"For you," he said modestly and happily like someone presenting a gift.

The note said merely: "Not sure when you're arriving. I've gone to the club to bathe; if you're in time, come along. If not, I'll be back early from office. V."

"Tea?" asked Mohammed.

"Yes, tea." He sat in an armchair in the darkened room and read Viola's note two or three times. He was uncertain whether he wanted to go to Zamalek or not. He thought:

"I'll see how I feel," and tossed the note aside. He stretched himself, conscious of nothing very much beyond a sense of leisure. He wanted to see Viola again, but with no urgency. His marriage was a matter of a lifetime. He would see her sooner or later.

After tea he decided he would go out. He wandered gently through the hot, dusty evening, across the bridge to Zamalek. The gardens by the river were full of Egyptians in their whites and pinks; the women squatting in groups on the grass, the children running barefooted. He took the water-side path that led beside the garden railing, and as he went he looked over the railing and saw, through the heat haze of evening, the very tall trees and palms, the heavy flowers and the creepers that grew up to the distant branches and fell in garlands with yellow trumpet-shaped flowers or flowers like silver lilies. The river moved slowly. Down among the lumpy and root-broken soil at the verge, a boy was washing himself, slapping up the water as his ritual demanded but keeping his genitals covered with extreme care. He looked up anxiously as he heard Geoffrey's footsteps and Geoffrey, averting his eyes, stared over the water at the barracks on the opposite side. The barracks, at once formal and Oriental, glowing a ginger-red in the late light, always had for him the quality of a Victorian print. The palms, the still water, the square, low-lying buildings, the Empire, the Queen-Empress, the opulent East . . .

His thoughts trailed on until the path ended. Here he had to enter the gardens where the long shadows of the palms lay across the dusty grass. The sun had sunk out of sight before he crossed the road into the drive up to the Sports Club. He went into the central hall where the chairs stood about empty. Only a few Egyptian girls and officers on leave were there, jumping into the swimming pool, swimming its short length and getting out again.

They were making as much noise as they could but the place had the deserted look it wore during office hours.

Geoffrey felt lost now. He had been walking towards Viola as to a goal, but she was not there and he did not know what to do. He wondered was there another club? Yes, he knew there was another club. He could not have said where it was, but he felt its position somewhere within the fogs of his brain. He set out again, taking his bearings from the block of flats that stood up like a prow by the Sports Club gate. If he could reach a main road, the gate of the other club would be somewhere on his right hand. He went towards it unfailingly and passed into the garden. The club building was a large bungalow. He walked round it, looking into the lighted windows but not entering. There were a few Egyptians inside and some English civilians at the bar, but no Viola.

The safragis in the cool of the twilight were carrying chairs and tables out on to the lawn. Geoffrey took a seat, again leisured, indifferent now to the failure of his search. Viola almost forgotten, he gazed across the drive to the lawn of another club where some European officers moved against a prospect of enormous trees. Limelight was playing from the club house, giving the greens an acid brilliance and touching the bandstand so that it glittered like a silver bird-cage. An orchestra was playing Italian opera music and the officers, with flashing epaulettes, moved as in a ballet.

Geoffrey was scarcely aware he was watching a real scene, so closely did it resemble the occasional bright, visionary memories that often came into his mind. Usually his past was hidden as by a curtain against which shadows appeared but disappeared before he could recognise them, and he felt only that somewhere behind it there was a region of the imagination in which he once existed. His fear seemed ridiculous to him now. Of the period of his mental sickness he could separate clearly only a memory of sitting in a garden somewhere and contemplating the lost reality of life with passionate nostalgia.

And here was that desirable reality. He looked up at the sky that in the last few minutes had become richly dark and peppered with summer stars; he breathed in the perfumes from the flowers and trees—but he could relate nothing to himself. Someone had stopped beside his table.

"Well," said Clark. "Don't you recognise me?"

"I think so—yes, of course."

Clark took the chair opposite: "What about a drink?" he called a safragi. "Two whisky sodas."

Geoffrey, recalling Clark's looks and movements, felt momentarily oppressed—but nothing about Clark could account for his feeling.

"Well, and how are you?"

"Quite well. Ready for work. I got back this afternoon. I've been looking for my wife."

"She'll be at her office now."

"Of course. I'd forgotten," Geoffrey laughed.

"I hear Bagshot wants you back?"

"Yes. I like Bagshot. Very easy to work for."

"But, you know, you could go home if you liked."

"Home!" Geoffrey stared at the match with which he had lit a cigarette. He was certain Clark had some motive other than friendship for telling him that but he had no idea what it might be. He repeated the word: "Home," and no picture came into his mind: "England, you mean! But my wife couldn't come with me?"

"No, I suppose not."

"Then there's no point."

"To tell you the truth," Clark spoke confidentially, "you could get your discharge."

An instant's apprehension flickered across Geoffrey's face, then he laughed: "Why? I'm all right. I'm fine. I've got a job to do."

"And what about your painting?"

"There are other things more important, I'm afraid."

"Winning the war?"

"Of course. After that, life can begin again."

"We hope."

"What are you doing here?" Geoffrey asked after a pause, "weren't you in Palestine?"

"I was posted to Alex; now I'm on leave, but I expect to get home this year. Lister's gone to Cyprus."

"Lister!" the name did not fill the blank in Geoffrey's mind. He was finding it difficult to keep his attention on Clark's remarks. Everything seemed to enhance the emptiness in himself and his attention slid away to the people who were beginning to fill the chairs around him. He thought that at any moment now Viola would appear and bring like a gift a sudden clarification of the past. Clark, for some reason, was still speaking of Lister, but Geoffrey found it easier to listen to the two young officers talking loudly at the next table. They had just heard a news bulletin on the club radio.

"Good show!" said one. "Good show! Good show! Another little drinkie to celebrate a jolly good show."

They were both handsome young men, sunburnt—too young to have known any profession but that of arms—already very drunk.

The other one said: "And when we've finished with these bastards, whose turn next?"

"Anyone you like. Keep the show going. This is the life!"

As Geoffrey picked up his glass, Clark's voice returned and, at the same moment, the world seemed to solidify around him. He felt come, like a physical weight on his shoulders, consciousness of reality, and he wondered why, during the months of his illness, he had so longed to return to it.